HER MAJESTY'S
MISCHIEF

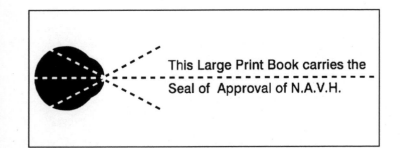

This Large Print Book carries the
Seal of Approval of N.A.V.H.

A SIMON & ELIZABETH MYSTERY

HER MAJESTY'S MISCHIEF

PEG HERRING

THORNDIKE PRESS

A part of Gale, Cengage Learning

Farmington Hills, Mich • San Francisco • New York • Waterville, Maine
Meriden, Conn • Mason, Ohio • Chicago

GALE
CENGAGE Learning·

Thorndike Press® Large Print Clean Reads.
The text of this Large Print edition is unabridged.
Other aspects of the book may vary from the original edition.
Set in 16 pt. Plantin.

LIBRARY OF CONGRESS CATALOGING-IN-PUBLICATION DATA

Herring, Peg.
    Her Majesty's mischief : a Simon & Elizabeth mystery / by Peg Herring. —
Large print edition.
        pages cm. — (Thorndike Press large print clean reads)
        ISBN 978-1-4104-8322-5 (hardcover) — ISBN 1-4104-8322-3 (hardcover)
    1. Large type books. I. Title.
    PS3558.E75478H48 2015b
    813'.54—dc23   2015020249

Published in 2015 by arrangement with Peg Herring

Printed in Mexico
1 2 3 4 5 6 7 19 18 17 16 15

HER MAJESTY'S
MISCHIEF

CHAPTER ONE

Susan Maldon hurried into the shop, small fists tight on the broom she'd been using to smooth the threshold. "Father! There's a man outside, and he's everywhere blood."

Setting down his mortar and pestle, Simon rose from his stool. "Go to your mother and stay until I call." Eyes large with distress, the girl disappeared through the curtain that separated their living quarters from the apothecary shop.

Stepping from the dark workshop into the bright June sunlight, Simon squinted until his eyes could take the light. Before him, Blackie Mather grasped a porch post, barely holding himself upright. Bright blood stained his chin and shirt front, and his eyes pinched with pain.

"Goodman Maldon, I must —" A spate of blood gurgled from his throat and he coughed, choking.

Sliding his good arm around Blackie's

back, Simon helped him inside to where he'd been grinding skullcap seeds into headache powder. Blackie slumped against the wall, limp. "I'll mix some herbs with vinegar," Simon told him in a reassuring voice. "Chervil to settle your stomach and yarrow to stop the bleeding."

Despite the healer's tone, Simon saw that whatever he gave Blackie would not delay death for long. Disease caused by a lifetime of drink and hard living was beyond an apothecary's skill, even a physician's, if Blackie had been able to afford one.

Blackie, so called because his teeth had darkened and rotted when he was a boy, waved a weak hand. "No physic." He paused for breath. "I — confess."

Simon's brows rose, making his long face even longer. "I'm no priest."

Blackie wheezed a short laugh. "No . . . priest. No . . . puritan prattler." A racking cough spewed blood down the front of his clothing and onto the rough plank floor. The smell of death hung on him, undeniable and unavoidable. "You've ever been . . . good to me, Master Maldon."

Reaching for the vinegar-soaked cloth he used to clean the tables, Simon gently wiped Blackie's face. Though only a little older than Simon, Blackie looked ancient, with lanky, gray-streaked hair, a deeply lined face, and sallow skin. Because they'd grown up together, Simon tried to help when he could, providing medicine, a listening ear, and advice at times when Blackie seemed receptive. Now, Simon guessed, the man sought company as he neared death, someone he might call a friend.

Except it was more than that. Though he found it hard to breathe, Blackie fought to speak. "Your sister . . . widow."

"Annie?" Simon's other sister was married, but Annie was twice a widow.

"Her man . . . murdered." No longer able to hold himself up, Blackie slid off the stool and onto the floor. Another cough, weaker this time, sent bright blood running down his cheek.

Wiping Blackie's face again, Simon sat down beside him and took his head onto his lap. "Rest now. I'll stay with you."

Blackie sank into unconsciousness, and Simon watched as he struggled to breathe. Tumors in the lungs, he thought, taking up the space needed for air. He spoke soothingly every few moments, hoping to make passage to the next world easier. As Blackie wheezed, Simon wondered why his sister Annie had come to the mind of a dying man.

His sister's first husband had died eight years ago of the same plague that carried off their parents. When she'd married Will Clark, friends and family said how wonderful it was Annie'd found happiness a second time. But Will had been stabbed to death for the purse on his belt.

Simon still mourned the passing of his brother-in-law and friend, and the image of Will's corpse flashed through his mind. Blackie'd been there, pointing into the crowd and shouting he'd seen the cutpurse make his escape.

Blackie spoke again, making Simon start. "He . . . made me say . . . I saw it."

Simon leaned closer. "Who?"

Another spate of coughing, then, "No cutpurse. . . . Him."

Looking into the man's face, Simon saw truth. "Who? And why?"

Blackie's lips moved, but he was too weak to answer.

"I don't understand. Someone murdered Will?" He looked toward their living quarters, where Hannah attended to household tasks. Maybe she could decipher the dying man's cryptic comments.

When he looked down, however, Blackie's body was slack, his chin sunk on his chest, his eyes fixed on the floor. He could say no more.

"He said it wasn't a cutpurse who killed Will." Simon had told it twice already, but he said it again, trying to make sense of it.

Hannah gestured dismissively, splashing soapy water from the tub where she scrubbed a shirt against itself to remove a stain. "Simon, who would murder Will Clark?"

Henry, hovering in the doorway like an unwelcome guest, surprised Simon by asking a question. "Why would Blackie lie about what he saw?"

"Not lie," Hannah said. "Imagine. He was mad with pain and afraid to face God's judgment. He imagined he might do some final good, but it was only that: imagining."

Henry seemed ready to say more but apparently thought better of it. Simon wished for the hundredth time that his wife and son were closer. Like Henry, Hannah was an orphan, so it seemed to him they should understand each other. Instead, they communicated little, and then with cool politeness. Hannah was kind to Henry because she was never otherwise, but she seemed to stand back from him. For his part, Henry was reserved with his adoptive mother, as

11

he was with everyone except Simon himself.

"Blackie saw what happened," Hannah said. "We all believed him then."

"But the description he gave of the thief was vague, now that I think on it. It might have fit a score of men." Simon wiped his face with a hand. "I wish I could have questioned him further!" The wish was useless, for Hannah had wrapped Blackie in a length of cloth and Simon and Henry had laid him on the shop worktable. "Why would he lie to protect a murderer?"

Again Henry spoke. "Someone forced him to. He said that, didn't he?"

The boy's eyes were hard, and Simon felt a stab of pity. Henry knew about the pressures an evil man put on those too weak to resist.

"I don't believe it, nor should you," Hannah said sternly. "Blackie's mind was ever addled with drink, and pain and fear turned his thoughts to nonsense." Pointing a finger first at Simon and then at Henry, she ordered, "There'll be no word of this to Annie from either of you. She's only now begun to smile like her old self and to notice the men practically standing on their heads to catch her eye."

Simon's brows met over his nose. "My sister thinks of marrying again?"

Wringing the water from the garment with strong hands, she tossed it into a basket at her side. "One cannot grieve forever, Simon."

From her tone, he guessed Hannah was pushing his sister toward marriage, believing, as most did, that every woman needed a man to complete her. Like every matchmaker ever born, Hannah believed pressing Annie to marry was in her best interest.

The thought brought England's queen to Simon's mind. The council, the common people, and several foreign governments had for years now urged Elizabeth to marry, both to provide an heir to the throne and to gain the advantage of a man's strength and wisdom. But Simon remembered a long-ago day when she'd told him, "I shall never marry. Never."

It was difficult to guess how Elizabeth felt about marriage these days. Was Hannah correct that every person needed a mate to be content? Certainly he was happy as a husband, with Hannah and two children, not their own but as dear to him as if they were. Would Elizabeth find happiness as a wife and mother if she let herself consider it?

Hannah was listing the reasons Annie

should remarry, but Simon's woolgathering had distracted him. "— doesn't take them seriously. She says Paul the chandler is too grumpy to live with and Andrew the grocer would soon make her a widow for a third time." Rolling her eyes, she added, "Even the constable shows interest, though I doubt that one has marriage in mind."

"Fenman?" Simon asked. He noticed Henry's frown of disapproval.

Hannah tilted her head at Susan, who had crept in, her blue eyes shining with interest. "Annie let him know she is not the sort he imagined her to be."

"Good," Henry muttered, apparently unaware he'd spoken aloud.

It was unusual for the boy to enter a family discussion. Hannah found his reticence frustrating, complaining, "He's so . . . blank! It's as if he has no feelings at all."

More than once Simon had explained that the women Henry knew as a child had treated him as a nuisance or worse. Still, Hannah was hurt when the boy didn't warm to her over time, didn't smile and joke and laugh easily the way Susan did. The more Hannah smiled at Susan, the more Henry retreated into himself.

Once the property of an outlaw who'd used violence, intimidation, and murder to get what he wanted, Henry used silence as a wall of protection from others. Though it was true he seldom showed emotion, the boy had a quick mind and a deep sense of right and wrong. Will's death had affected him deeply, and apparently the news it might have been murder had spurred him to comment, even in Hannah's presence.

Hannah had a final word on Annie's future. "If your sister chooses to marry again, Simon Maldon, you'll smile and say it is well. Too few chances come to a woman of her age, and with four children, too!" The argument seemed like one she'd made before, probably to Annie herself. Simon guessed his sister wasn't as anxious to marry as his wife was to see her married.

Handing the basket of laundry to Susan, Hannah turned to stir the soup simmering over the fire, tasting it and nodding. "All this has nothing to do with Blackie Mather, unless you think someone murdered Will and waited five years to begin courting his wife." Wiping her hands on her apron, she turned to Simon earnestly. "If you repeat Blackie's words, Annie will face the grief of Will's death all over again. Do you think that's any sort of kindness?"

"But if it was murder —" His argument died on his lips. If it was, then what?

Sensing her advantage, Hannah pressed it. "Blackie was not in his mind. He was dying." She put a hand on Simon's arm. "Let your sister have the little peace she's found."

Blackie had spoken what he thought was the truth. Simon was certain of it. Like a sneeze that tickles inside one's head, an urge rose he hadn't encountered in a decade: the desire to investigate a crime. *A possible crime,* he corrected. Hannah might have the right of the matter, but they didn't know that yet. Shifting his shoulders, he said, "I'll see to his burial."

Hannah peeped at the bread baking on a shelf at the side of the fireplace. "Poor man! A sad life and a sad end."

"What did you put in the soup?" Simon asked. "It smells wonderful."

As Hannah began a recitation of ingredients, he nodded without really listening. Her world was small these days: the house, the shop, the children, and the women she helped through labor and childbirth. He saw no sign she missed the days when they solved murders together. For his wife, things were simple: Life was good, so one shouldn't borrow trouble.

Simon, however, missed the times when he and Elizabeth Tudor had poked their noses into crime. This puzzle had literally appeared on his doorstep, though he hadn't gone looking for it. While he didn't want to stir memories that would cause his sister pain, should he let murder go unpunished? It couldn't hurt to look into it. If he found Blackie's claim might be true, he'd set the matter before the authorities and let them pursue justice.

Looking up, he saw Henry watching. The boy's head moved slightly in understanding. Henry, as usual, was on his father's side.

Leaving Hannah to supper and Henry to mind the shop, Simon went to the church to arrange Blackie's burial. The building was new, finished only at the front, where the central pulpit demonstrated the importance of preaching in the Protestant church. The rest was bare and raw-looking, but there were plans to make it a suitable place of worship as money became available.

The preacher was raking the dirt floor level. When he learned what had happened, James readily agreed to perform a simple ceremony of committal.

"Blackie had no family," Simon warned, "and he had rejected the church."

"We will do what we can for him, then," James replied. "God will decide what becomes of his eternal soul."

Simon liked James, who took upon himself only what he believed was suitable for Man and left the rest to God. He pressed some money into his friend's hand, knowing the church was always in need of funds.

On the way home, Simon pondered the dying man's confession. He'd known Blackie all his life, watching with dismay as he slid from youthful indolence to adult idleness to eventual dissolution. A cheerful acceptance of his own unworthiness had made Blackie a likeable sort, though not one who could be trusted. Given a coin to deliver a message, he was liable to spend the coin for drink and forget to deliver the message.

When Will died, Blackie's report that he'd witnessed the crime had surprised those who knew him well. "Odd he came forward," a neighbor remarked. "Blackie usually stays well out of the way of the law."

"As he should," the man's wife had added, tapping her lip as if to stop herself from criticizing a fellow human being.

The story Blackie had told was simple and convincing, and, for once, no one doubted him. On a cold November day in 1558, their little community had gone with the rest of the city to see the new queen, Elizabeth Tudor, ride into London. It had been an exciting time, though a little frightening, as a change of monarchs often was. Would the Catholic council allow the last of Henry Tudor's children to peacefully take the throne, knowing she was likely to lean toward Protestantism? Would some powerful family put forth a different candidate, as the Dudleys had when they tried to set Lady Jane Grey on the throne in place of Elizabeth's half-sister Mary? Would Elizabeth force her religion on all Englishmen, as "Bloody Mary" had done?

Despite their questions, there was a feeling of optimism that day. So like her father that it was impossible to believe those who claimed she was illegitimate, Elizabeth had spent the years of her sister's reign in dignified seclusion, coming to court only when invited. It was said she'd accepted the crown humbly, declaring she would be queen only when the nation accepted her and she was crowned by the church. After years of governmental mismanagement and uncertainty, Englishmen hoped Elizabeth, born of English parents, would lead the country out of debt and into prosperity once more.

Simon recalled standing on the roadside as she rode by on a magnificent horse. When last he'd seen her, she'd been locked in the

Tower of London, pale and afraid, but that day she looked every inch a queen, dressed in purple, confident and gracious. Behind her Robert Dudley rode, his handsome face composed but his eyes lit with energy. He, too, had escaped death in the Tower, and Simon guessed "Robin" would be indispensable to the new queen.

Elizabeth would not have seen Simon in the huge crowd, even if she'd been looking for him, and he could not have been on her mind that day. She probably seldom thought of him, but he was proud of their past association and what she'd achieved thus far.

There were cheers for the last of Henry Tudor's children, her name called over and over, followed by loud huzzahs. In those moments, according to the story Blackie told later, a thief stepped up behind Will Clark and tried to take his purse. When Will turned and grabbed the man by the collar, the thief reached down, took Will's own knife from his belt, and stabbed him. It happened so quickly, Blackie claimed, he'd had no time to stop it. The cutpurse escaped into the crowd as Blackie hurried to Will's side. He'd found him dead.

Now Simon reconsidered the event in light of Blackie's claim of murder. Will wouldn't have been suspicious if someone he knew pulled him to the back of the crowd on some pretext. Everyone's gaze had been focused on their new queen. The unknown person could have stabbed Will and simply stepped back into the crowd. It would take nerve, but once it was done, the killer would merely have pretended to be as shocked as everyone else when the corpse was discovered.

But why? Will had been employed as a searcher, hired by the guilds to monitor merchants' practices. That might have caused resentment, but Will had been fair to all and honest as a man could be. He had no enemies Simon knew of, no reason for someone to kill him in the bright light of day. Still, would Blackie lie with his last breath? Sudden anger at Will's death built in Simon's chest and seized his whole body, closing his throat and tightening the muscles of his jaw. Blackie had come to him for justice. Will had been his friend. He would right the wrong that had been done if he could.

"I don't know where to start, though," he told Henry later as they crushed Solomon's seal roots to make physic for broken bones and wounds. The shop smelled of lilies, but neither noticed. "It will do no good to question Annie, for she wasn't even there that day."

He'd been the one who had to tell her, and Simon couldn't erase the image of his widowed sister pulling her newborn child to her breast as he spoke, as if the infant could somehow shield her from the terrible news.

Hannah had stayed at Annie's house for a while, letting her weep or talk or stare into space as her grief played out. While Simon minded the shop and their children, Hannah had provided the support his sister desperately needed, seeing to the housework, the older children, and gently reminding her when it was time to feed the baby. Simon was grateful to his wife for her tender care in those days, when they'd feared Annie might lose her mind.

Finally Hannah had come home. "She slept last night," she told Simon, "and this morning she began to consider how she will live without him. My presence now is more hindrance than help. Annie will go on."

One did go on in such cases, because there was no alternative. Annie buried her grief, though Simon knew it went deep into her heart and seared it beyond healing. She'd begun augmenting her modest widow's pension with baking and took a loan from the guild so her oldest son could enter training as a pepperer. Young Jacob had finished his apprenticeship and was now a "journey-man," traveling from shop to shop in order to learn what different merchants could teach him. Once that was done, he could apply for guild membership and perhaps someday open his own shop, though that required luck. Simon himself might still be an apprentice if his master had not left him the business and his house as well.

"If someone murdered Will," Simon said for the third time, "I see no reason for it."

Henry didn't have time to answer, for a man in bright livery stepped through the door, his expression slightly disdainful of the humble shop and its inhabitants. "Simon Maldon?"

When Simon nodded, he said in a peremptory tone, "I am to conduct you to the queen, who has some business with you."

Simon set aside his tools and said to the man, "I am ready."

CHAPTER TWO

A light rain fell as the two men made their way southward from Old Change, Simon's neighborhood, into the center of London. Beyond saying the apothecary need not bring his bag, the man seemed uninterested in conversation, so they walked in silence. Since he seldom went into the city these days, Simon took note of small changes: a new shop, a new twist in the road, a new noise added to the cacophony of sound. London was alive, and there was a growing sense of optimism that brightened the very aspect of it. Religious strife was largely ended, trade was up, relations with other nations had settled into tolerance, if not amity. A man could make a living, and it was all most Londoners wanted of a monarch.

Damp and slightly winded after the brisk walk, Simon entered Whitehall Palace, stepping aside at the gateway so a party of women of gentle birth could pass. It was good that his guide knew the way, for the place was a warren of rooms and anterooms, many of them changed since Simon's last visit some years ago. Whitehall was, however, as busy as always. In every room they passed through, people worked at various tasks or conversed noisily with those around them. Most hardly spared the newcomer a glance.

When they finally reached a mid-sized room paneled in oak, he was disappointed to find that Elizabeth was not there. Instead a man sat at a table, examining papers with a pair of lenses set into a wire frame. Behind him the draperies had been pulled away from the window, letting in the gray light and revealing a garden bursting with flowers of every hue. He recalled Elizabeth loved flowers and felt glad she could have all of them she wanted these days.

When the door closed softly the man at the table looked up, and Simon recognized Robert Dudley, Elizabeth's long-time friend. They'd met several times over the years, and though Dudley didn't know all of what Simon and Elizabeth had done to search out murderers together, he'd no doubt made it his business to learn what he could.

Dudley's name was inextricably linked

with the Queen's these days, and there was constant speculation among the English, and foreigners as well, as to whether Elizabeth would dare to marry the man she was obviously in love with. There were many arguments against it.

First was Dudley's wife, Amy Robsart. As a person she was no longer an impediment to marriage, since she'd been dead for three years. However, some said Dudley had arranged Amy's death in order to become Elizabeth's consort and the power behind the throne.

The Dudleys in general and Robert in particular were an ambitious lot. Gossips said he'd hired someone to push his wife down the stairs of their home, but the coroner had declared it an accident. Rumors persisted, making the great man a poor candidate for a queen's consort. In fact, Hannah reported the rumor that he'd taken to wearing light chain mail under his shirt to protect himself from some of his fellow courtiers.

"Master Maldon." Dudley set his reading lenses aside, rising and coming around the table to clasp Simon's hand with what seemed like real affection. He looked older, which of course they both were, but Dudley's aging seemed more to do with strain than time. He was still handsome, still straight-backed and dark. His eyes, however, revealed past suffering.

"Your Worship," Simon said with a bow. "We were grieved to hear of your wife's accident." Though he saw appreciation in Dudley's eyes for the implied vote of confidence, it wasn't meant as flattery. Simon had little talent for fawning on his betters. He simply didn't see Dudley as the sort of man who would kill an innocent person to get what he wanted.

"I thank you." Dudley turned to business. "Her Majesty is sending a delegation to Scotland, and I am to ascertain that your health permits you to be part of it."

"Scotland?" Simon was dumbstruck. "What would I do there?"

Dudley rapped his knuckles on the oaken table edge as if something bothered him. "She will herself instruct you further. I am merely to assure you are in health for travel."

"I am well, but —"

"And your wife is well? She can mind the shop for a time?"

"She is, and my son is capable, but —"

"You will be well paid, of course. Return in two days at noon, when you will meet your party and begin the journey." He turned back to his table, signaling the interview was complete.

"My party?" Simon asked.

"Her Majesty's ambassador, Thomas Randolph, leads the delegation."

"Thomas Randolph." He sounded like a lackwit as he struggled to grasp the magnitude of Dudley's news. He was to travel to Scotland on some mission, probably secret. He shook his head. He had a family to care for, a business to run — a murder to solve. Taking a step toward Dudley he said, "Your Worship, it is inconvenient for me to leave London at this time. Please convey to Her Majesty my thanks for the honor, but beg her to find another for this journey."

Dudley's expression showed complete understanding as well as grim humor. "You misunderstand, Maldon. Her Majesty does not make requests. She gives commands, and we obey." Including himself in the statement was telling. If Robert Dudley, Elizabeth's favorite and possible lover, was unable to refuse her requests, how did a mere acquaintance from her youth hope to escape the demands of the woman who was now his sovereign?

"Scotland!" Hannah was aghast. "Why would she send you there? They live like savages, in huts dug into the hillsides!"

"Who told you that?"

"Your mother's brother went there once, to fight for King Edward."

"And you believe my mother's tales? Hannah, she used to claim Anne Boleyn flew from the palace each night, visited her lover, Henry Percy, in Northumberland, and returned before dawn." Simon waved a hand to dismiss silly rumors. "The Scottish queen was raised in France. I'm sure her palace is well-suited to civilized folk."

Still unhappy, Hannah lifted the pan of ashes she'd gathered from the fireplace to hip level, sending up a light cloud of gray. "Who is this Mary, and what have we to do with her?"

"She is Her Majesty's cousin, daughter of the Scottish king and Mary of Guise, who was Henry VIII's niece. She has some claim to the English throne, and being Catholic, is an attractive candidate to some."

Hannah's expression grew concerned. "Her Majesty might be deposed?"

"Not likely," Simon sniffed the air. "Elizabeth's moderate path has stilled all but the most ardent zealots on either side. What's this?" He took the lid off a pot that simmered over the fire, earning a slap from his wife. "Ow!" Rubbing his arm, he finished,

29

"The question of succession is troubling. Who will rule should Elizabeth die, as she almost did last year?"

"Do you think that's what this mission to Scotland is about? The succession?"

Simon prodded the fire with an iron rod. "They say Her Majesty considers silencing her critics by naming the Queen of Scots her heir."

Hannah swept a live coal back into the hearth with her foot and shifted the ash pan to her other hip. "Why does she not simply marry, as everyone wants her to do?"

He didn't tell Hannah his theory that Elizabeth was reluctant to share power with anyone, even a man she loved. "If she chooses one suitor from the pack, she'll anger the rest," he replied. "The English themselves are divided on the question, though most prefer she not marry Dudley."

"I think he'd make a dashing consort." Hannah met Simon's eyes. "He's very handsome."

Simon smiled to acknowledge her teasing. "His enemies fear he would exact retribution for the executions of his brother and father."

"Do you think that's true?"

Simon shook his head. "I can't say what any man would do with great power, but it

30

seems to me Dudley's wise enough to see that the past must be the past if England is to thrive. He has in his circle Catholics, Calvinists, and those in between. That means, I think, he agrees with Her Majesty that the function of government is not to look into men's souls."

Hannah set her free hand on her hip. "None of it helps me see why you must go to Scotland."

"I shall learn that day after tomorrow." Simon turned toward the doorway to the shop. "Though I will try to explain, I must also be ready. We both know Elizabeth can be stubborn when she's made up her mind about something." He added with a rueful smile, "And these days, she's no longer a powerless princess, as she was when you knew her."

"I will do as you say," Henry said for the fourth time, making an effort to keep impatience out of his voice. "You'll be late, and the queen cannot be kept waiting."

His father smiled to indicate he recognized his own fussiness. "I know you'll do well in my absence." He rose from his stool, setting aside the pestle he'd used to crush garlic into a strong-smelling paste. Plague season was nigh, and he'd demonstrated how to

31

make poultices of butter, onion, and garlic to treat the disease, though Henry had seen it done a score of times before today. Simon puttered a bit longer, obviously torn between leaving and staying. "Will you walk with me part of the way, son?"

Henry glanced at the work he'd planned to do this morning. Though it would be hard enough to keep up with his father gone, he could never refuse Simon anything. "Of course."

While Simon went into the house to say goodbye to Hannah and Susan, Henry remained in the shop. Though he admired his mother, he thought it was easier for her to love Susan, whose mood was almost always sunny. Though she treated him well, Henry saw how carefully Hannah held her face when she spoke to him.

When Simon returned, his eyes were damp. Any long journey held unknown dangers: storms, sickness, bandits, and beasts. If he didn't return, his family might never even know why. It angered Henry that his father had been given no choice in the matter. Though Simon spoke of the queen with affection, Henry thought she might have found someone other than a middle-aged man she hadn't seen in years for this unknown duty.

Straightening his shoulders, Simon picked up his pack with his good hand and slung it onto the shoulder of his other arm, crippled from an accident at birth. He followed Henry out the door, and they made their way down the lane, toward the noisy, crowded High Street that went south, to the city's center.

"Do you recall the night you came to us?" Simon's voice was casual as he asked the question, and he looked ahead, not at Henry.

"I do."

"I almost lost Hannah that night."

"Yes."

"She's a good woman."

"Yes."

Simon stopped, nearly causing the peddler behind him to drop his sack of goods. "I know you will take care of her should —"

"Father, the queen would not send you into danger. You are her friend."

Simon's smile was sad. "A queen has no friends, Henry, and if she did, it would not be a poor apothecary from the north of London."

Henry turned in surprise. "We're not poor. Our home is warm and we never go hungry."

"In Her Majesty's eyes, our home is a hovel and our meals pitifully small." Ignoring Henry's doubtful look, Simon returned to his point. "Elizabeth will use whoever she must to serve England's needs. I will do my best for her, but I have no doubt there is danger in it. She has no one she can trust, else she would not have sent for me."

Henry didn't like the sound of it, but Simon began walking again. "I don't mean to frighten you. I merely want you to understand."

Knowing he was asking Henry to support Hannah if he didn't return, he said, "Don't worry. Hannah and Susan will ever be in my mind."

At the wall, Simon hugged Henry tightly, holding him close for a few moments. Henry felt the rough fabric of his father's tunic against his neck. "I regret this parting," Simon said in his ear. "I wish —" He didn't finish, and Henry wondered if he was thinking of Blackie and the possibility murder had been done.

A second hug followed, this one quick and final. "Keep well. I will return as soon as possible." Apparently determined to dispel his earlier tone of dread, Simon turned with a jaunty wave and walked away as Henry stood looking after him.

"I shall do everything you asked, Father," he said under his breath. "And more, for I will find Uncle Will's killer if I can."

CHAPTER THREE

The High Street was clogged with people, and Simon's progress was slow. Frustrated and sweating, he hurried through the gateway, sure Elizabeth was tapping her foot, furious with him for disrupting her schedule. The thought caused him to sweat even more. Would the princess he once knew forgive her old friend for being late?

He gave his name at the entry and was allowed inside. A servant led him to an anteroom, where he waited for an hour with several other impatient men, most dressed far better than he. So much for disrupting the queen's schedule, he told himself, chuckling inwardly at his mistaken assumption that he mattered.

Finally an officious-looking fellow in slightly baggy hose came to the door and called, "Simon Maldon!" He hurried after the man as they navigated a succession of corridors and rooms filled with people busy at various tasks. When they reached another anteroom, Simon was left to wait, this time alone. With nothing in the windowless room but a small table, he spent the next hour examining the paneled walls, the patterned ceiling, and even the tiled floor. Through two high doors opposite the one he'd entered, he heard sounds of conversation, movement, and even laughter, but there was no sign the queen was aware of his presence.

Eventually the heavy oaken doors opened, and a different man came to lead him into the next room. "Simon Maldon, Your Majesty," his guide called in a voice much too loud for Simon's comfort. Every person present stared as he stopped just inside the door, unsure what to do. Taking no chances, he bowed low and stayed there, his face toward the floor as he peeped through his lashes to see who was in the room.

Elizabeth sat at a table, two stacks of papers before her. Behind her stood Dudley and two others, one of whom was no doubt her trusted advisor and Secretary of State, William Cecil. At two tables a respectful distance from the queen sat the members of her council, and in the rest of the available space stood the less exalted: clerks, messengers, and other functionaries. On every face except the queen's and Dudley's, there was curiosity. Who was this stranger who'd been invited among them?

"Ah, Master Maldon," Elizabeth said off-handedly. "We shall be at leisure to speak with you shortly. You may wait over there." As she nodded toward an alcove with a padded stool, he caught a glimmer of humor in her eye. "Sit if you will, for I think you are far older than I."

The men in the room caught the teasing note in her voice and relaxed a trifle. Bowing even lower, Simon backed toward the alcove and stood beside the stool, feeling like a donkey at a horse show. He stared at the floor and put on a blank expression, which Hannah, who'd once served the princess Elizabeth, advised was the proper thing to do while waiting. Noblemen and women generally ignored those below them in rank, assuming they were too stupid to follow a conversation. Simon knew, however, if Elizabeth wanted him here, he was supposed to be paying attention.

"I repeat," Elizabeth said in a clear, firm voice, "we must be united in this. If we offer the Queen of Scots what she desires, we must achieve our desires as well."

"Your Majesty," said a man with a hound-like countenance, "one hears your cousin attracts plots as a flower attracts bees." He leaned forward, palms pressed against the table. "Simply by sitting prettily and smiling at suggestions, she encourages rebellion in England."

People said the Queen of Scots was beautiful, but then, court language was prone to exaggeration. Every king or prince was splendid and daring, every queen or princess surpassingly lovely. Mary had been raised in France, where a woman could not rule and was generally a decorative addition to the power held by a man. It was no surprise her beauty, not her political acumen, was what most concerned the English council.

"She is our cousin," Elizabeth said. "We recognize her royal blood and wish her no harm."

A slight pause and some hushed shifting of feet hinted that some in the room did wish the Scots' queen harm. As long as she ruled, so close in distance, so close in blood, the chances for war with Scotland and the possibility of rebellious plotters in England were strong.

"As most of you know, this day we send a delegation to secure her agreement to quell any who approach her with plans to disrupt our peace."

"Which we have done before," Dudley said, earning a warning glance from Elizabeth for the interruption. He pressed his lips together as if forcing himself to refrain from further comment.

Elizabeth turned from Dudley to the man who must be William Cecil. Tall and thin, with a high forehead, a long chin, and eyes that seemed to see everything, Cecil looked like the decisive type he was rumored to be. Meeting his eye the queen said, "We have a proposal we believe will please my cousin, once she has time to think on it."

A signal passed between them and Cecil took up the topic in a surprisingly low voice. "If Mary Stuart, who needs our support against her own strong-willed lords, consents to marry an Englishman, Her Majesty is prepared to name the Queen of Scots her heir."

There was a slight stir in the room. Succession had been uncertain for decades, and if Elizabeth would not marry and produce an heir, the matter had to be put to rest some other way.

"Your Majesty, shall religious matters be considered?" someone asked.

Elizabeth waved the question away with an impatient hand. "There are both Protestants and Catholics in Scotland, and

Mary seems content to let them be." She looked to Cecil again, and he continued as if the interruption had not occurred.

"The queen believes her cousin might be persuaded to take up residence in England. Our court will no doubt be more attractive to her than the rough life in Scotland. Her council would rule, as it seems to do despite her presence, and she —" Cecil paused to clear his throat. "— and her husband will enjoy the company of the queen, her kinswoman."

Cecil's tone sounded odd, but Simon kept his face lowered, not daring to show interest.

One of the younger men said in a voice that betrayed curiosity and perhaps hope, "This man will have to be an attractive prize, to make a queen leave her kingdom behind."

Elizabeth fingered the decorative stitching on the sleeve of her gown as Cecil answered, "We feel Lord Dudley is a suitable candidate, and he will receive additional honors to raise him to a level appropriate for a queen's consort."

Unable to hide his interest, Simon glanced up at Dudley. For a moment he looked as if he'd been struck with a mallet. The surprise on his face turned briefly to anger, but he mastered both emotions. Robert Dudley had watched his brother die on the battlefield. He'd been imprisoned in the Tower of London under sentence of death when his father and another brother were beheaded. After a lifetime of facing benefit and adversity with measured control, he didn't betray himself now, though it was clear this announcement was the last thing he'd expected.

The men in the room began discussing the idea among themselves. Simon wondered how many of them realized Dudley had not been consulted. It was difficult to tell now that his courtier's mask was back in place. However, standing at the side of the room, Simon could see Dudley's left hand. His fingers drummed against his thigh in the same way he'd noticed a few days before when Dudley admitted he didn't know why Simon was being sent to Scotland.

In the first few years of her reign, Elizabeth had treated her old friend well. He was almost always by her side, and he spoke for the queen when she was unavailable. Rumors in the city said they were intimates, that he came and went from her chambers at all hours from his own rooms next to hers. Though spicy bits of gossip passed from one person to another, Simon tried to ignore them. The queen's private matters were no one else's business, and the Elizabeth he knew would never do anything that would harm England, no matter what her feelings were.

When Dudley spoke, his voice was slightly higher than normal. "Majesty, I beg a few moments in private to discuss this matter."

"What should we discuss?" She didn't look at him. "You are a widower, are you not?"

"I am." The admission came through lips that barely moved.

"And you will do what is best for England?"

"Yes." Dudley's gaze dropped. Any argument he made would seem petty and possibly traitorous.

"Well, then." The queen looked to Cecil, who pursed his lips before beginning again.

"Master Randolph, you have your instructions." A middle-aged man whose pointed beard disappeared into his high collar stepped forward and bowed to the queen with practiced ease.

"Thomas is well acquainted with the Scots and their ways," Elizabeth said. "We trust him to present our proposal at an opportune moment." A rumble of approval went through the room. After years of fruitless argument, something was finally being done about the succession.

Elizabeth had not looked at Dudley directly since the announcement. He made a small movement toward her, and she glanced sideways, though she kept her face turned away.

There was discussion of particulars before the meeting ended and a man in a deep green doublet announced they were dismissed. Benches scraped against the stone floor as members of the council stood to go. At a gesture from Elizabeth, the man in green bent forward, and she said something only he could hear. As the men filed out, he stopped Thomas Randolph, indicating he should stay. A glance from Elizabeth told Simon to remain where he was as well. Soon there were only five of them in the room: Elizabeth, Cecil, Dudley, Simon, and Randolph.

"Master, I add to your party Simon Maldon, who serves at my pleasure. You will find him useful, for he is a trained apothecary as well as a sharp observer." Randolph nodded to Simon, who bowed politely. "You may go. Master Maldon will follow anon."

With an elaborate bow, Randolph backed

out of the room, and the door closed behind him. Elizabeth met Cecil's gaze and he, too, bowed and left the room, retreating through the doors behind the queen. That left only three, and Simon felt like an unwelcome chaperone. As soon as the door closed behind the secretary, Dudley spoke.

"Majesty, is it your true wish that I be married to your cousin?"

Elizabeth's face was expressionless. "It would serve the nation well."

With a glance at Simon, Dudley said, "Shall we speak on this in private?"

Her smile was grim. "Oh, I have no doubt we shall speak on it, Robin, in private, in public, and everywhere between. Nevertheless, I have decided on this course." She raised a hand as he drew breath to argue. "The proposal might come to naught, in which case your fretting is useless. Even if she agrees, it will be years before a ceremony can be arranged. In the time between, you shall strive to convince your wife-to-be that happiness lies here in England. If you are successful in that endeavor, you shall have everything you have now and more, including your nation's eternal gratitude — and mine as well."

Dudley's lips moved as if to form arguments, but in the end he must have decided to forgo them for the present. "As Your Majesty knows, I stand ready to serve, for I love my nation and my queen above all else in this world."

"We are pleased to hear it." She still looked away. "Now leave me with my old friend."

Adjusting the ruff at his neck, Dudley gave Simon a pleading glance, bowed, and left the room. *What does he think I can do to help?* Simon wondered. *I don't even know why I'm here.*

Once they were alone, Simon became more nervous than before. Elizabeth looked different: more rigid and haughty than the girl he'd known since she was thirteen. Her body was armored in cloth that admitted no softness, no femininity. Her face was heavily powdered, her brows a thin line high above her eyes. The rich fabric, the deep colors, and the extensive jewelry, so different from the simple, colorless clothing she'd worn as a princess, signaled a vast change. This Elizabeth wasn't the girl he'd known but a formidable figure, almost less than human.

For some moments she waited, as if challenging him to say something. He remained silent, knowing the interview would be entirely under her control. When she glanced out the open window, he saw at the side of her face a pale, round scar, a remnant of the smallpox that had almost killed her a year before. There were hushed sounds outside the room, a bird calling in the garden below, a woman laughing somewhere far away, and the scrape of feet on stone in the anteroom. Someone else waited to see the queen. Simon guessed there was always someone else, always another decision to be made. Finally she spoke. "You are well, Simon?"

"I am, Your Majesty."

"And Hannah?"

"Well, too."

"They tell me your shop prospers."

He tried a small joke. "Men are ever hopeful someone can help them live to old age in good health, though it is God's doing, not mine."

She didn't smile. "You are wondering why I send you to Scotland."

Simon folded his good hand over the crippled one. "I must admit, I have little taste for travel, Your Majesty. In addition, some family business arose lately, and I beg leave to see to it."

Her brows rose. "Business that prevents service to the crown? I would like to hear of it."

He knew he should drop the subject. The murder of one man was not the queen's concern, and she had no time for stories. Still, she'd joined him in the past to bring criminals to justice. Perhaps if she understood, she'd send someone else to Scotland. He told her everything.

When he finished, her comment went straight to the point. "You have no proof of this."

"Why would Blackie lie? He was dying."

"Drunkards often imagine things, I'm told. Or he might himself have been the cutpurse who murdered your kinsman, and his conscience bothered him at the last."

In earlier times, he would have argued. Now he said only, "It's possible, Your Majesty."

A long look from pale blue eyes told him his apparent meekness was not convincing. Rising from her chair, Elizabeth went to the window, and Simon wondered what he was supposed to do. Approach? Move back? Offer to adjust the window for her? Leaning her elbows on the sill and gazing out over the city, she ended his quandary. "Your business must wait. I have need of your skills on this journey."

"Your Majesty, surely there are others who would gladly go —"

48

Elizabeth's eyes hardened, and he felt as if he'd been stabbed. "Are you sovereign then, Master Maldon? Would you decide what is England's good and what is not?"

"No, Your Majesty," he said hurriedly. "I am ever at your service." In a burst of honesty he added, "You are the best monarch England could have in these trying times."

Her gaze softened slightly. "Since you never learned to flatter, Simon, I shall accept you speak your true feelings." He bowed again, and her eyes lost their sternness. "You think for yourself. That is why I need you."

Somewhat at sea, he said, "Thank you, Your Majesty."

Elizabeth put a hand over her mouth, fingers slightly spread, and for a moment she looked like the girl he'd known. "When we are alone, you may call me Highness, as before."

"I thank you, Highness," he said with a smile. "It comes easier to my tongue."

The atmosphere in the room warmed somewhat, and they became less monarch and subject, more Elizabeth and Simon. She told him a little of how things were for her, though he sensed the things she didn't mention. He guessed the crown weighed heavily on her brow, both literally and figuratively. Though she'd longed for it, the task of righting England's course after years of ruinous bickering and reversals was herculean. The nation she'd inherited was weak, financially and militarily, and the people were tired of wrangling leaders. They'd watched to see if Elizabeth favored Protestants, as her brother Edward had, or Catholics, as Mary had. She received advice from her council, but it was slanted to each member's beliefs and desires. Since she was a woman, they expected her to be obedient to the will of men.

None of that had anything to do with him. Why should he go to Scotland, of all places?

"I am much vexed in the matter of my cousin, the Queen of Scots," Elizabeth said as if she'd read his mind. "I've sent men to meet her, but not one of them seems able to discern her true nature." She paced the room, folding her fingers together as her skirts rustled against the floor. "I want to meet her myself, but events intervene, and it has thus far been impossible."

Simon tried to read the message underlying the words. Elizabeth had always longed for the affection of her family. She'd worshipped the father who'd ordered her mother beheaded and often ignored her.

She'd adored the brother who removed her from her rightful place in succession. She'd remained loyal to her sister Mary, who'd imprisoned and considered executing her. Now they were all dead. It was no surprise she longed to know what her cousin was like.

She turned again to the open window, watching the bustle of activity outside. "I must deal with Mary Stuart both as a fellow queen and as my kinswoman, yet I know little of her. Some claim she is a scheming plotter with eyes fixed on my throne, and at times her actions seem to confirm that. Others, however, describe a delicate, saintly woman who would not swat a fly, much less plot against me. It's maddening."

"Their emotions color their perceptions."

"Their emotions, their politics, their religion — all of it. What I need is —"

"A spy?"

She chuckled. "No doubt there are spies enough in the party. I need an honest man."

Simon ran a finger around the neck of his tunic. "Highness, I —"

She raised a hand to stop his protest. "I want your opinion of her."

"But I have often been wrong in my

perception of people. Remember the baroness —"

She shook her head at his lack of understanding. "Simon, listen! Those closest to me are loyal, but each has —" She paused to find the right word. "— prejudices that color his advice."

"Cecil wants Dudley to marry the Queen of Scots, and Dudley wants — He doesn't want to." Though he amended his words in time, he saw from her glance that Elizabeth knew he'd almost said, *Dudley wants to marry you.*

"Each man in the delegation is to some degree allied with one of them or the other." She fixed her gaze on him. "Only by sending my own man can I get a true picture of the queen."

Simon almost argued that he should not judge one so far above him in rank, but Elizabeth went on, "You had a fine education. You are a person of careful thought. I have not known you to judge nations, religions, or philosophies as evil or wrong simply because they are different."

He began to comprehend. His observations, imperfect as they might be, were valuable to Elizabeth simply because he had no reason to view the Queen of Scots as good or evil.

He couldn't help but sigh. "I understand."

Sensing victory, she handed him a roll of vellum from a stack on the table before her. "This will supply anything you need. A servant waits without with money and a disguise." When Simon looked surprised, she explained, "I recall you have a talent for such things. You will travel as Randolph's surgeon, since I did not think it wise to send you to Scotland as a woman."

She referred to a time she'd dressed him as one of her maids, and taking the smooth roll from her, he grinned despite his misgivings. "That was not my finest hour. Farewell, Highness."

"Farewell, Simon." He thought her eyes looked misty, but he told himself it was his vision, which had faded somewhat with age.

Simon felt little concern about posing as Randolph's surgeon. His father had been a physician, and but for his withered arm, he might have followed the same profession. The role was within his abilities so long as a real emergency didn't arise, and travelers who could afford it often brought their own medical men rather than have no help or take a chance on a stranger's ministrations. Randolph could claim a condition that required special medication or occasional bloodletting.

In the parcel he was given, Simon found a belt hung with vials of ground toad and common herbs as well as a waxed cloak designed to protect from disease-causing miasma. It was heavy and cumbersome, but at least they hadn't seen fit to include the long-beaked hood many physicians wore along with it. The beak, filled with herbs to purify the air the wearer breathed, was meant to keep out the plague, but it made a fellow look like a large, pale bird. Simon wore instead the close-fitting coif that signified membership in the surgeon's guild. The cloak would at least protect him from rain, which he'd heard was plentiful in Scotland.

Also in the pack he found clothing suitable for a royal emissary. Simon put it on, extracting a promise from the clerk to keep his own clothes somewhere for him. Hannah had made each item with loving hands, and he felt more comfortable in galligaskins and a tunic than in hose and doublet, no matter the fabric was softer and finer than his usual clothing.

Shouldering the pack, Simon followed his guide out of the palace and down to the quay where a vessel waited. Unlike the brightly painted ferries surrounding it, the two-masted hoy, meant for trade along the coast, had space for cargo as well as passengers. Randolph, already aboard, stood between two men. One of them seemed interested when Randolph nodded at Simon and made a brief comment. The other acted as if he hadn't heard.

"Master Maldon," Randolph greeted him as he stepped over the rail. "This is Samuel Eliot, one of our party."

Eliot was a large man, probably an ex-soldier, though he wore clothes as rich as the law allowed those without a title. Handsome and confident, he reminded Simon of some Spanish smugglers he'd once met, slightly dangerous but friendly enough. "Maldon," he said, offering his hand. "A pleasure." For some reason Simon recalled Elizabeth's comment about spies in the party. To whom might Eliot report what happened on the journey?

Randolph turned to the other man, in every way the opposite of Eliot. Light-haired and light-eyed, he was dressed in clothes much like the ones Simon had left behind at the palace. "This is Sholto Munn, our Scottish guide. Simon Maldon, my surgeon."

Munn gave only a brief jerk of his head to signal acknowledgment. A twitch of sardonic humor moved Eliot's lips, but the humor wasn't shared, even after Munn moved away.

Randolph led Simon around the ship, introducing the rest of the group. They were twelve in all, and he soon lost track of who was who. He had plenty of time to get to know them before they arrived in Edinburgh. Most were minor figures like himself, sent for a specific purpose: to arrange travel, to see to supplies, or to record events. A few of the older men were advisors meant to help Randolph decide on the political niceties of meeting with the Scottish queen. Two of them had brought along their sons, probably as a way of training them for service to the queen and perhaps with an eye to broadening their view of the world.

Activity picked up as the ship's crew made ready to depart. The passengers huddled together at the bow, trying to stay out of the sailors' way. Randolph made conversation, asking about Simon's home and background. Simon answered truthfully but minimally, aware he was a cipher to his supposed employer. His actions and comments would be analyzed and discussed over the next few weeks. It was best, he decided, to do as Elizabeth had learned to do at a very young age: trust no one fully.

"Your place is there, next to Munn." Randolph indicated a spot on the deck protected somewhat by a tarp stretched between masts.

"You'll be glad of the shield," Eliot commented, "for by God's feet, this time of year we'll see rain every day, and more as we near Scotland."

The prediction was correct. It rained off and on the whole trip, though most afternoons the sun appeared for a few hours, providing drying and warmth. Simon was pleased to find he was a good sailor. The only other long journey he'd ever taken had been on horseback, and he'd hated every step. While the boat was crowded and damp, it didn't try to bite him, and his backside went un-blistered. The air was clean and fresh, and he loved watching the flow of water at the bow, breaking and channeling along the side before coming together again at the stern with a constant, gentle swish. He fancied the water forgetting them as soon as they passed, returning to its usual state with no memory of the meaningless creatures that had traversed through it.

From time to time they passed fishing villages built on convenient coves where folk moved about, seeing to daily tasks as the ship made its way to the sea, then northward. They hugged the coast, pulling to shore at night, where the passengers could sleep on land if they liked. Simon chose the deck, enjoying the gentle rocking and the lap of waves against the ship.

Munn chose the shore, which Simon tried not to take as a personal insult. The Scotsman avoided all of them but seemed especially gruff with Simon, pulling back abruptly if they touched accidentally on the tiny deck. He sometimes muttered to himself about last-minute additions to the party who never truly explained what they were there for. Often Simon looked up to see Munn glowering at him across the deck. It wasn't fair, since he'd done nothing to offend the man, but at least Munn's choice left more room for Simon to stretch out on the deck.

The third morning when they woke, the taciturn Scot was gone. "The scoundrel!" Randolph exclaimed when he was told. "I paid him in full to escort us to Edinburgh."

"Our captain will take us there," Eliot soothed. "We need no Scot to show the way."

"True," Randolph allowed, "but it's helpful to have someone who can communicate with the folk along the way who don't or won't speak proper English."

One of the older men said, "We'll make do, Thomas, for we must."

Simon guessed they would, but he wondered, too, why Munn had left. His small bag of possessions still lay on the deck, and Simon opened it to look inside. It contained only an extra shirt, some bits of leather, and a letter Munn had obviously carried with him for some time. From what Simon could tell, in spite of tattered edges, heavy creases, stains, and unfamiliar words, it had been written by a priest on behalf of Munn's mother to say a girl he meant to marry had died of fever.

There was much discussion of Munn's betrayal, with many theories offered of his motives and current destination. Simon wondered if he would use Randolph's gold to return home, to visit the grave of his beloved and be comforted by his family. Why, though, had he neglected to take with him the letter that seemed to have meant so much to him?

They journeyed on. Every morning brought rain, sometimes a drizzle, sometimes mist, but always wet. The benefit of so much moisture was a vista of vibrant greens on the shores they passed. The detriment was it was often shrouded in fog, and the green turned misty gray and at times disappeared completely.

Only Randolph knew Simon was not what he seemed, at least as far as he could tell. He didn't know what the ambassador had been told about his reason for coming, but there was little time for them to speak privately. A careful man, Randolph was almost prim in his behavior, and he treated Simon as he treated everyone, with grave dignity. Eliot was friendly in a rather condescending manner. Simon thought he detected the contempt of a whole man for a cripple, for Eliot often looked at his arm rather than his face.

The youngest of the party, a lad named Philip, had come with his father, James Coulston, who had accompanied Randolph on previous trips and served as his adviser. Philip was a little younger than Henry, and Simon guessed he'd been named to honor Mary Tudor's husband, now king of Spain. Philip often sought Simon out, and together they watched the shore pass as the young man talked of things important to him.

Once the subject of Eliot came up, and Philip reported in a low voice, "He's able with a sword and he's been to Scotland. It makes him the perfect bodyguard for Randolph, Father says."

"Bodyguard?"

Philip leaned closer. "Who's to say the Scots want to hear our message? Or that someone in this party hasn't plans to stop us?" Before he could stop his tongue, he added, "They distrusted you for a time, but Randolph says the queen herself sent you. And besides, an assassin wouldn't have —" His brain finally caught up with his mouth, and he didn't voice the argument that Simon was no threat due to his withered arm.

"So Eliot's task is to guard Randolph's life?"

"No one says it aloud, but why else is he here? Father says he offered to travel with us because he was about to be arrested for murder."

"Murder!"

"It's only a rumor," the boy admitted. "He seems friendly enough."

Simon glanced at Eliot, who was talking with one of the sailors. They were an odd assortment: a fastidious emissary, a few old men, a possible murderer, some green boys, and an apothecary unsure how to accomplish the mission he'd been given. At least his companions no longer thought him an enemy. In fact, they invited him to join the games they played to pass the time. He quickly grew tired of cards and dice, however, and he suspected his companions grew tired of the wagers he made, always the minimum allowed.

CHAPTER FOUR

"Sergeant, Her Majesty commands you attend her at this afternoon's council session."

Calkin looked up from mending his tunic. "She asked for me?"

"By name." The messenger seemed as curious as he about the order. A long-time veteran of the palace guard, Calkin rarely pulled such tedious duty as routine council meetings, where the queen's guardsmen were required to stand at attention for hours.

"Very well." He worked the needle a little faster, pushing it through the thick fabric with strong fingers. "Put Lammond on duty with me."

Lammond, newest of the guardsmen at Whitehall, was a good lad who could be counted on to do as he was told and keep his mouth shut. If Elizabeth had asked for Calkin personally, she was up to something. *But then,* he reminded himself as he rose to make sure the rest of his uniform was in perfect condition, *she always is.*

The meeting was, like all council meetings in Calkin's opinion, overlong and boring. The two guardsmen stood impassively near the doors, alert but apparently not listening. The guard, created by Henry VII and initially made up of Welshmen loyal to him, was charged with protecting the Tudor family. When Elizabeth, the last of them, died, they might be out of a job, but in his years of service, Calkin had put money by to live on. At least, if he didn't live too long.

When the meeting finally ended the members filed out, breaking into smaller groups of like-minded individuals, eager to discuss the matters that had been addressed. As usual, Dudley and Cecil stayed behind. A brief exchange was conducted in low tones, and Elizabeth listened to both men, nodding from time to time. Cecil spoke as a father might, in a faintly authoritative but gentle tone. Dudley's manner was more intimate. He smiled into the queen's eyes and even touched her arm at times. The discussion ended when Elizabeth made a wry comment that caused Cecil to smirk and Dudley to frown. Then she excused them.

When the doors closed behind her two

closest advisors, Elizabeth turned to the guardsmen. "Calkin, attend me. Your companion may wait outside."

It was against orders, but then, who made the orders? The queen had ultimate say over when she would be protected and when she would not. If Calkin stuck a knife between her ribs, Lammond would be executed for dereliction of duty. Calkin smiled at the younger man to signal he had no such intention. Lammond left the room, his brow furrowed.

"Are you well, Calkin?" Elizabeth asked when he was gone.

He bowed. "As well as age and past events allow, Your Majesty." In truth his feet troubled him from standing long hours in attendance on Henry, then Edward, then Mary, and now Elizabeth Tudor. Still, Calkin liked his job and the Tudors, despite their faults and eccentricities. He counted the last twenty years well spent.

"I met some days ago with Simon Maldon."

Calkin's respectful expression broke into a smile. "How does the lad, Your Majesty?"

Elizabeth raised an eyebrow. "He's past thirty." She herself was near thirty, twice the age she'd been when Calkin first met her.

"I think of him as forever young," he said with a bow. "Like yourself, Your Majesty."

"None of us grows younger, Calkin." She seemed distracted from her purpose for a moment. "Yet you have not taken a wife."

The dichotomy of Calkin's life was that he had known many women and come to know none of them. "I've been too long on my own, Your Majesty. I'll likely stay that way."

"One becomes accustomed to it." Folding her hands, Elizabeth set them against the stiff bodice of her gown, resting her elbows on the layers of skirting that bulged around her. "I sent Simon to Scotland on an errand, but he was less than willing to go. It seems a death in his family some time ago was blamed on a cutpurse, but he recently learned it might have been murder."

"How did he come upon such information?"

As she recounted the story as Simon had told it to her, Calkin noted Elizabeth's skill at recalling detail and her talent for cutting through to the essence of a matter. He supposed such a mind was invaluable in a monarch, but it struck him as odd this monarch took as much interest in the death of an ordinary citizen as she did in the affairs of France or Spain.

When she finished telling Simon's story, the queen's expression turned mischievous. "I thought we might surprise him, you and I. If I arrange for you to investigate the crime, when Simon returns we can report that we've settled the matter."

A dozen arguments sprang into Calkin's mind. The case was years old, which meant there'd be no clues to examine. His particular skill, remembering details of a crime scene he'd seen, was no help here. There were differing stories from a witness now dead who, even if he were alive, sounded unreliable. Added to that, Calkin was a stranger in Old Change, which teetered on the farthest edge of London, more village than city. He'd be as noticeable there as an elephant in a herd of cows.

He amended the number of arguments. There were a score of reasons why this was a fool's errand. None of them would change a thing, however. If the queen ordered investigation, his duty was to obey. "I will do what I can, Your Majesty."

"Good." Taking up a pen, she scribbled a brief note. "How will you begin?"

God's knuckles! She'd put her nose in the matter, too! "I will visit the local constable —"

The queen stopped him with a gesture.

"Some onion-eyed gudgeon who'll babble in the alehouse the queen's man is on the trail of the murderer? We must be discreet, man!"

His sense of dread grew. Along with managing marriage proposals, threats of war, and financial instability, the queen intended to direct his investigation into a crime that was probably exactly what it appeared to be. Did she think to become his partner in sleuthing, as she'd been Simon's in times past?

In a flash of understanding, Calkin saw that Elizabeth missed the excitement of hunting killers. Dangerous as it had been, she and Simon had been a successful team. In her current role, matters waxed and waned but were seldom solved, and justice was difficult to achieve. A simple problem of right and wrong was irresistible, especially since she might at the same time pay Simon back for his efforts on her behalf over the years.

"You must approach it with finesse," she said. When Calkin looked confused, unsure what the word meant, she added, "Indirectly."

He spread his hands in a plea for understanding. "Your Majesty, I am no Simon, going about in disguise and asking

68

clever questions to reveal men's sins."

The queen put a hand to her chin, regarding him gravely. "That's true. You're a soldier, and no beholder would take you for anything else." She seemed momentarily stymied, and Calkin hoped he might escape, until she smiled. "We must think of a suitable falsehood."

Ten minutes later, Calkin left the room with Elizabeth's directions ringing in his ears, each one bringing arguments to mind he'd dared not say aloud. "You cannot simply appear," she cautioned, "for Hannah will wonder why you are there. Tell her I have sent you on secret business. She'll understand the need for discretion, and she will speak to her children."

When did women and children ever keep secrets? Trudging along the corridors with head down, Calkin saw only trouble ahead. If he didn't tell Hannah what he was really up to, she'd be angry when she learned the truth. If he did tell her, he'd have two unhappy women to explain to when he failed to find the killer, which, he thought glumly, was almost a certainty.

The English delegation stopped at a nameless village on the border between Scotland and England. As the ship's crew unloaded trade goods and carried fresh supplies aboard, the passengers walked along the rocky shore, stretching their muscles. Randolph explained as they walked there was no actual border, only a wide swath of land between the two nations called the marches, where lawlessness was more prevalent than peace.

"Some of the landholders are no better than outlaws," Randolph said in a disapproving tone. "They make their living by robbery, seldom caring if their victims are Scot or English."

"Is there no law to control them?" young Philip asked.

"The marches are overseen by wardens who organize patrols, watches, and garrisons to deter raiding. They can cross the border to recover loot and to arrest raiders, called reivers."

"Are they successful?"

Randolph shrugged. "Many wardens are corrupt, favoring their countrymen and relatives. Others are overwhelmed by the duty of maintaining justice in the midst of such thievery."

"It's impossible with so many places to hide and so few wardens," Coulston commented.

Randolph went on, "The march wardens

have tried setting up times when men may meet to discuss differences and settle claims. These Days of Truce are much like fairs, with entertainment and socializing."

"That seems a good idea," said Matthew, one of the younger men.

"In theory," Randolph replied with a dry smile, "but in reality, it's not unknown for violence to break out before the Days of Truce conclude."

Philip shivered. "I'll be glad to pass the border marches and reach proper Scotland."

His father muttered a comment into his beard, and Simon, being nearby, heard it. "He'll find the Scots are not always proper, even at court."

When the others turned back, Simon walked on along the shore, playing idle games with birds that showed little fear and darted away only when he came within steps of them. Tiring of their boldness, he stood looking out at the seemingly endless sea, wondering what it would be like to live here, never without its sounds and smells. As he let his mind wander, it came as usual to Hannah and the children. He missed home, having spent few nights away since he and Hannah married and never as long as this.

"Wishing you were elsewhere, Maldon?"

Turning to see Samuel Eliot standing at

his side, Simon gave a rueful smile. "The voyage is pleasant thus far, but I'm not one who loves travel."

"A man does what he must for queen and nation."

"Yes."

"You came along rather late." Eliot's brows rose, making the statement a question.

"It was indeed a late decision, but I hope I may do my part."

"One hears you met in private with Robert Dudley recently. Do you know him well?"

He probably should have lied, but Simon said, "We have met from time to time."

"You served him in the past?"

He thought of his former contacts with Dudley, when they'd joined forces to preserve Elizabeth's life. "Our purposes are at times similar, and we have helped each other."

Eliot's expression turned slightly scornful, and Simon realized he didn't seem like the sort of man Robert Dudley might seek out for help. Rather than try to explain he said, "Her Majesty sent me on this mission in concern for Master Randolph's health."

His companion gave a sarcastic snort. "Thomas is as fit as I am. He's never had a surgeon trailing his steps, and he needs none now."

Unable to argue that point, Simon turned toward the sea. The queen had made her wishes known, and all of them, whether they liked it or not, had to accept the situation.

Eliot stepped closer. "Whether you're Dudley's man or Cecil's matters not to me, Maldon. If, when a question arises in the group, you cleave to my opinion, you will be richer for it when we return to England. Do you understand?"

Simon understood he was being asked to take Eliot's side in some future debate. Unable to agree without knowing the specifics, he shrugged. "I take your meaning."

Eliot clapped a large hand on Simon's shoulder, apparently satisfied. "It is well, then."

What was Eliot's aim? Had he been sent to see a Catholic monarch never sat on the English throne again? To ruin Dudley's prospects for marrying the Scottish queen? Whatever his mission was, he appeared to think Simon might get in his way. Recalling Philip's comment that he'd killed a man, Simon wondered what Eliot would do if he opposed him. Taking in the vast amount of water before him, he couldn't help but think it would be easy to arrange an accidental drowning, especially when the victim was an untried sailor with only one good arm.

Calkin left the palace and journeyed to Moorgate at a determined pace and with a stoic expression that revealed to any who knew him that his errand was one of necessity. When he neared his destination, a cacophony of sounds greeted him, none of them pleasant. Female voices argued inside the ramshackle house, rising and falling pettishly but without any real emotion. From the back, a cock crowed over and over, as if trying to drown out the noise of his human companions. Utensils carelessly used and tossed aside clanged in accompaniment. There was no peace here, no welcome for him or any guest. His mother's house was a place of anger, and it was duty that brought him, with perhaps a small slice of pity.

He paused on the earthen threshold for a few moments, gathering himself. *I will be patient,* he told himself silently. *I will not let them upset me.* Squaring his shoulders, he knocked once then pushed the ill-fitting wooden door open and went inside. The smell of soiled linen struck him like a slap in the face, and a baby, startled by his entrance, began to cry in protest. A woman beside the fire turned toward him, her face betraying irritation. A second woman, sitting at the rough wood table, didn't seem aware of either the crying child or his entrance.

Calkin's mother sat in a corner, hands folded over her protruding belly, back so curved it took an effort to look up. She squinted toward the doorway. "Who is it, Betty? Who's there?" The seated woman stirred sluggishly on her stool, turning and focusing with some difficulty on first her brother's feet, then his torso, and finally, his face. Her mouth moved, but she didn't seem able to form a reply.

"It's Rich, Mother Calkin," his sister-in-law answered. She stirred at a pot, leek soup from the smell, adding in a sarcastic tone, "Ain't we privileged? It's still three days till Sabbath."

Ignoring Kat's barb, he approached his mother. "I came to tell you I will be away for a while on the queen's business." He reached into his pocket. "Here's money for a fortnight."

Betty rose with surprising quickness and stepped toward him, her hand extended. Calkin gave her a warning glance before setting the bag in her palm. "See it lasts until I return."

"We try." Her thin face pinched even thin-

75

ner. "But you know how dear things is."

Noting her red eyes and beery breath, he sighed but said nothing. His sister's drinking made things harder for all of them, but he understood her desire to dull her senses. He and his brother had left what passed for a home as soon as they were able. Betty had stayed with their timid, ailing father, caring for him lovingly when his wife would not. What he hadn't foreseen was that their demanding, loveless mother would suck all the joy from Betty's life, leaving her a shell of the girl she'd once been.

The sons of the house had left with high hopes for a better future, but Gerald had died in Scotland with an arrow in his throat. Richard had for a time wanted to die there, too, but life doesn't offer death on a wish. Soldiers go on, despite loss, and he'd done his duty.

When he returned from war with a position in the King's Guard and a little money in his pocket, he'd found his father had finally died of his cough, his mother had fallen along the Thames and broken a hip which never healed correctly, and his sister had begun drinking.

He often wondered if things might have been different if he'd stayed at home, but he doubted it. It was more likely they'd both have drowned in their mother's acid, and he'd have become a bitter man. Betty, who'd once toddled around behind him asking endless questions and depending on him for everything, was still dependent on him, though much less lovable. While he told himself he wasn't to blame for Betty's decline, he couldn't help but feel that he was.

The child, a boy of perhaps a year, had stopped crying, and he stared at the visitor blankly. "Whose child is that?"

"I mind him while a neighbor sells goods from a cart," Betty replied. "She gives me a little." Glancing up she added, "Not much," and he saw she was afraid he'd expect her to earn her own way in the world.

"Just as well she brings in something," Kat said, her mouth a line of disapproval. "She's no use at all to your mother — hurts her any time she touches her."

It had been a mistake to let his sister-in-law stay in the house after his brother was killed. He'd thought she would be a help to Betty, and she'd insisted she would be, but Kat was a spiteful sort who soon took to complaining about the trials of caring for a cripple. She had no talent for invalid care nor a desire to develop any. Not that his mother enkindled warm feelings in anyone,

Calkin thought grimly.

He'd made a hundred suggestions for different arrangements, but they refused to hear them, preferring what they already knew and, he suspected, enjoying their own shared misery. The three of them lived in a constant state of enmity and poverty, the younger women needing a place to live, and his mother needing — though resenting — their assistance. His part was to support them, but Betty's drinking, Kat's spite, and the old woman's complaining were a constant trial.

"Richard!" Her voice was like a nail run up his backbone. "Why must you go away?"

"I have said," he replied patiently. "The queen orders it."

She sniffed derisively. "And I'm left here with two sluts! My daughter, a lumpish baggage, and this beef-witted harpy your brother married! They're no help to me whatever!"

He heard Kat take breath to screech an insult in return, but he quieted her with a glare. "Mother, you must be content. The girls do what they can, and I'll warrant you are as large a plague to them as they are to you."

"I don't believe Her Majesty sends you anywhere," she said, the *s*'s whistling through the gaps where teeth had once been. "You're off on some adventure." She'd never forgiven him for leaving Moorgate, finding a decent position, and earning the money she now depended on. "Always one to go off on your own, never telling folk where or why. Your father said you were an independent sort, but he was more fool than man. 'Independent?' says I. 'He ain't independent, not Richard Calkin. He's a churlish, boil-brained, joithead who will do for himself. Doesn't trust anyone, doesn't confide in anyone, doesn't need anyone, since he was as tiny as a cabbage.' " Her withered lips pulled inward. "Got cabbage for brains, you do."

And who caused me to depend on myself? he thought. *Who taught me not to trust others?*

He kept silent, repeating to himself the promise he'd made at the doorway. He would not let his mother's bitterness, his sister's drunkenness, or Kat's peevishness affect him. His duty was to the queen, and the money he got in return for his loyalty provided a living for the three of them. They weren't grateful or even understanding, but as one of his mates in the Queen's Guard often said, a man who expects fairness from life should plan on a lifetime to wait for it.

He didn't kiss the old woman but patted her shoulder in farewell. "I'll see you when I return, Mother." He didn't speak to the others. Kat had turned her back, and Betty had returned to her stool and dumped the coins he'd provided in her lap. She didn't look up as he left, and the last glimpse he had as he closed the door with a scrape, she was bent over them, counting.

CHAPTER FIVE

Calkin started early the next morning, riding through the crowded streets. People might jostle a man on foot, but they knew enough to make way for a horse. When he reached the neighborhood known as Old Change, however, he dismounted and led the animal, trying to get a sense of the place. Though he'd visited Simon a few times over the years, he hadn't paid attention to the neighborhood the way he needed to now.

Old Change was neither poor nor prosperous, part of the city but separate from it. In central London, trades tended to gather together, and there were streets or even whole sections dedicated to apothecary shops, grocers, tailors, or smiths. Old Change was almost rural, with one or two pliers of each trade stretched along the narrow street or down lanes that ran a short way before ending in fields or woods.

After the noise of the city center, the place

seemed very quiet. There were sounds, to be sure, but they were individual and could be deciphered, unlike the constant roar he knew. As he passed through, Calkin picked out the thump of a cobbler's hammer, the laughter of two women at the well, and the hum of a potter's wheel.

He passed three churches, none of them very grand. A swift-flowing river crossed the area slantwise, and from the smell, he guessed there was a slaughterhouse along it somewhere to the north. There was probably a mill, too, providing grain for the local people. He guessed many inhabitants seldom left the boundaries of Old Change, making a life for themselves with what was there and avoiding the crowded heart of London.

Calkin first took a room at the inn so he could refuse Hannah's inevitable offer of a place to stay. It was actually an alehouse with two chambers to let upstairs, but that suited his purpose well. He paid for a week, telling the owner he might remain longer. The man was so curious about the purpose of his visit that he all but asked outright, and Calkin concluded strangers seldom stopped for more than a night.

He told the story Elizabeth had suggested — *ordered* was a better word. He was a recently retired soldier whose uncle had asked him to locate a cousin with a tendency to go missing. "Someone claimed they saw him near here a fortnight ago," he explained. "His name is Denis." He rubbed a hand over his freckled face. "He looks a lot like me, only not so handsome."

The host smiled politely but said he didn't remember the name or the man.

"I'll speak to your constable," Calkin said. "He'll know of strangers in the area, I trow."

"He will," the innkeeper said, adding, "if this Denis is a troublemaker, he's already sent him on his way. We do not suffer knaves in Old Change, and our constable knows his duty."

Calkin shrugged. "I'd say Denis is more idle than bad. My uncle is anxious to find him and see that he enters apprenticeship for a trade."

The innkeeper nodded agreement with the nonexistent uncle. "Work is the salvation of wayward men. I hope you find him."

The English delegation's departure one morning was delayed by the discovery of damage to the hull of their boat. The day had for once dawned sunny, and the wait was almost welcome. The delegates spread their belongings on rocks, hoping to dry them completely for once. Simon laid his cloak and doublet out flat, then sat down on a large rock, letting the warmth of the sun bake the damp out of the garments he wore. He dozed lightly, dimly aware of the sound of saws and hammers as repairs were made. Once that work was done, sounds changed to mild grunts as sailors replaced barrels and bags that had been moved out of the way. There were heavy thuds as they dropped into place on board.

When an unfamiliar voice called out, "Master, a word!" Simon opened his eyes, but the stranger hadn't spoken to him. A man approached Randolph, who turned, his expression polite.

"It is hard to know in Scotland who is important and who is not," he had commented at the outset of the voyage. "One who looks like a creature of the forest might be of gentle birth, at least according to their view of things."

The man who closed the gap between himself and Randolph was no forest creature. Barrel-chested and sandy-haired, he was dressed as well as any of them. Well armed, clothed, and fed, he stood out from the local villagers, who were wretchedly poor.

"Might ye be sent fro' th' English queen?"

the newcomer asked in a throaty burr.

"We are."

He stopped, one hand on the hilt of an over-large sword at his side, but it was more habit than threat, since he bowed formally and spoke in a pleasant tone. "I am Dickie Muir, steward t' the laird o' Duns Tower." He gestured westward. "A day's ride from here."

"Who is this laird you speak of?" Randolph asked.

"Geordie Kerr doesna go oft t' court," Muir said. "Still, we're not s' rural we dinna hear o' doings there. I'm told ye seek the Queen o' Scots."

Randolph paused with his usual caution, but he apparently saw no harm in answering. "We are indeed on the way to Holyrood for an audience with Her Majesty."

Muir stepped closer. "But she isna there. She's on a royal progress, inspectin' her lands."

A tightening of Randolph's lips revealed irritation. "She is not in Edinburgh?"

A monarch on progress moved frequently, visiting the homes of her lords. It might be weeks before they caught up with Mary. Simon shared Randolph's dismay, for finding the queen would undoubtedly require horses.

Muir spread his hands, his smile broadening. " 'Tis is a boon for ye I happen t' be here, for I can save ye miles o' journeying."

Randolph's head rose with interest. "How?"

"The queen is at ma master's tower house, or if she isna, she soon will be." He bowed gallantly. "I am willing t' guide ye there, if 't serves yer purpose."

"Your offer is most kind." Randolph never spoke or acted hastily, which Simon supposed was a good quality in an ambassador. "I will confer with my companions. Where shall we find you when we have made our decision?"

"At the inn there, with th' blue door." Muir pointed to a building hardly large enough to be called a house, much less an inn. "We leave early i' the morning, for ma master waits for the wine he sent me t' fetch." His eyes twinkled with humor. "Though I ken his wish for speed, I choose a hot meal and bed o'er a night on the trail wi' nae softness but ma playde." He touched the long piece of rough, brown fabric draped over one shoulder and under the opposite arm.

Randolph thanked him again, and the steward went on his way, whistling a jaunty tune. His position was one of trust, making

Muir responsible for much of what went on at the estate. Simon imagined he anticipated a night without duties to perform, without his laird watching and perhaps criticizing his every move.

Randolph called a meeting on the shore. "I've been informed the Queen of Scots has gone on progress." The others sighed, muttered, or growled in response, but he went on, explaining Muir's claim that Mary was presently either at Dun or on her way there.

"How do we know the fellow is truthful?" Bartholomew Empton asked, his overlarge jaw jutting. "We cannot go galloping into the marches on the word of a stranger." A few rolled their eyes, for Empton found something negative in every situation, but Simon thought, for once, Empton made a reasonable argument.

"I cannot see why he'd lie, but he is a Scot, after all," Coulston said, only half-joking.

Randolph listened as everyone had his say. "I agree we must verify this Muir's claim," he said. "James, take Philip and visit the alehouse. Bartholomew, speak to whatever sort of law officer they have in this place. Samuel and Simon, see what you can learn in the village. I will ask the ship captain what he knows of Geordie Kerr."

The party spread out over the hamlet, Eliot and Simon visiting shops hardly worthy of the name. Most were simply huts where one might buy whatever the inhabitants made, caught, or grew. Apparently gifted with a cast-iron stomach, Eliot bought and consumed a meat pie that smelt spoiled, a bit of dried fish, and some bread Hannah would have given to her pigeons. In each instance, he struck up a conversation and brought it skillfully to the subject of Geordie Kerr, Dickie Muir, and Duns Tower.

They learned very little. The people knew Muir, since he often came to meet ships and collect supplies. He liked a good time, one man reported. He paid in gold. That was all.

At the third place they stopped, the woman who'd made the stale bread mentioned a "grand lady" currently staying with a local widow. Eliot's interest kindled. "Who is this lady?"

"I canna say," the woman answered with a shrug. "She come on a ship, all by hersel', and she's waiting."

"Waiting for what?"

"I canna say." She went back to her knitting, watching her needles click together.

Simon was surprised this unusual event brought such a mild reaction, but when he mentioned it outside the shop, Eliot sniffed derisively. "These folk scratch out their living, like dogs. It kills their curiosity and even their wits." He looked around, his expression disdainful. "Peasants are the same everywhere. These know boats, nets, and tides. In other places they know cattle, corn, and planting times. England and Edinburgh are as far away to these folk as the moon, since they might never in their lives journey even as far as the next village."

Recalling some of the people he knew back home, Simon had to agree.

"Who do you suppose this grand lady is?"

Mocking the woman's tone, Eliot replied, " 'I canna say.' " He turned, surveying the area. "But we will do our best to find out."

The widow's house was a little better than most, with three rooms and well-fitting doors in front and back. She had, she told them after some shameless flattery from Eliot, rented a room to a young woman from Edinburgh who was at present out for a walk. The widow pointed out the direction the lady had gone, and Eliot started off, leaving Simon to bid her good day.

It didn't take them long to find the lady, for she stood out from everyone around her. She was apparently on her way back to the house, and when she saw them her expression revealed surprised interest. Modesty prevailed, however, and she turned her eyes to the ground.

She was beautiful, with perfect skin and hair so dark it shone blue in the sunlight. Her gown, slightly heavy for the season, was made of expensive fabric and elaborately decorated with pearls that clicked together softly when she moved. Her loveliness would have been better served with simplicity, Simon thought, for the dress seemed like gaudy baubles hung on a rose.

Eliot approached her, stopping at a respectful distance. "My lady, I pray, do not be offended that I speak so boldly. We are travelers from England, and when we learned of your presence in this remote place, we feared it must be due to some misfortune. If there is any way we can assist you, please state it candidly, and we will do our best to help."

The lady said something to her maid, an elderly woman dressed in dusty black who looked at them fearfully and turned away. The lady spoke again, but the woman hid her hands in her skirts and dropped her chin to her chest. With a disgusted look at her unwilling maid, the lady finally spoke for herself. "I thank ye for your concern, goodmen, but I require no assistance. I must journey inland, and I'm told 'tis unwise to do so without an escort. I have only now found a man who agreed t' guide and protect me on the journey."

Eliot glanced at Simon. "Is the man called Dickie Muir?"

She looked surprised. "Why, yes. Do ye know him?"

"We met him only today when he offered to guide us to Duns Tower."

"Why, that is where I must go." She touched the pearls at her neck, setting them dancing.

"Might we ask your purpose?" Eliot asked. "I assure you, it is not idle curiosity."

She considered the question before answering. "I go t' meet my lady, the Queen o' Scots, who is on her way t' visit Geordie Kerr, the laird of Duns."

Begging the lady's pardon, Eliot took Simon aside and ordered, "Go to the wharf and tell the others. I will ascertain the details of the queen's plans." Simon went, guessing Eliot's purpose was at least partly due to a desire to spend a little more time with the beautiful lady.

Most of the party had returned, and they compared information. The people of the village confirmed Dickie Muir was indeed Geordie Kerr's liegeman, and while no one praised his character, none suggested he was a liar, either. The exact whereabouts of the queen were unknown, but rumors of a planned progress during the summer months had reached the village.

Muir had indeed come to purchase several casks of wine from the ship that carried them north. "The captain says he claims it is for an important guest," Randolph reported.

When it was Simon's turn, he told them about the lady. "She came to meet the queen and will travel inland with Muir on the morrow."

Eliot joined them as he finished and Randolph asked, "How does this lady know the Scottish queen's whereabouts?"

"She is one of Mary's inner circle," Eliot replied. "Her name is Agnes, and she sailed down the coast hoping to intercept the queen at Duns, bringing only a manservant and a maid."

"A woman alone?" Empton said in disgust. "Has she no father to instruct her?"

Eliot shrugged. "She has waited here for three days, eager to rejoin her mistress, perhaps fearful of losing her place if they are apart too long."

"Why is this woman not with the queen if she's one of her circle?" Coulston asked.

"She was ill when the queen left the capital but has since recovered." Eliot gave a sly smile. "She says she will appreciate travelling with a dozen stout Englishmen." That earned him a disgusted snort from Empton and amused looks from several others.

Simon, who had read everything he could find on Scotland before starting on the trip, thought he recalled Mary's closest companions were four women, all named Mary. However, the queen might have added Agnes to her circle recently. Agnes might not be as close to the queen as she claimed. Or the newssheets might have been wrong, as they often were.

There was a lull as everyone waited for Randolph to reach the decision in his deliberate manner. Squaring his shoulders, he delivered an opinion. "We have confirmed Muir works for this laird, and a second source tells us the queen is either at Duns Tower or soon will be. Are we agreed we save ourselves a trip to Edinburgh?" The decision was his, but he sought consensus, as any wise leader might.

More discussion followed. Matthew wanted to see Edinburgh, having heard much of the forbidding castle that shadowed the city below. Coulston consoled him.

"Edinburgh Castle is a great sight, but a smaller holding will be less formal, and the laird is likely to go to great pains to entertain his queen. There will be sights to see at Duns Tower, I trow."

In the end they agreed, and Randolph turned to practicalities. "Matthew, find horses and a cart for the morning. Philip, unload our baggage from the ship and set it ashore. John, get what supplies you can for the journey. There should be dried fish hereabouts." He added in a mutter, "God knows when we shall find decent food again!"

Simon was assigned no task, but he offered to help Philip move their possessions to the narrow beach. In the process, he found the bag left behind by their missing guide, Munn. There was nothing inside worth much. He gave the contents and the bag to the sailors, keeping back only the letter that told Munn of his sweetheart's untimely death. He'd probably carried it with him for years. Why, Simon wondered again, had he not taken it when he stole away in the night?

The rest of the day was simply waiting, which left Simon's mind free to wander. Would the queen be at Duns Tower when they arrived? Would the horse he'd be given be amenable to amateur handling? The only thing he didn't question about the near future was that he'd arrive at Duns with a sore backside.

CHAPTER SIX

After his father went to Scotland, Henry spent his days mixing, packaging, and displaying their goods. As required by the guild, he worked at a table in the center of the room, in full view of customers. Behind him were shelves of raw ingredients, stored in jars, boxes, and paper cones. Against the west wall, a long table held merchandise for sale, including sweets Hannah and Annie made, pynade, gingerbread, and spiced fruits in almond cream.

Simon had installed a window at the front of the shop to let in light, and, though the glass distorted the view somewhat, customers could look in and see a table of cosmetics for sale. Susan was in charge of making an eye-catching display, but her work was slowed by her need to examine each jar and box. Henry watched fondly as she paused to inhale each aroma appreciatively, occasionally testing a concoction with her finger. Though she was fascinated by the enhancements available to women, Susan needed nothing to complete her beauty. At ten years old, she already brought interested looks from men. Hannah had recently moved Susan's bed from the loft to the main floor, and Henry guessed it was because of him. Despite Hannah's fears, he loved Susan only as his little sister. He admired her open, carefree manner, while he, with his silences and downcast eyes, generated only suspicion.

Susan chattered to Henry as she added to the window display, apparently not minding that he said little in return. Conversation was Susan's natural state, and Henry's tendency to silence provided a good listener.

After covering the topic of their father's absence, the baker's sick dog, and the story she'd just read in one of Simon's books, she brought up a subject that had apparently been troubling her. "Do you think someone killed Uncle Will on purpose?"

Henry believed in truth. "I do. But you mustn't worry on it, Poppet."

He couldn't take his own advice, though. While Henry knew firsthand how unfair life could be, the idea Will Clark's death might have been murder made his insides roil with anger.

"He was such a jolly man," Susan said. "And he said I should call him Uncle Will, though Grandmother always said we're not really part of the family."

He was surprised she remembered Mary Maldon's slights, for she'd been dead for years. Odd, too, that sunny little Susan had sensed the old lady's resentment at having to accept two orphans into the family. "Simon says we're his children, no matter what others say."

Susan's mother died just days after she was born, but Hannah had taken her to her heart, becoming her mother in all but blood. Henry, a skinny waif from the worst part of London, had no one to care for him until Simon Maldon took him in. In spite of this, Simon's mother had never stopped suggesting this herb or that amulet in hopes Hannah would become pregnant. She'd never truly accepted them as her grand-children, calling them "the boy" and "the girl." In those early days, Henry had prayed Hannah would never bear children, lest he be cast aside. It took a long time, but he'd finally become convinced his place here was permanent. Now he sometimes felt guilty, wondering if his prayers had kept Hannah barren. The thought came in church, in those brief moments when the preacher almost convinced him God answered prayer.

"Will took you fishing, lots of times," Susan was saying. "He liked to fish, didn't he?"

"He did." Will had often stopped by to invite Henry along when he took his own sons fishing. Will never minded he didn't say much, never urged him to "Speak up!" as others did.

Had Will known how much Henry liked him? He'd never said it, finding it hard to leave the shell he'd built as protection from life's buffets. Henry knew he seemed cold and unfriendly to most people, but reticence was part of him. Will had understood, as Simon did.

His sister was still talking, but typically, she'd wandered from Will's death to the subject of Annie's future. "Mother says Aunt Annie should marry again," she said, tying a ribbon around the neck of a pomander. "A woman needs a man to keep her, as a man needs a woman to love."

Annie was indeed lovable. Like her husband, she'd looked into Henry's eyes and seen the boy inside the solemn shell. "Poor lamb," she often said. "We must fatten you up, or you'll blow away in the next storm!"

Though Henry had never become fat —

or even plump, as Annie herself was — she always had something for him in her apron pocket. "Eat this," she'd say. "A growing boy needs food."

"I'm going to marry Matthew Taylor," Susan announced. "He'll have a shop, and I'll greet the customers and arrange the wares while he makes fine clothing."

"That will be a good life." Henry was distracted by thoughts of murder. Though no one had questioned the account of Will's death at the time, Blackie's revised version rang true the minute Henry heard it. Hannah's claim it was delusion came from her desire for peace in their lives. Simon's doubts stemmed from his desire to believe the world's evil did not stalk good men. But Henry had lived with evil. He knew goodness was no protection from ruthless men.

"You should think about the kind of girl you'd like to marry," Susan advised, her expression earnest. "It's an important decision, you know."

He couldn't help but smile. He was undersized, spoke seldom and bluntly, and had no idea who his real parents were. What girl would want him? Despite that he promised gravely, "I'll consider it, Poppet, if you will see the pigeons have enough water."

Susan hurried away, blond curls bouncing

as she went. Almost as soon as she disappeared, a man stepped into the shop, ducking his head to avoid bumping it against the frame.

"Calkin!"

"Henry, you grow taller each time I see you," Simon's old friend said. "Hannah must stop feeding you so well, or you'll not fit in your bed."

"I'll tell her you're here."

"Do that." Calkin gave him a playful push toward the doorway. "Ask if she has a morsel of food for a starving man."

Though he didn't visit often, Calkin was always welcome at the Maldon home. The guardsman and Simon had been friends for years, and though he'd been ill at ease around Hannah at first — Simon said because he hadn't been around many decent women — he'd become used to her and could converse with only occasional pauses to censor his language. Henry listened eagerly as they rehashed stories of the old days, when Simon had apparently had some part in chasing down criminals. He guessed Calkin was the major figure in these events, since his father was much too gentle to go about battling desperate men.

Hannah always urged Calkin to take a wife, and he always grinned and said marriage was not for him. His visits generally ended with the two men going outside to throw knives at a target behind the house, which led Hannah to comment they were too old for such things.

When Henry told her of Calkin's arrival, Hannah adjusted her cap, smoothed her apron, and went into the shop. "Calkin! It's good to see you. Simon is away, but come in!"

Ordering Henry to pull up the best chair, she ladled out a bowl of garbage, soup made from chicken heads and feet. As she told their guest about Simon's trip, she cut a generous slice of fresh bread and set a tart she'd made that morning on the table before him.

As Hannah fussed with preparations, Calkin teased Susan about how tall she'd become. Why did grownups always comment on a person's height? Henry wondered. Susan seemed pleased to be noticed, however, and he supposed that was the purpose.

Between bites, Calkin told them the reason for his presence in Old Change. "I'm sent by the queen to investigate a merchant who cheats on the price of goods sent to the palace."

"The queen takes note of such things?"

Susan asked in amazement.

Calkin looked uncomfortable, but Hannah said, "She notices everything. I never knew anyone half as clever, and certainly no woman."

"They say her grandfather was a careful man with money. I suppose it's in the blood." Henry thought Calkin was relieved Hannah had accepted his statement so readily.

A bump sounded at the back door, where family and friends came and went. Annie Clark entered, her back to them as she carried a cloth-covered object in her hands. While Simon was tall and thin, like their father had been, Annie had her mother's short stature. A barbe, a linen band that often signified widowhood, framed her pretty face. "Oh!" she said when she turned and saw a stranger in their midst. "I didn't know you had company."

"Annie! Please come in. This is Simon's friend . . . Calkin." Hannah seemed to realize for the first time that after years of acquaintance, she had no idea what the rest of his name was.

"Richard," Calkin supplied, rising from his chair. "Richard Calkin."

"My sister-in-law, Annie Clark."

Annie set down a dish she'd carried in,

and Henry caught the aroma of apple cake. Hannah was a good cook, but Annie baked the best desserts of anyone he knew. In the shop, her goods were imprinted with an oak leaf to distinguish them from Hannah's. Annie received the money from the sale of her goods, and the two families split what didn't sell by the end of the day. The practice suited Henry, since he had, Hannah often said, an amazing capacity for food.

"You've no doubt heard us speak of Calkin," Hannah told her sister-in-law. "He and Simon have been friends for many years, though we don't see him as often as we'd like."

"I was thinking that very thing on the way here." Calkin looked at Annie as he spoke. "I should make a greater effort to see my friends the Maldons." His voice sounded odd, the tone lower than it had been a minute ago.

Hannah offered Annie a tart, which she politely refused. She was, she explained, halfway through a spiced custard when she'd discovered she had only a few raisins left. Hannah rose to get some for her. "I could do without them," Annie said to Calkin, "but they add to the flavor."

"I am one who would have raisins in everything," Calkin said. "And currants, too."

Annie seemed to find that humorous, and she giggled the way Susan did when the apprentice down the street told her she was pretty.

Hannah returned with raisins wrapped in a cloth, but Annie lingered despite her earlier claim she was in a hurry. In response to her question, Calkin said he'd come to Old Change to locate a missing cousin, catching Henry's eye in warning as he said it. Henry didn't like Annie being lied to, but the guardsman's mission was apparently not one he could admit to everyone.

"Where will you stay?" Susan asked, and Henry waited, hoping Hannah would invite him to stay with them.

"I have a room at the inn." He added with a comical grimace, "The fellow in the stable suggested I take my meals elsewhere, since the food is worth neither the price nor the eating."

"You must take your meals with us," Hannah said.

Calkin shook his head. "No, though I thank you. I'm an old soldier, and I've learned to eat where I happen to be when I get hungry."

Annie was horrified. "You must have at least one meal each day, or you'll grow weak. My house is only a short walk from the inn, and it will be no trouble if you share our mid-day meal while you are here."

"You'll not be disappointed in Annie's cooking," Hannah put in. "She is a marvel." Annie blushed at the compliment.

Calkin considered. "I agree, if you let me pay you a fair price." When Annie drew breath to argue, he raised a hand. "I have funds for expenses, so it's not my money you'll be taking."

There was some polite haggling as Annie named a figure too low and Calkin offered one she claimed was too high. In the end Hannah quoted what she thought was reasonable, and the two agreed. Once that was settled, Annie turned brisk. "I must go. My two youngest will be tearing each other limb from limb."

Finishing his second tart, Calkin rose and brushed the crumbs from his lap. "I, too, must be on my way." Turning to Annie, he bowed slightly and said rather formally, "I'm pleased we finally met, Goodwife Clark. Simon never told me his sister was so fair."

Henry caught the smile Hannah quickly hid as Annie covered her embarrassment with a businesslike tone. "Anyone can tell you the way to my house. I'll expect you tomorrow." Sidling past Calkin, she took the raisins she'd come for and left, giving them a farewell wave.

Calkin's gaze remained for a while on the door where she'd exited. It was almost as if he was thinking of Annie, but Henry dismissed that thought. Calkin was close to forty years in age. His aunt, almost as old, had four children. What had seemed like flirting in their parting glances must have been something else.

"Well, Richard," Hannah said teasingly, "I trust we will see you again while you are here, even though you chose to stay at an inn and dine with my sister-in-law."

Calkin turned at Hannah's tone. "I mean no offense to your hospitality, but this business of mine is best handled without involving you." He put up a hand as her eyes widened. "I foresee no danger, but to be safe, I will be only an old acquaintance of Simon's. Leave it there." He turned his gaze to Henry. "Do you understand?"

He might as well have said: *I have a man's work to do, and I don't want a boy's interference.* Henry nodded. Calkin's presence didn't change his plans. His uncle had been murdered, and he wanted to know who'd done it. What did he care about the queen's business?

■ ■ ■ ■

Calkin left the apothecary shop slightly discontented. He disliked lying to Hannah, the children, and the widow of the victim, who was pretty and quite lively, too. Though he knew it was best to banish emotion when delving into crime, he liked the Maldons. All of them.

The queen's suggestion — again, *demand* was more precise — had been he should first determine who'd benefited from Clark's death. That, he figured, was the present searcher. A stranger who asked questions was unlikely to get answers. Calkin needed to establish a reason for his presence, then let time make him a familiar face in Old Change. Seating himself at a table in the alehouse, he told anyone who'd listen he was looking for his cousin, Denis Crooks. Once that was known, he hoped the local folk would be less suspicious of him. After a few rounds, some were bound to become talkative, and when the talking began, informative bits slipped out.

The first night Calkin talked a lot, paying no mind to the minimal answers he got. He spun a tale that Denis had been friends with a man named Blackie. "If I can find the fellow tomorrow," he said, "he'll surely tell me where my cousin has gone."

After a pause, the host told him the bad news. "Blackie died, perhaps a seven-night ago."

"There's ill luck for both of us," Calkin responded. "Did he have a wife or family that might be able to tell me something?"

"None," a man across the room answered. "To say truth, it was difficult to tell how he lived, with no income, no family, and no friends."

"A scoundrel, was he?"

The inhabitants seemed to recall as one that Calkin was not one of them. No one answered, and he retreated, making an innocuous comment about the weather. That led to discussion of the river level, which brought up the price of goods. That touched a nerve in one man, who voiced the opinion prices were high due to the guilds that controlled every trade and business.

"But don't the guilds work for the good of us all?" Calkin asked innocently. "To see we're not cheated or poisoned with bad food?"

"They should." The man buried his nose in his bowl of ale. Knowing a pregnant pause when he met one, Calkin waited expectantly. Sometimes all a person needed was a patient listener. After a gulp of ale, the rest of it came out. "If honest men run things, then all is well."

He said no more, but Calkin deduced there was dishonesty in the workings of the local guilds. He didn't push, but said instead, "This talk of guilds reminds me. Searchers are in and out of many places, and yours might have seen my cousin in his travels."

The man glared at the table. "Our searcher notices nothing that doesn't put money in his pocket." He went on, as if compelled to speak his dislike aloud. "John Dodgson couldn't tell the truth if it stood beside the Devil and he had only to choose between them."

Well, well, Calkin thought. *I have the searcher's name, and it seems he's dishonest.*

At a surprisingly early hour, the inn's patrons went off to their homes, and the serving wenches put away the bowls and wiped the tables. Taking the hint, Calkin retreated to his room upstairs, but he had trouble falling asleep. Sounds from below diminished and ceased, and the place went silent as a tomb. The absolute darkness of the room felt empty and vaguely threatening. In the barracks there was always light, always someone to talk to, something going on. How, he wondered, did a person sleep when it was dead quiet, and how did a man feel safe and at ease without the brash, easy company of soldiers around him?

CHAPTER SEVEN

When the party travelling to Duns Tower assembled at daylight, they were almost twenty: the Englishmen; Muir and two servants who handled the cart with the wine kegs; and Lady Agnes and her two attendants. Agnes seemed shy among so many men, but upon seeing how lovely she was, several in the group were anxious to run any errand she might wish done.

Muir paid no attention to Agnes whatsoever, but organized their departure in business-like fashion. Randolph deferred to him as an expert in local matters, and they worked out an orderly train: a half-dozen men in the lead, including Muir, Simon, and Randolph; the two carts with their goods; the lady, who rode sidesaddle as her dour manservant led the horse and her maidservant trudged stoically behind; and finally the rest of the men as a rear guard against bandits. "The path is bumpy,"

Muir explained as they set out. "Laden carts hae a difficult passage, but ma men are skilled at repairs."

They started along a wide, smooth path that led from the seacoast village into the marches. The way soon narrowed and roughened, however, crossing barren tracts that had, Muir informed them, once been forested. "Tha were cleared over th' years for firewood and buildin' materials. The crown sends out pleas tha' we plant trees where we can, for wood is verra dear. The birds and beasts eat both seed and seedlings, sae what's harvested doesna grow again."

There were wooded areas along the way, dark and thick and silent. After the warnings he'd heard concerning the marches, Simon couldn't help but imagine each tree held bandits, waiting in the branches to drop on them like predatory birds. None appeared, but unable to shake the prickles at the back of his neck, he often glanced upward and behind like a frightened child.

The open areas were rocky and uneven, and he worked to maintain his seat as the horse sought its way. Luckily his mount was a placid sort, uninterested in being either leader or last. She was the best Simon could have hoped for in equine equipment, ambling along with the other horses, never shying or offering to bite. Some of the others chuckled to see Simon dismount, however, for due to his weak arm he dropped clumsily to the ground and often staggered several steps backward before regaining his balance.

The morning's journey was dreary, with the sky above them an unrelieved gray and the land not much brighter. Muir, in the lead, tossed comments over his shoulder, difficult to hear due to Simon's position and hard to understand due to the Scot's pronunciation. Simon had to think for a moment when their guide pointed west and said, "Ye micht clap een on deer thonder." He thought that meant there were deer in the spot indicated but learned later that Muir used "deer" in the old sense, meaning any wild animal. With time, the Scot's dialect began to make sense to him. Since the vocabulary was much the same as English, he only missed occasional words.

At mid-day, Muir's forethought paid off. With a terrible crack, the cart Matthew had procured in the village broke an axle. "Tha' cheated ye, o' course," the steward said with a shrug as he surveyed the splintered wood, "but it's nae matter."

And it wasn't. His men uncovered an array of tools and materials, including a spare axle, and went to work, putting it into place in short order.

While repairs were made, Simon tethered his horse to a tree and walked the length of the train, exercising his tired muscles. As he passed, Agnes's maid was unfastening the foot-strap that allowed a lady to maintain her seat on a sidesaddle. Turning aside for sake of her modesty, he nevertheless offered his good arm as a steadying point as she dismounted.

"I thank ye," Agnes said, straightening her skirts. He bowed, noting again her shy manner. Though he'd heard the Scottish court was backward, he'd never imagined a queen's lady-in-waiting would blush and look away from one so lowly as he.

Lady Agnes wore another sumptuous gown, though its sleeves were too long. The hem dragged the ground, too. Having read that Queen Mary was taller than most women, Simon guessed Agnes had received it as a gift from her mistress. Apparently the girl had no one to adjust it to fit her, and she looked a little like a child playing dress-up.

The two women disappeared into the trees, reminding Simon this was a good time to do the same. Taking the opposite direction and going just far enough to be discreet, he relieved himself. Before making his way back to the group he stopped, considering the vast emptiness of the land they were crossing. Used to having a shop or cart nearby where he might purchase almost anything, Simon found it odd to think the bag of coins Elizabeth had provided were worthless here. There were no goods to buy for miles and no one to sell them, though there might well be, he thought with a shiver, men eager to steal the money.

The cart was repaired quickly, and they started off again. The rest of the day was uneventful, and Simon grew used to the sound of grinding cart wheels, the smell of damp horses, and the ache of thigh muscles locked in an unfamiliar position.

At dusk they climbed a long, low hill that sloped sharply downward on the other side. Below them was a pretty little lake, a "tarn," according to Muir. On the far bank, jutting from the hillside like a rocky fist, stood a formidable stone structure known as a peel tower. It was surrounded by several other buildings, the largest also of stone, the others of lesser materials and size. Geordie Kerr's holding. It took a while to reach it, since they had to skirt the lake, so Simon had plenty of time to take in the character of the place, which seemed stark and unwelcoming.

"On the borders, protection coomes before decoration." Muir said, sensing his visitors' dismay at the aspect of the place. "Dun's Tower was partly burned during the Rough Wooing."

A dozen years earlier, English troops had invaded Scotland in an attempt to force a marriage between Mary Stuart and the English king, Edward VI. The conflict had ended with the Treaty of Nordham, which essentially returned matters to where they'd been when it began, but estates near the border had taken the worst of the disagreement.

Simon tried to see past the dour aspect of Duns Tower and consider it as the home of a Scottish laird and his people. It was quieter than he'd expected. Randolph noticed, too, reining his horse to gaze at the adamant structure. "Not a lively sight, for all the queen is a-coming."

Simon agreed. Either the party had not yet arrived, or Mary traveled without the parade of courtiers and servants that exited London when an English monarch left the city.

"Her Majesty knows we are simple folk," Muir said with a shrug. "Wi' such as us she'll expect no fripperies. She'll gie a bed, good food, and —" He tilted his head at the casks on the cart behind them. "— wine tha' compares well wi' what she was served i' France."

As they neared, clouds above them broke apart and the moon appeared, hanging over the tower like the ghost of some long-dead laird. The rectangular structure it illuminated was obviously defensive in purpose. Judging by the arrow slits, the tower had four stories and allowed a full-circle view. Only about twelve meters square, it was too small for daily living but undoubtedly useful as a refuge in times of trouble. The second level had an addition the others didn't have, a covered walkway with a half-wall surrounding it. Along it would be murder holes, trapdoors through which defenders could drop rocks, hot tar, or other discouraging substances on attackers below.

Linked to the tower was a hall house, living quarters for the laird, his family, and their servants. A courtyard Muir called a "barmkin" was edged by a low stone wall, and a ditch on its inner side could probably be flooded to further slow an enemy assault.

As they passed, Muir looked up at the tower and saluted. Simon couldn't see anyone, and no welcoming voice responded.

There was only chilly silence.

They dismounted under a large, red sandstone arch, where two small boys took charge of their horses. Following Muir through double doors, they entered a vaulted room that served as the tower's base. There was a shallow well, some cattle stalls, and a pigpen, all empty. A dozen chickens pecked at the floor in search of food, crooning at the interruption.

Simon compared the inside with what he'd seen on approach. When invaders came, the tower's basalt rubble walls, sturdy and thick, would become a haven for the family, their servants, and the peasants who lived in huts scattered along the lake shore. They would desert their homes, bringing their animals and what food they had time to gather. Entering the tower, they'd close the heavy wooden doors behind them, making Duns conquerable only by siege, which would require more effort than the result could justify.

The tower was not their present destination, however. Muir turned right and opened a second doorway, ushering them into a house less defensible than the tower but much more comfortable. They came directly into the hall, a large, open room with a fire-pit in the center. Through the smoke, Simon's eye was drawn to a jumbled mass of tapestries that covered the walls haphazardly. Though colorful, some were dirty, others torn, and still others frayed at the edges. They overlapped, and some hung sideways or even upside down. He guessed their purpose was insulation, not adornment, and in truth the hall was chilly, despite the time of year.

Beside the fire, on a raised platform that held only an elaborately carved stool black with age, a lone figure sat, turned away from them as if, Simon thought, to present a noble profile.

Clearing his throat, Muir announced, "Ye hae guests, m'lord." The laird remained another moment in position, apparently in deep thought, then turned and regarded them with what was no doubt meant to be grave dignity. It looked more like dyspepsia, and Simon suppressed a smile, wondering if he should offer a calming physic.

Kerr was a man of unremarkable features, a plain face, pale eyes, and a rather weak chin under a mouth that turned slightly down at the edges. The most remarkable thing about him was his hair, tied at the back, mere wisps about his ears and on his chin, but a huge loaf of reddish fluff on top. It leaned out from his brow like the figurehead of a ship, pointing whatever way he turned. Though Simon tried to look him in the eye, the lump a few inches above almost screamed for attention.

Gesturing theatrically, Muir raised his voice. "Ma liege laird, masters, Geordie Kerr." Surprised that Muir had not mentioned the lady, Simon turned and saw that Agnes was no longer part of the group. There was no time to wonder where she'd gone, however, for their host, apparently satisfied he'd achieved a bold impression, rose, stepped down from his platform, and came toward them, sloshing liquid from the bowl he held as he raised his arms in greeting.

"Welcome, friends! Ye're most welcome!"

Randolph bowed. "We thank you, Your Worship. I am —"

"I ken who ye are. We're most pleased t' receive Elizabeth's delegation. Most pleased." Setting his bowl on the stool, Kerr shook Randolph's hand with both of his then went on, greeting each of them. When his turn came, Simon noticed the man's hands were like ice. *Too much phlegm,* he thought. *His humors need balancing.*

Glancing around the room, Randolph said diffidently, "We were given to understand that your queen would be in residence, sir.

While we are most grateful for your welcome, we will not tarry if the information we received is incorrect."

"She will coome, masters. She will coome." Kerr gestured widely. "Ye hae seen fer yerselves how treacherous the roads are hereabout, wi' the cursed rain. I expect the watchers'll sight her party tomorrow, and she shall dine wi' us at mid-day."

"That is welcome news." Randolph turned to practical matters. "May we prevail upon your hospitality until her arrival?"

"O' course, o' course!" Kerr raised his voice. "Nettie! Tavish!"

As if she'd been waiting, a young woman appeared in a doorway behind Kerr. Moments later a young man slid into place at her side, dwarfing her. Both wore shapeless, tattered tunics, and the girl had put one over another, presumably because modesty demanded it. From their similar look, Simon guessed they were sister and brother. Though the girl was slight and the youth oversized, their coloring and facial features were much alike except for an ugly scar that paralleled the man's right eyebrow. He stood expressionless, but his fists bunched as he awaited the laird's command. The girl's eyes remained downcast, but she brushed a hand against his arm as if in warning.

"We hae guests. Nettie, fetch food. Tavish, bring oot the boards." Simon felt a wave of gratitude. Kerr was not obligated to feed them so late, but the dried fish they'd brought along had turned out to be almost inedible, and he was famished.

With a glance at Tavish that seemed half plea and half warning, Nettie disappeared, presumably toward the kitchen. Like a figure made of wood magically gifted with movement, Tavish went to a corner and pulled two trestles out, setting boards across them to make a table. As he worked, Kerr warned, "I can offer nae more than a place here in th' hall fer yer beds."

"We will be grateful for it," Randolph replied, though he glanced at the rushes strewn on the hard-packed floor. They looked as if they'd been in place for some time, and Simon wondered if the Scots had different bugs than those he was used to.

Nettie returned with a tray of bread and a soft concoction the laird called crowdie. Explaining that it was a local cheese, he urged them to help themselves. Following Kerr's example, each man tore off a piece of oat bread, dragged it through the soft stuff, and tasted it warily. Simon found it excellent, though he wasn't sure if it was the flavor or his empty stomach that approved.

The girl, who had hurried out as soon as she set down the tray of food, returned with a pail of strong-smelling beer. Tavish set out bowls, and the men dipped them into the bucket, serving themselves as they washed down their bread and cheese.

As they ate, Kerr talked, something Simon quickly concluded he enjoyed more than most. He'd become laird of Duns Tower only a few years before, he said, and he lived by raising sheep and cattle. "I am nae a wealthy man." He pulled at the belt encircling his ample waist. "But when God wills 't, we dinna gae hungry."

The host's modesty rang false in Simon's ears. He wore clothing of a quality far above what one might expect in such a rural region, though his outfit seemed unplanned, a mix of silks with rougher, warmer fabrics. Observing the rags the servants wore, Simon concluded there was some wealth at Duns, but the laird chose not to share it with his people.

Kerr was full of stories of his own grand exploits. He'd been a soldier, he said, adding with a chuckle, "the son of a man who lived like the wealthy and died a pauper." A noble father who left his son penniless was a common enough story. Kerr was probably lucky to have secured this holding, poor though it might be. He might easily have spent his life as a sword for hire, living in this country or that and fighting nameless wars for petty princes.

When the rush lights began to sputter, Kerr said his goodnights and left the hall. Tavish put the boards and trestle away again, clearing space for them and the rest of the household to sleep. Each man of the party made himself the most comfortable bed he could manage, using what he had to pad the hard, cold floor. As Simon spread his doctor's cloak out, Nettie passed with the empty beer bucket.

"I trust the lady was offered food and drink," he said.

Nettie stopped, looking directly at Simon, and in the light of the banked fire he saw that one of her eyes was ringed with fading bruises and suffused with streaks of blood. "The lady?"

"Agnes, who arrived with us," he explained. "I suppose she was given a private room."

Her blank look was replaced by something else, and she looked away. "Ah, Lady Agnes. Yes, she will sleep in a fine bed this night."

"Good, then. I thank you for your kind-ness."

Nettie seemed surprised, but Simon didn't explain that his wife had once been a servant like her. Such women received little thanks for the hard work they did, and he suspected in this remote place, Nettie's lot might be worse than most.

CHAPTER EIGHT

It took Calkin some time to find the searcher the next morning. No one he asked could say where he was or might be at some point. He supposed, since searchers monitored merchants' business practices, it was wise for them to avoid an established schedule or a known route.

Finally a woman said she'd seen Dodgson enter a shop a few minutes earlier. She pointed the way, saying, "Look for a rooster of a man."

It sounded odd, but the moment he saw Dodgson, Calkin admitted she'd found the perfect description. In a slightly run-down grocer's shop he found two men, and the grocer's wife. One was paying for items he'd bought, and he chatted with the woman as he stowed them in a bag slung over his shoulder. The other stood off to one side, watching. He was almost a miniature, no more than five feet tall, with shiny, dark eyes and a face that seemed to have been shaved to a beak-like point. He wore a well-made suit but no cap, and his hair, which was reddish and stiff, stood up at the crown in a way that suggested a cockscomb.

Calkin played the role of waiting customer, examining the asparagus and sniffing the rhubarb. The shop was dark, and the corners smelled moldy. A flash of movement along one wall looked suspiciously like a rat. Though he'd been in worse places, he wouldn't buy here, given a choice.

The woman behind the table glanced nervously at Dodgson every few seconds, though she maintained a friendly exchange with her customer. Hannah Maldon wouldn't have been seen in a dress as dirty as the one the shopkeeper wore, and her cap was even worse.

Dodgson's bright eyes moved briefly to Calkin when he entered, but his interest soon returned to the sale in progress. When her customer left, the woman turned to Calkin. "Good day, master. Is there aught I can help you find?"

"I was hoping for limes, but I thank you." Leaving the shop, Calkin stopped near the door as if waiting for someone. By standing aslant, he could see the two people inside peripherally and watch their exchange, though he couldn't hear what was said.

The woman and Dodgson had a lengthy conversation, and a tone of argument in the woman's voice carried to the door. Dodgson's voice remained level but slightly threatening. In the end he gestured first with one hand and then with the other, indicating a choice. From the woman's expression, she was unhappy with both options.

From the corner of his eye Calkin watched closely, almost certain he'd soon see money change hands. Having seen the condition of the shop, and recalling what his companion at the inn had said last evening, he guessed the owners paid the searcher not to report them. Dodgson was probably negotiating a better deal. The practice was all too common, for while the guilds paid searchers well to discourage bribe-taking, there were some who did it anyway.

In the end, Dodgson glanced at the doorway, saw only the apparently inattentive Calkin, and leaned toward the woman. Glaring, she fumbled in her apron pocket. There was a clink of coins. Dodgson bowed mockingly and left, smiling with satisfaction.

When he'd disappeared around a corner,

Calkin went back inside, took up a handful of dried cherries, and took them to the woman, who stared out the door, tight-jawed and angry.

"I'll have a penny's worth of these." Pretending to notice her expression for the first time, he asked, "Is something wrong, goodwife?"

She smiled, but it took effort. "A headache, that's all."

"I hope that man did nothing to upset you."

"No," she said quickly. "I have no complaint of him, nor he of us, I trow."

"He seemed a man of importance, at least in his own mind," Calkin said in a joking tone.

Her face relaxed slightly. "He's our searcher, so his favor is important to us."

"He seems young for a searcher."

She shook her head. "Our last one was much the same age."

"And was the job not to his liking?"

"He died." Her eyes widened with the eagerness of one with a lurid story to tell. "A thief killed him for his purse, which held only a few coins. And he with a wife and young children!"

Calkin feigned dismay. "There are thieves

hereabouts who will kill a man for his purse?"

"It were some years ago," she said soothingly. "It was the day our blessed Elizabeth came to London, after her sister the old queen died."

"Oh. Did the authorities find the killer and punish him?"

She frowned. "I think not. But our constable is watchful. He suffers no evil men, and those who seem idle or dangerous are soon sent on their way."

Calkin brought the subject back to Dodgson. "So the man who is now the searcher got the post when the former searcher was killed?"

She thought about that. "Not until later. For some time there was no searcher. Then one day Dodgson — that's his name — came through on his way to somewhere else. When he heard about the position, he went to the guild house and showed letters saying how he'd done the work in Lincoln, and they took him on." She finished with a hint of triumph, "We've had no bad reports since he came. None."

Thanking the woman, Calkin left the shop, tossing the shriveled cherries he'd bought to the birds. Dodgson wasn't the culprit, since he'd arrived after Will's death.

Though he'd formed an immediate aversion to the man, he reminded himself not everyone he disliked was a killer.

Waking on the floor at Duns Tower, Simon felt the damp had seeped into his very bones. The rushes indeed contained an assortment of insects. Yesterday's ride had left his legs feeling rubbery, and he found that Scottish beer stimulated his bladder the way English ale never had. The doors had been bolted for the night, so twice he'd had to rise, tiptoe among the huddled bodies on the floor, and relieve himself from a window at the far end of the room.

Embarrassed to see that everyone else was up and gone, he went outside to find Randolph and Coulston with their heads bent in conversation. "Good morrow."

They turned. "Good morrow, Maldon." Randolph seemed cheerful, at least, for Randolph. "If all goes well, we shall soon be able to see to our purpose."

Coulston straightened his doublet as if readying himself for an audience. "We must pray that all goes well and the cursed Scottish rains don't delay the queen another day."

The weather was better than yesterday, meaning the sky was a pale gray rather than gray-black. The laird's workers moved about, some tending a garden just outside the wall, others driving a few cattle onto a grassy spot on the south slope. Four children played near a waterfall that flowed from the rocks above, and an older girl passed them with a pan of bread crusts, sprinkling them across the ground as she called softly, "Here, chick, chick, chick! Chick!"

Randolph and Coulston discussed for the hundredth time how best to approach the topic of marriage between Mary Stuart and Robert Dudley. Randolph contended they should speak highly of Dudley for a few days before suggesting him as a bridegroom. Coulston argued they should begin with the idea of marriage to an English lord, keeping the identity of the candidate secret until the queen had agreed in principle to such a match.

Simon interrupted as something struck him. "No preparations."

"What?" Randolph looked surprised, Coulston, faintly irritated.

"If the queen is to arrive today, shouldn't they be sweeping and arranging sleeping quarters?" He indicated the peaceful scene. "These people should be busier."

His companions surveyed the quiet

courtyard. Then, without a word, Randolph turned and went back into the house. Eliot followed, with Simon taking up the rear.

They found their host seated on his one-man dais, a small table with a bowl of porridge before him and a bowl of beer at his elbow. He wore a heavy cloak of velvet, and his legs were wrapped in strips of fur. Beneath his feet were bricks that had been warmed in the fire. Simon realized the platform was not for visual effect but to keep Kerr's feet off the stone floors that probably never warmed. He wondered how the man coped in winter if he found the cold so unbearable in June.

Behind his master, Muir stood drinking from an elaborately carved bowl, one foot resting on the platform in a way that struck Simon as intimate for a servant. Either he'd finished breakfast or he preferred beer to porridge. "Good morning, masters," Kerr said when they entered. "Ye rested well, I trust?"

"Yes, I thank you, my lord," Randolph answered. "We are grateful for your hospitality. Have you had word of the queen's arrival?"

Kerr's expression turned rueful. "I hae, but I fear t'will dismay you. She has been delayed."

"Delayed?"

The laird waved a hand. "A matter o' a day or twa, nae more. They stayed on at Lammermuir due t' some entertainment th' host planned. Gracious lady she is, th' queen sent word that I might not prepare too early. O' course, she didna ken ye hae arrived fro' England."

"I see." Randolph glanced at his companions.

Simon murmured, "Perhaps we should journey onward and meet the queen."

"Nonsense!" Kerr's voice was loud, and he waved a hand as if to settle the echoes.

Muir shifted his feet. "Ye should wait here in comfort rather than wander through rough country and mayhap become lost."

Kerr set his meaty fist on the table with a clatter. "Masters, I hae a proposal. We shall dine together at mid-day, and afterward we'll go hawking. I hae a wonderful bird, a credit t' ma falconer's skills. Tomorrow or the day after, the queen will come. Ye may trust me, masters."

It was agreed, though it was clear Randolph was not satisfied, and Simon was thinking he mistrusted men who spoke of how trustworthy they were. The rest of the delegation had begun to file into the hall, and the host invited, "Come, masters! We shall ken each other better." Raising his voice, he shouted, "Tavish! Set the benches there, by the window."

Tavish appeared and obeyed, as Kerr ordered, "Sit! Sit! My people even nae prepare our meal, and afterward, ye shall see ma lands. Sit ye down, all. Sit."

A long morning of listening to Kerr's exploits followed. Some were new, and some they'd heard the night before. The stories grew more and more unbelievable, and Simon had all he could do not to roll his eyes. Randolph, schooled in diplomacy, muttered admiring phrases. Eliot seemed to enjoy the more violent tales, murmuring appreciatively. Some of the younger men took to staring out the windows, and Coulston dozed, arms folded and back against the wall.

Simon's salvation was the aroma of food that began to permeate the place. Despite their host being a braggart and a liar, it had been days since he'd had a decent meal, and Kerr's monstrous ego would be forgiven if the food was half as good as it smelled.

Finally a bell rang somewhere at the back of the house, and the hall became a buzz of activity. Though Simon had never shared a nobleman's table, he'd heard about formal meals from Hannah. Watching the room turn to a banquet hall, he guessed Kerr had ordered the most impressive meal his servants could devise. He couldn't help but wonder why a small party of untitled Englishmen merited such treatment.

Kerr answered the question with a casual comment. "My children are nae accustomed t' fine meals, but it's best tha become so." After a moment he added, "Wi' the queen on her way."

If their meal was practice for the royal visit, Kerr had left it late. Hannah, knowing such an event was in the works, would have been planning and practicing for months.

The rehearsal went well, however. Tavish and three other men formed the trestles into a "C" shape and placed the boards atop them. They brought benches and stools from all over the house to provide seating for everyone. Muir hovered in the doorways, watching and giving orders here and there. Tavish did as ordered but never spoke to or even looked at the steward.

Once the table was in place, a young boy placed trenchers before each seat. Most were simply rough slabs of wood, but the host, his family, and the English guests got plates of metal, mismatched but superior for dining. Servants, each as ragged as the next, brought in platters containing dried fruit and small bowls of salt or ground herbs and spices the diners could sprinkle on their food as they liked. These were set at the center of the main table and at the head of each side section. The highest in rank would serve themselves first; if there was no salt left when the bowl reached the end of the table, the lowest of them would go without.

At a nod from Nettie, Muir called an invitation. As he directed the diners to their seats, Kerr went to a doorway at the back of the room and called, gesturing impatiently when the summons was not answered immediately. Three women appeared, huddled together, and he said in an off-hand manner, "Masters, ma wife and daughters." His tone changed when he introduced the final member of the group. "Ma son and the heir to Duns Tower, Kenneth."

Simon watched with interest as the women and Kerr's son took seats at the host table, wearing what was probably their best clothing. They seemed unsure of themselves, and the two girls, not much older than Susan, bent their heads toward each other and giggled nervously as the company waited politely for them to sit.

The Englishmen had been directed to a table on the right. Randolph took his place nearest the host, and the rest took seats as each saw his own importance. Simon held back, but Randolph caught his eye and nodded to the bench opposite him. No one objected when he sat down next to James Coulston, who faced Samuel Eliot.

The table on the other side of the room filled as at least two dozen of Kerr's henchmen entered and sat. Guessing that at least that many men would be elsewhere on the estate, Simon thought Kerr maintained a surprising number of men for such a small holding. They were hard men from the look of them, and they seemed pleased to be seated as a group. One asked, "What's this?" and pointed at bowls of water set on the table with a scrap of cloth beside each.

"For washing your hands, you lout," replied one of the older men, and the rest laughed loudly. Their mirth sounded forced, as if they were aware they were supposed to make a good impression but weren't sure how to do it.

"Is there no place for the Lady Agnes?" Randolph asked.

"The lady is fatigued from the journey an' begs we proceed without her," Kerr said. "She'll rest in her room for the day an' join us on the morrow."

More likely Agnes was uncomfortable with so many men, Simon guessed. She'd no doubt feel better when she was reunited with the queen.

The meal they shared was more elaborate than either guests or hosts were used to. The English party was comprised of men who served royalty but were not themselves royal. Randolph and Eliot had probably shared banquets with their masters, but the others seemed as perplexed by the succession of courses as Simon was. The laird's daughters were subdued, watching their mother and doing as she did. The son, Kenneth, seemed disinterested, eating only when the sister next to him urged it. Even the servants seemed nervous as they brought in trays and set them within reach of the most important person at each table. Nettie could not keep still, peering constantly at dishes that might need refilling. When she reached past Simon to pick up an empty tray, he saw four clear finger marks on the white skin of her forearm. He turned to meet her eyes, but Nettie hurried away, head down.

A young boy stood at the end of each table, holding a jug of what turned out to be excellent mead. The lads kept each guest's bowl full with all the care of priests serving communion. They glanced at Muir anxiously every few seconds, and if he so much as twitched, hurried to see if anyone's bowl needed filling.

After the first course of vegetable broth and bread was served and eaten, the host made a little speech of welcome to his guests, alluding to the coming of the queen "tomorrow or the day after." His vagueness seemed to bother Randolph, whose feet shifted under the table, bumping Simon's. When the host finished, however, he rose and made a polite speech of thanks for the hospitality of the laird of Duns Tower and his people. His taut lips were the only sign that Kerr's lack of specifics about the queen's whereabouts concerned him.

After the second course, salmon in a thin sauce, servants brought in the first remove, crystallized fruit designed to cleanse the palate for the remaining courses. This led Simon to conclusions about Kerr. Though he didn't believe the laird's stories of his honorable past and his peaceful present, the man had some acquaintance with good living and the demands of etiquette. Kerr had not always lived on the marches, and Simon guessed Muir, too, had been in fine homes.

The first remove traditionally called for entertainment, which came in the form of a second speech from the host explaining his wife's pedigree. "Lady Anne is the daughter of the old Earl of Menteith." Though she was no prize for looks and most likely illegitimate, since Kerr made no mention of her mother's name, an earl's daughter was a coup for a minor laird like Kerr. Randolph muttered softly that the earl was a potent force in Scottish government.

There followed a long recitation of how Kerr had met and wooed the lady, but Simon, watching her struggle to keep her expression pleasant, guessed most of it was pure fiction. When Kerr finished, he leaned toward her in apparent fondness, and she froze, her smile a parody.

Nettie and two serving boys arrived with the next course, slices of venison, steamed and roasted vegetables, and frumenty, a hearty barley stew to which the cook had added currants and almonds. These dishes were followed by a second remove, sugared almonds and gingerbread.

The entertainment for the second remove was a formal recitation of the family's lineage. The bard was practiced and tuneful, though Simon suspected his account was at the very least exaggerated, and at worst completely falsified. The guests sat politely, listening to all the ways Kerr and his lady were connected to the Scottish throne. There seemed to be many.

When the bard's recitation reached the preceding generation, Kenneth whispered something to his father. Looking at him sternly, Kerr shook his head. A short while later, the youth spoke again, putting an insistent hand on his father's arm. Kerr shook it off, his scowl a warning. The son's lips curled into a pout, and he sat back in his chair, arms folded angrily.

A short while later he spoke again. This time Kerr pounded the table in an angry response. The heir's chin jutted in anger equal to his father's. As the bard went on with hardly a pause, Lady Anne nudged the daughter next to her, who rose quickly, went to her brother's chair, and whispered something that changed the pout to a smile. Rising so fast he sent the stool crashing behind him, he followed his sister out of the room. Kerr appeared not to notice.

The final course, called the *banquet,* was snow pudding made with four pints of cream and eight egg whites; a moise made with apples, rosewater, and cinnamon; and a subtlety made of small, round cakes stacked into the shape of a dragon. The guests exclaimed over the cleverness of it, though the cakes had sat out too long and were stale. Simon saw young Philip dunking his in his beer, but the cake fell apart, making a soggy mess.

When the meal was over, Kerr ordered his people to clear the tables. "Be quick, for I want the hall t' m'self." His command was obeyed with an alacrity that spoke volumes, for men and women almost tripped over each other in their haste. Last to go was Muir, who watched to see it was done to his satisfaction. When Nettie collected the last tray of dishes, he followed her out with a nod to his laird that seemed more amused than respectful.

"My men prepare for our hunt, Master Randolph, but I would hae some conference wi' ye and one or two o' yer trusted men afore we set out."

Simon was surprised when Randolph dismissed everyone but him, Coulston, and Eliot. The others left the room reluctantly, sensing something interesting was about to happen. A few looked doubtfully at Simon, who was himself unsure why he'd been singled out.

Once they were alone, Kerr said eagerly, "Ye harkened to the bard, did ye not?"

They formed expressions of appreciation with varying degrees of success. Simon thought Coulston suppressed a grin, but training won out, and he said gravely, "Yes, Your Worship."

Kerr raised his hands, palms up. "Then ye must see it. My son's blood is evera bit as royal as the queen's." That was hardly true. On the other hand, Scottish kingship had been based more on strength than on blood all the way back to Macbeth and Duncan, who'd taken the crown rather than wait for it to be offered. What did this minor laird's obvious fascination with bloodlines have to do with the English delegation?

Kerr meshed his fingers and shook them, indicating firmness. "As man and wife, Kenneth and Mary will form an unshakeable government for Scotland."

"Is the queen aware of this proposal?" Randolph asked, his tone devoid of emotion.

"She has received letters fro' ma son tha' express his admiration for her beauty an' wit." Kerr smiled fondly. "They're finely done, masters, finely done. A lass canna help bu' tak note."

Simon was glad he wasn't spokesman for the group, for he had no idea what he would have said to that. The petty laird thought his son a suitable match for the Queen of Scots?

Things grew worse, for Kerr added, "In some years, when th' English ken the strength of this union, they'll nae doubt want it for themselves."

"You would claim the English throne as well?" This time, a little cough interrupted Randolph mid-sentence.

"Mary has more right than yon Elizabeth!" The tone was abrupt, but Kerr quickly changed his tone. "I ken it's no fault o' yers, masters, for ye must serve as yer council demands. Still, Scotland's queen, descended from auld Henry Eight's sister, is truly sprung o' royal blood, while Elizabeth is some musician's whelp, foisted o' th' English people by deceitful men."

Simon was angered at this dredging up of old gossip. Anne Boleyn's trial and accusations she'd been unfaithful to the king had been a travesty. Anyone who looked at Elizabeth would admit the gossip was lies — unless he *wanted* to believe otherwise.

The shock must have shown on their faces, for Kerr waved a calming hand. "Dinna fret, masters. My son an' his wife will hae much t' do in Scotland afore they turn their attention t' England. I will —" He caught himself and began again. "Bishop Oglethorpe duly crowned the Boleyn woman, and th' English accept her as sovereign. T' save trouble betwixt our nations, we pledge t' wait 'til Elizabeth dies before acting on our claim." As Randolph stood mute, Kerr raised his brows. "Is tha' nae what ye've come to propose? That Mary be Elizabeth's heir?"

Randolph answered carefully. "There has been some discussion of that possibility."

Kerr smiled. "Then our desires meld. Ye need an heir t' the English throne. Scotland needs a wise man t' help its queen. I can provide what each nation needs." He chuckled at the silence. "It is much t' ken, is it nae? Think on 't, and we will speak further tomorrow."

"When the queen arrives?" Randolph said with a slight challenge in his voice.

Their host nodded vigorously. "O' course! When the queen arrives. Now, let us see what ma falconer has arranged for yer pleasure."

As the others followed Kerr outside, Simon remained behind, hoping no one would notice only ten showed up for the hunt. He was determined to either confirm or ease the niggling doubts building in his mind, and he guessed Randolph would approve and cover for his absence. Finding a small room used as an office, judging by the papers piled on a table, he waited until he heard the hunting party leave the courtyard. When the house went quiet, he began to explore.

CHAPTER NINE

Henry often delivered medicines to those who could not or would not come to the shop themselves. Over the next few days, he saw Calkin on the streets from time to time. He always greeted him politely and went on, as Calkin had instructed. Still, he'd begun to think the guardsman's presence was a golden opportunity for him. Surely someone who'd actually dealt with crime and criminals could advise him how to find Will's killer.

As he watched Calkin chat casually with this person or that, picking up bits and pieces of information, a question began to flit through his mind. Why had the queen sent one of her guardsmen to secretly investigate improper business practices? The usual way of dealing with such things was to arrest the suspected criminal and question him until he told the truth. Since stealth had been chosen over the more efficient method of torture, the case must be unusual. Henry decided Calkin's purpose was more than he'd admitted to, perhaps treason or a brewing revolution. Wise monarchs were always watchful for such things, and danger to the throne seemed a more likely explanation for Calkin's sudden appearance in Old Change.

He didn't really care about Calkin's secrets if the man could help him find out who'd murdered Will Clark. He'd considered every motive he could think of, but nothing seemed right. No one had benefited directly from his uncle's death. Though some might dislike the searcher's oversight, there'd been no indication anyone hated Will. A merchant who wanted so much to avoid charges that he'd kill the searcher was unlikely. In the first place, Will had always given shopkeepers time to correct any problems he found with their business practices. In addition, it was hardly worth killing a man to avoid a fine or a day in the stocks, the usual result of a searcher's bad report. Henry had seen merchants who went right back to their old ways after the punishment, joking about having had a day off.

He'd considered the suitors who vied for Annie's hand in marriage as possible killers, but none of them seemed likely. Constable Fenman had showed interest in Annie only in the last few months, according to Hannah. Paul the grocer had been dividing his attention between two women since his wife's death, and everyone knew he simply wanted a woman to help him raise his seven children. Andrew the chandler had been somewhat unseemly in his haste to pay court, waiting only a few weeks to start hinting he needed a wife, but Hannah's view was probably correct: "At his age, a man has no time to waste."

That left Henry with no suspects, which was why he wanted advice. If he assured Calkin he wouldn't interfere with his current task, maybe the guardsman would make a few suggestions.

With this in mind, Henry went to his aunt's house as the sun came directly overhead. He found Annie's second son, John, hoeing tiny plants in the well-tended garden. The house was small, but there was pride of ownership in every aspect, down to colorful flowers that served no purpose except gladdening the hearts of grower and passerby alike. The door was freshly lime-washed, and it stood open to allow the bright sunlight inside, where Annie stood mixing something, the bowl tucked under her arm. When she saw Henry, her face lit with a smile. "Why here's another guest to make our home that much happier. Come in, Henry! Have you eaten?"

It was a question she always asked, but the answer hardly mattered. Annie would insist any visitor eat something, even if he'd just left a banquet. Henry entered the house, stopping a moment inside the door to let his eyes adjust.

Calkin was seated at a heavy wooden table with a boy on either side of him: Arthur, almost five, and Aaron, seven. John followed him inside and took the place across from Calkin, effectively surrounding the guardsman with boys.

"Take Jacob's place," Annie directed. "He's staying in Fairfield this week." Henry sat down at the head of the table, feeling a little uncomfortable, but Annie smiled at him as she took her place at the opposite end, her face pink with warmth from bending over the fire.

The meal was relaxed and lively, with Calkin telling stories of his childhood that brought gales of laughter. He seemed to enjoy himself, and he certainly did justice to the meal Annie served. He didn't linger when it was finished but thanked Annie for the food, taking leave of each boy by name

151

and commenting on something specific to him. They were pleased at the attention but, being polite children, didn't follow him on his way.

Henry did. Promising he'd be back shortly, he hurried to catch Calkin before he reached the main street. "I want to ask a favor."

"After your aunt's cake, I'm in the mood to grant favors," he said, rubbing his stomach. "The woman can cook, I tell you, and she gave me a bit to keep for later, for I said yesterday that I like a bit of sweetness before bedtime."

"That was good of her," Henry said, impatient to get off the subject of Annie's cooking. "Some years ago, my uncle — Annie's husband — was killed. At the time they thought a cutpurse was the culprit, but lately we heard it might have been murder."

Calkin turned to him with a look he couldn't read. "Who would have done this deed?"

"That's the thing. I've tried and tried to figure it out, and I cannot." Gratified that his story hadn't immediately been dismissed as a boy's tale, he listed his theories and his reasons for rejecting them. When he finished, Calkin merely looked at him. "I don't ask you to do anything," Henry said, hating the pleading tone in his voice. "I only want advice as to how to proceed."

"My advice is to forget the whole thing." Calkin's tone was peremptory.

"Simon meant to look into it." Henry hoped his father's name would add weight to his argument.

"And what would your father say about you taking on this task alone?" Henry hung his head, dreading the lecture that was to come. "I'll say what Simon would say, were he here. You have enough to do to help your mother keep the shop. You have no experience with murderers and could put yourself in danger. And your uncle cannot return to life, even if you discover who stabbed him with his own knife." Calkin went on, leaving Henry standing dejectedly at the gate.

When he returned to the house to thank his aunt for the meal, the boys had retreated to separate corners, working on the lessons their mother set for them each day. Annie had already cleared the table and was cleaning the dishes. When Henry came in, she asked, "Do you think Richard enjoyed the meal?"

"Very much." Behind her, John rolled his eyes at Henry, indicating it wasn't the first time she'd asked that question.

"Does he like a sauce on his asparagus, I

wonder? I plan to cut some for tomorrow."

Henry shrugged. "I don't know. He did say you are a wonderful cook."

"Wonderful? Is that what he said?"

"His very word." He wasn't sure he'd quoted Calkin exactly, but Annie seemed pleased.

"We enjoy his stories." She looked down at her work. "Does he have a family?"

"None that I know of. Why?"

"No reason," Annie said, but her cheeks went pink. "He says little of current matters, only that an uncle sent him here. I asked myself if that uncle is all he has left in the world."

"He's been a soldier, I think."

"I see." Annie tucked a curl back inside her cap. "You must tell me if he mentions a certain thing he'd like for his meals, or something he doesn't want another time." As Henry backed out the door she added, "Or he could stop by and tell me himself."

Henry shook his head as he left. Calkin and Annie *were* interested in each other! He replayed the meal in his mind, collecting evidence he was correct. It was only when he examined his conversation with Calkin that he realized the guardsman had given something away. Henry had never said Will was stabbed with his own knife.

Somehow, Calkin had already known it.

With the men out hunting and the servants presumably preparing for the queen's visit, Geordie Kerr's house was quiet. Stepping from the tiny room where he'd hidden, Simon oriented himself. The hall had four entrances: the large double doors that led outside; a door at the back that led to the kitchens; the doorway he'd just come from; and a passageway that probably led to the family's living quarters. Beginning there, he went down a low-ceilinged corridor past a series of rooms. The first had three pallet beds, each with a large trunk at the foot. A few feminine garments and keepsakes indicated the daughters slept here. Simon wondered where the third was, since she hadn't appeared with the others at the meal.

The next room had a wooden bed with a brazier beside it, a large rug on the floor, and a small table topped with a washbasin and ewer. In one corner a chest stood open, and a jumble of clothing spilled out as if the owner had dug for something he wanted, leaving a mess behind for someone else to put in order. Stones lay on every surface, some big as a melon, others small as a pea, but each apparently interesting to the occupant, who Simon guessed was the son,

Kenneth.

The last bedroom was larger than the others, with comfortable furnishings. The bed sat on a raised platform, and heavy curtains surrounded it, though they were tied back now to air the space. Pegs on the wall held both male and female garments, though the feminine ones were plainer and fewer than the man's. It was the master's bedroom, with only a few indications of the mistress's presence.

The corridor ended at a sunny room where large windows had been opened to let in light and fresh air. Near one of them, four women sat sewing, their stools arranged in a circle to allow conversation as they worked. One of them looked up as Simon appeared in the doorway, and he recognized Kerr's youngest daughter. From the gasp she made, he wondered if he'd grown a second head in the last half hour. Kerr's wife turned to squint at him. Rising, she stepped forward as if to put herself between him and the girls.

"What d'ye want?"

Simon bowed politely, though her tone was anything but welcoming. "I felt slightly unwell and decided not to accompany the hunters."

"Oh." Anne Kerr was stout, with a

splotchy face and an oddly lumpy chin. It was obvious she didn't know what to do with him. "Nettie can make ye a tisane."

"I think quiet, away from hounds and men, is what I need," Simon told her. "I'm sorry to interrupt your work, but I was curious to see your fine house."

The two young daughters were obviously curious about their visitor. One leaned toward the other, puffing her lips as if she might explode. The second rolled her eyes at the first. The third girl, taller than the others, sat stiffly, her face turned away. She seemed familiar to Simon, but for some reason he imagined her slight figure clothed in silk.

Anne Kerr apparently came to a decision. "Girls!"

All three stood as if pulled by wires. Two moved off reluctantly, with sly glances backward. The third kept her face averted and pulled nervously at her cap as she hurried out of the room. Simon wondered if some facial deformity caused her to remain apart from others. Having a crippled arm, he knew how uncomfortable it was to meet new people and see the shift in their expressions when the infirmity registered.

As they went his hostess said ungraciously, "My daughters dinna meet wi' strangers."

Simon remained in the doorway, asking innocuous questions in an attempt to put the lady at ease. Kerr's wife had few conversational skills, and she answered his queries in as few words as possible. He despaired of trying to get her to speak of her husband, his work, their children, or even the weather. When he asked about the history of Duns Tower, however, she seemed to find the topic safe. "Long ago," she said, nodding wisely, "a famous scholar lived hereabouts."

Putting the name of the place together with what he knew of Scottish philosophers, Simon asked, "Was it John Duns Scotus?" The philosopher's view of the nature of God, Man, and the Universe had created discussion and dissention among scholars for the last few centuries.

The lady waved a hand. "I dinna know all his names, but they say he was verra wise."

Simon expressed admiration, and she relaxed, speaking a little of her life at Duns. In her comments he heard longing for the days when she'd lived in the city. "We have few visitors here, being sae far from anna real road," she said. "It is dull —" She stopped herself. "But women are easily bored, ma husband says."

"I suppose it's quite different from

Edinburgh."

"Aye." She touched the sewing beside her. "There's work t' be done, o' course, but we hae no entertainments sech as I had as a girl."

"Then the queen's visit will be a delight."

"The what? Oh, aye, the queen. Tha' will be a delight." Wiping her hands on her apron, she repeated weakly, "A delight."

"You no doubt have much to do to prepare. I would not keep you from your work."

She waved vaguely, apparently as anxious to have him stay now as she'd been a while ago to have him leave. "Muir handles such things. Ma husband says I am too light wi' the servants. Dickie knows best how t' deal wi' them."

He thought of Nettie's black eye and bruises. Was that Muir's way of dealing with her?

"Nevertheless, I will disturb you no more." Bowing, he backed out of the room. The laird's wife was not like his Hannah, who would have been up to her elbows in preparations had a queen deigned to visit her home. It was indeed a steward's job to run the household for his lord, but most wives took more interest, especially with a royal visit pending. Anne seemed a little

159

slow, which was probably how a penniless soldier like Kerr had managed to marry her. Husbands had to be found for the daughters of important men, even slow, illegitimate daughters.

He'd seen all sections of the house but one, so Simon took the only exit he'd not yet explored. A narrow wooden tunnel led to the kitchens, separate from the house due to fears of fire. Here several servants, including Nettie, were at work cleaning up the remains of the banquet. Looking up from a stack of dirty dishes, she said, "They've gone a-hunting."

"I have no interest in birds." She seemed unsure what to do with him, but she was also less tense without the laird or his steward present. "Have you always lived here?"

She regarded him for a moment as if trying to decide his purpose. Apparently finding nothing suspicious, she answered, "Aye, Tavish and me. Our mother served the auld laird."

"Kerr didn't say how he came to be laird of Duns. Was it a gift for service to the crown?"

Nettie's lips barely moved as she said, "He got it when his uncle died."

Simon noticed a shifting among the others, who kept their eyes averted but were certainly listening. Nettie seemed to want to say more, but she pressed her lips firmly together. Taking up a pail of dirty water, she brushed past Simon and went outside. When he followed her, Nettie gave him a glance half disgusted, half resigned.

Away from listeners, Simon asked, "Is he cruel to you and your brother?"

"What does it matter?" she asked, but her eyes were bleak.

Though he knew it was wrong, Simon said, "I might help you get away from here."

Nettie looked at him in surprise. "Where would I go?"

He paused. She was Kerr's property, and if she left, she'd probably be returned to Duns for the beating of her life. Seeing it in his eyes, she said, "I wouldna leave m'brother."

He thought of his coming audience with the queen. She might remove Kerr from his position if he could give her cause. "Is Kerr an honest man?" he asked Nettie.

The laugh she gave him was bitter, and it was the only reply he got. After shaking the bucket, she went back inside, slamming the door in his face.

Walking around to the front of the house, Simon entered and strolled the hall, examining the motley assortment of tapestries. His observations were gelling, leading to a theory, and the tapestries were part of the evidence. From the variety of colors and weaves, he concluded they came from many different places. Not one family's belongings, but the property of many families, used to ease the cold that plagued Kerr.

Simon at first told himself that stories of border bandits had fired his imagination, but Nettie's manner, Lady Anne's revelations, and the hard-eyed men he'd seen at dinner added fuel to the fire. He pictured raiders carrying these beautiful woven pieces out of burning houses and bringing them here as spoils.

Leaving the hall, he went to the tower, where he was pleased to find the ladder down and the hatch open. He'd never been inside such a structure, and the view from the top must be impressive. There would be men on guard, but he could simply claim he was curious. No telling what might be concealed there to reveal Kerr's activities.

Climbing to the second level, he put his head cautiously into the opening. Bows, muskets and the accompanying ammunition were piled in every corner. That was no surprise, since this was the main point of defense for the estate.

A second ladder rested against the opposite wall, leading to a second hatch overhead. Climbing, Simon entered a room stocked with food: bags of grain, tightly closed boxes, and jugs sealed with wax. Provisions laid in for a possible siege.

Eyeing the ladder that led to the next level, he heard the murmur of voices. Above him a woman spoke in a tone of fitful command. He couldn't make out words, but the answer was male laughter. He was about to retreat when the woman cried, "Ow! That hurts!" A moment later he heard a scream that ended abruptly, as if someone smothered it with a hand.

Launching himself up the last few rungs, Simon lunged through the narrow opening and pushed himself upright. The room held more siege supplies: pallets stacked against a wall, wooden boxes piled in two corners, and between them, several large earthen jugs.

In the corner opposite the trapdoor, a man and woman sat side by side, their backs to the wall. The man was Kenneth Kerr, and he looked up as Simon appeared, an impish grin freezing on his face. The woman, who struggled to remove a lock of her hair from his grip, was Agnes, who'd journeyed to Duns with them, claiming to be a lady who attended the Queen of Scots.

Simon stood uncertainly, feeling foolish and confused. A laugh from above made him look up, and he saw two of Kerr's men looking down at them, wide grins on their faces.

"Trouble, Agnes?" asked one. "Can't handle the heir's teasing, eh?"

"Get back t' yer watch," Agnes ordered, "or I'll tell ma father ye're neglecting yer duty."

The trapdoor closed, but sounds of muffled laughter persisted above.

Agnes returned her attention to Kenneth. "Let go of my hair, laddie," she said coaxingly. "Be a dear and let it go. Let — it — go." As she repeated the phrase in a soothing voice, Simon got a different understanding of Kerr's only son. He'd thought him handsome, and that was true. Kenneth had the face of an angel, though a dark one, with black hair and deep brown eyes. His shoulders were wide and his frame muscular. His legs, splayed before him in relaxed ease, were long and well formed. Many a gentleman at Elizabeth's court would have envied those legs, able to fill out a stocking without resorting to padding, as some did.

But the enjoyment he took from tormenting Agnes revealed that Kenneth's physical perfection was not matched by mental acuity. His expression was child-like, his enjoyment of his sister's discomfort obvious. As she pleaded, Kenneth loosened his fist enough to allow her to remove her hair, inch by inch, giving it one last yank before letting go completely. Agnes yelped, rubbed her scalp fiercely, and stood to face Simon.

Noting her plain woolen dress and the cap lying at her side, he realized something. "It was you below, sewing with the others."

"Kenny," she said, "will you look all around and see if the wardens are coming? Your eyes are better than mine."

The young man immediately turned to the arrow slits, his manner focused and serious. Agnes said, inclining her head at Kenneth, "He went missing, and I know he likes to come up here." She frowned at Simon. "We thought you'd all gone hunting wi' father."

Simon had been reorganizing things he'd noticed recently into a different pattern. His earlier sense that Agnes lacked sophistication. Her ill-fitting clothes. Nettie's grim amusement at his concern for the woman who'd arrived with them. "You're not the queen's lady."

Her expression turned wistful. "I hope t' be someday." Looking at Simon

165

speculatively she asked, "Have ye been t'court?"

"I've been to the English palace."

"Do they dance there?"

Simon had no idea, but he said he thought they did.

"Your queen allows this?"

"I believe so."

Agnes' brows descended. "Ye said ye hae seen her."

"I have not seen her dance."

"Ye're not sae important, then."

"I am not." Some might consider solving murders together more important than knowing if the queen could dance, but he guessed an adolescent girl would not. "Why did you lie to us?"

Agnes's gaze swept the room as if looking for the proper answer. "I do as my father bids me, as does any good daughter." Her hands went to her shoulders, as if Simon might strike her.

He saw the plan, though he wasn't sure what it meant. Kerr had wanted the delegation at Duns, and he'd arranged it quite cleverly. If Muir had been the only one to report Queen Mary was coming, they might have rejected his story. Agnes's presence had convinced them.

"Tell me everything." He made his voice

commanding, guessing she'd followed orders all her life. Seeing her fear he softened, adding, "Your father will never learn where I heard it."

Agnes glanced at Kenneth, who moved from one slit to the next, pressing his eye to the opening. Satisfied he was focused elsewhere, she said, "We were in Edinburgh, Father and I, and he learned o' yer coming. He put me on a ship, tellin' me t' wait a' that village till ye arrived, meet ye somehow, and say I was the queen's lady, bound t' meet her at Duns." Her eyes filled with tears. "I was frighted half t' death, and a' alone except for th' twa half-wits he sent wi' me."

"Agnes, why —"

"There's no one out there." Kenneth had returned his attention to them, and he noticed tears on his sister's face. "Ye made Agnes cry!" He lowered his chin, glaring at Simon from under heavy brows. Though the voice was masculine, the comment had a childish tone.

"My name is Simon, and I am a surgeon from England."

Agnes hurried to add, "It's all right, Kenny. I'm all right now."

Sticking out his chest, Kenneth said, "I am Kenneth Kerr, heir t' Duns Tower an' descendant o' kings!" He turned to Agnes. "Did I get it right?"

The girl cast a glance at Simon before answering. "Yes, love, that was exactly right."

He grinned happily. "Father will be glad t' hear it, will he nae?"

"He will." Brushing dust from her skirts, Agnes said brightly, "Let us show our guest yer hounds, Kenny, for he hasna seen them."

"I hae four new puppies," Kenneth said excitedly. "The muther likes me, and she lets me touch 'em if I'm careful." Leading the way down the ladders, he asked, "What happened to yer arm?" Without waiting for an answer he went on, "I hurt m' arm once when I tried t' climb down the wall on a rope. Father was angry, was he no', Agnes?"

"He was," his sister replied, adding in a low tone, "I got th' beating for 't."

Kenneth led the way to the kennels, where six sleek hounds and four fat puppies bounded forward and jumped joyously at them. Simon attempted to maintain a polite expression while a large female muddied his doublet and slobbered on his face. Agnes swatted at the dogs, ordering them to leave him alone. Kenneth returned their affection with abandon equal to theirs, rolling on the ground with a large female, holding its head in his hands as he spoke lovingly to it.

Things changed quickly when the dog, apparently unhappy at having its head squeezed, scratched at Kenneth with a paw. A thin line of blood appeared on his hand, and he roared in pain and surprise. With sudden fury, he punched the dog with his fist, sending it rolling onto the ground. Cradling his injured hand, he rose and kicked the nearest puppy, sending it flying to a corner of the pen, where it lay cowering against the slats.

"No, Kenneth!" Agnes shouted, catching his arm. The dog boy hurried over to restrain the hound, pulling her away and crouching protectively over her. Kenneth didn't see the handler's angry glance, but Simon did.

Holding her brother's shoulders, Agnes spoke calming words. "It's a' right, love. It's a' right." She touched the wound lightly. "It's but a scratch, and she dinna mean it."

"She hurt me!" Kenneth protested. "She mustna do that! I hurt her bairn t' teach her."

"She dinna mean it," Agnes repeated, wiping the tiny scratch with her apron.

Calming, Kenneth still insisted the dog was at fault. "She must learn she canna scratch me, but I am nae angry wi' her." In a sudden shift, he turned to Simon. "There are lambs i' the pen yonder. Come, I'll show ye."

After the lambs, Simon met horses, ponies, geese, and a sow with seven piglets attached to her teats. Then he had to inspect the outbuildings, each and every one. "This will a' be mine one day." Kenneth seemed unaware that the workers stopped when he entered and watched warily, moving away from him when possible. The heir's visits caused anxiety, and Simon guessed there'd been other incidents like the one he'd witnessed with the dog. How often did Kenneth's anger erupt suddenly and hurt whoever was nearby?

Agnes seemed to be her brother's keeper, and though she was uneducated and naïve, Simon liked her. From her soft words and promised treats, he guessed she was expected to control and protect Kenneth, all the while deferring to him as their father's son and heir.

Recalling their host's bold proposal, Simon considered the possibility of Kenneth becoming the queen's consort. If he never opened his mouth, he'd cut a dashing figure. His conversation, however, was limited to such topics as whether white ducks were prettier than brown ones.

The boy — it was difficult to think of Kenneth as a man — enjoyed showing his guest around, but Simon soon grew tired of his childish chatter. He had no interest in the rocks the laird's son had collected from the hills around Duns Tower or the feathers he'd implanted to decorate the west wall of the courtyard. Agnes caught his eye at one point and wiggled her brows as if to say, "This is how I spend my days!"

"Shall I show him the tarn?" Kenneth asked once they'd seen every building and corral.

Agnes's expression turned stern. "I am nae daft, Kenny, and I recall wha' ye did the last time we took a guest t' the tarn. Master Maldon can see at it fro' here."

Simon counted himself lucky she was there to keep a rein on Kenneth's behavior, since the youth's sly grin suggested he'd have ended up dripping wet. It was a relief to hear a shout and see the hunters returning.

"I must join my friends." He spoke to Kenneth, though he glanced at Agnes, wondering if she would try to stop him from revealing her charade. She shrugged as if she had no stake in the success of her father's scheme. As she'd said, she'd merely done what Kerr ordered her to do.

■ ■ ■ ■

After the meal at his aunt's house, Henry made his way to Hairless Moll's cottage to buy ingredients for medicines. Though she was a little frightening to look at, Moll had a gift for finding the shyest plants in the most difficult areas. Over the years Simon had forged a relationship with her that benefited them both. Moll didn't like to be among people, where she was teased and humiliated. Simon bought her plants and treated her kindly, taking sweets when he visited and staying to chat with the lonely woman.

Recognizing Henry from times he'd come with Simon, Moll consented to sell him the herbs he needed. They discussed the weather and the season, though Henry found it difficult to understand Moll's slushy speech and to ignore the facial twitches she couldn't control.

Henry left pleased with his main purchase, mandrake to mix with poppy and vinegar for local surgeons to use as anesthetic. Moll knew how to pluck the forked root from the ground without being killed by its curse. It was rumored harvesting was done by digging a trench around the plant, slipping a noose around it, then tying a dog to the other end of the rope. The harvester moved away a safe distance and called to the dog, which pulled the plant as it came, causing its telltale shriek as it left the earth. The dog would of course die, but once it was pulled, anyone could safely handle the root, which was powerful though dangerous medicine.

He'd bought other herbs, too, and as he walked, Henry made plans for their use. He paid little attention to his path until he came to the Caine River, which ran south to the Thames. Though smaller, the Caine was deep enough to require a bridge and swift enough to create the prospect of being swept away in its current.

There were two bridges over the Caine, one centuries old and one only a score in age. The old one, built of wood, was slowly rotting away. The new bridge was nearer to Old Change, wider, and built of stone. It was used by nearly everyone these days, but Moll's cottage, tucked away in the forest, was closer via the old bridge. Henry didn't mind its moss-slimed wood or the fact the handrail on one side was missing. What did bother him this day was Constable Fenman, who waited for him on the other side.

In his early years, Henry could not have imagined the life he now led in Old Change.

Even after ten years with Simon and Hannah, he was still surprised to wake up in a bed, in a home, in safety and comfort, with food enough to eat, and kindness rather than kicks and insults.

The serpent in Henry's Eden was Fenman, who'd taken a dislike to him from the first. For reasons Henry didn't understand, the constable harassed and belittled him whenever the chance arose. For years he'd endured rough questioning about neighborhood pranks, insistence "the orphan boy" was dishonest and sneaky, and frequent demands that he "move along" if he stood still for a moment to watch the sunset.

Once Fenman realized Henry didn't report his abuse to Simon, he became even worse, tormenting him with hurtful questions. "Tell me, lad," he'd ask when they passed on the street, "who was your father? And your mother — did she die in prison or on her back in a brothel?"

Henry never replied to the spiteful queries, having learned silence was best. It plagued him to have no answers to Fenman's questions that were satisfactory. His unknown parents had been at best feckless, at worst, criminal.

Simon often told his adopted son, "It's not where you come from that matters. It's what a man makes of himself that turns the world a little more to good or a little more to evil."

Henry tried to be on the side of good, as Simon was. Fenman, however, could upset him merely by appearing. Now he stood across the bridge, eyes lit with anticipation.

Everything about Fenman was medium: his build, his height, his coloring. He wore no badge of office and seemed to enjoy being unremarkable, adding to the effect by wearing only plain, brown clothing. The result was a totally forgettable man, except that the look in his eyes brought dread to those he chose to harass, ones who had no way to avoid him.

"Well met, Orphan," Fenman called in a cheerful voice. Henry considered turning upstream, willing to trek a half mile to the other bridge to avoid his tormenter. Fenman would only jeer at him about it next time. Instead, he made himself cross the bridge, face blank.

"Where has the man who pretends to be your father gone, boy?"

"Simon is away on business."

"And soon as he's gone, the woman who pretends to be your mother gets a new man."

He wondered how Fenman found out

everything that went on in their little section of the world, but the arrival of a stranger was always fodder for gossip.

"He is a friend of Simon's who stopped by, unaware he was away."

"And what does he want in Old Change?"

"I don't know."

"None of your lies, Orphan! He stayed at the apothecary for at least an hour, and now he shares the Widow Clark's table. He must have said something about his purpose."

"He says he's looking for a cousin who fell into drink and idleness. My aunt needs money, and he pays to take a meal at her house each day."

"No one recalls this cousin of his." Fenman leaned in, and Henry smelled the fish he'd had at his last meal. "What else do you know of him?"

He shrugged. "Nothing. We helped him for his friendship with Simon."

"Such a gentleman you are!" Fenman sneered. "All honor and courtesy outside, but we know what you are inside, don't we? The offspring of a bawd and a thief, or worse. You live among decent folk, but it's bad blood you've got. You're rotten inside, born of rotten stock!"

Henry tried to focus on Simon's faith in him, though the constable's hatred struck him like a spear. Fenman was no judge of goodness, only a man who used his position to indulge his prejudices. Henry's only defense was refusing to reveal that the jibes had an effect.

"If that's all, Constable, I must return to the shop."

"Go, then." Fenman stepped aside just enough to let Henry by, but as he passed, the constable dealt him a blow to the midsection that sent air whooshing from his lungs and bent him double. As he gasped for breath, Fenman pulled him close and spoke into his ear. "Know this, Orphan. I'm watching you, and your friend as well. If there's aught you've not told me, I'll find it out." Giving Henry a shove, he ordered, "Now go back to the house where you pretend to belong!"

Chapter Ten

The evening meal at Duns Tower was lighter and less formal, as was customary. Kerr circulated among his guests and retainers, speaking casually, but Simon saw him watching Randolph and knew what was coming. When Kerr inclined his head in invitation, Randolph looked to Coulston and Eliot, who moved to join him. Simon was surprised when Randolph took his arm as he passed. "Come along, Maldon," he said in a low voice. "We must face this lunatic as one."

Kerr led them into the room where Simon had hidden earlier that day. It was hardly big enough for five men, and he found himself backed against the west wall. It was made of wood, he noticed, unlike the other three, and it shifted slightly when he bumped against it.

Kerr took a seat at a small table facing the door. "I trust ye've had time t'consider what

I told ye earlier," he said in an unctuous tone.

Randolph replied, "My lord, the question is this: What is it you expect of us?"

Kerr pounded the table as if he'd said something hilarious. "Well said, Master! Well said! T' the point of it, then?" He leaned in confidentially. "Here it is. Ye're sent t' offer Mary an English husband." He patted his chest with one hand. "Howe'er, I intend t' leave soon for Edinburgh, where I will put before the queen ma ain proposal. 'Twill serve ma purpose well if ye delay yer arrival until I hae settled the matter." Leaning forward, he winked at them. "Yer queen will be disappointed, but travel i' Scotland can be treacherous, and 'twill be nae fault o' yers tha' ye reached Mary too late t' mak yer offer."

"The queen is not on her way here." Randolph's tone revealed more anger than Simon had so far seen him display.

"Tha's true." Kerr gestured toward the smoke-dimmed hall. "However, this is no' a bad place t' spend a week or twa. If ye consent t' ma will, we'll entertain ye wi' our best efforts." He leaned toward Randolph. "And ye'll leave somewhat richer than ye arrived."

Much of what had happened became

clear. Kerr proposed betrayal of their mission in exchange for money. Though Simon hadn't yet had time to tell the others exactly how Kerr had lured them here, it was clear the Scotsman would go to great lengths to set his son on the throne. They were isolated at Duns. If they refused to cooperate, Kerr might kill them and claim they'd been murdered by bandits in the marches. How would Randolph handle this?

He took the haven of the diplomat. "I must confer with my companions on the matter."

Kerr seemed content with that. "O' course, o' course! Tomorrow is time enow, but I leave the day after. Coome, then." Rising, he led them back into the hall. "Nettie!"

She answered immediately, "Aye."

"Bring more beer. Ye've let the bucket gae dry!"

The girl's face paled. "I am sorry, m' laird. I thought —"

"Do ye think anyone cares what ye thought? The bucket!"

As Kerr glowered after her, Coulston touched Randolph's arm. "Let us talk out of doors."

Randolph nodded agreement. "A walk beside the lake to settle the meal, I think." They passed along the narrow corridor, through the solar, and out the back doors, where they made their way down the steep path to the tarn's rocky shore. The evening was cool, and their feet crunched on the rocks as Eliot led the way. In the gloaming, Simon saw anger on Coulston's face, concern on Randolph's. Eliot's expression was harder to read.

"It is dangerous to speak inside," Randolph explained for Simon's benefit. "Houses hereabout often have what the Scots call 'laird's lugs,' the 'lord's ears.' "

"And what is that?"

"A hiding place above the hall where a man can lie and hear what is said below." Eliot bent and put a hand in the water of the lake, drawing back quickly. "Cold!"

"Edinburgh Castle, for one, has such a place," Randolph said. "It's best if we say nothing in the hall that should be kept in confidence."

"I see." Simon wondered again why he'd been included with the decision-makers of the group. There were men more prominent than he in the party, more versed in diplomacy.

Randolph seemed to read his mind. "You have the queen's trust, Maldon. If things go wrong here, if we are indeed delayed long enough our purpose is thwarted, we will count on you to attest to our best attempts to complete the task we were given."

In other words he was to serve as insurance against Elizabeth's anger. Bowing gravely, he said, "I shall confirm we were all surprised by this turn of events."

"The man's a lunatic!" Coulston said.

"Yet there's wealth here somewhere," Eliot observed.

"Yes," Randolph agreed. "The place looks barren and the servants half-starved, but Kerr and his men are well-clothed and fed. I'll warrant he's got goods hidden somewhere."

"Why does he hide it, then?" Coulston asked.

"Because it's ill-got," Simon answered. "Kerr is a bandit, I think. If he shows wealth in these parts, the wardens will arrest him, and he'll hang."

Randolph added his observances. "Mismatched tapestries, fine clothes that don't suit the wearer, an unexpectedly sumptuous meal. Kerr has wealth, but I'll wager it's not his own."

"The scheme is preposterous," Coulston fumed. "Their queen would never be foolish enough to marry one of her subjects, and even then it would not be an upstart from the marches!"

"Kerr is a cunning old fox," Eliot countered. "I, for one, would not bet against him." He spread his palms in a gesture of futility. "I ask you, friends, does it matter to us who the Queen of Scots marries? We face a simple question: Do we take his gold and let Kerr have his way, or do we oppose him and suffer the consequences?"

Randolph turned toward him in shock. "You would have me lie to our own queen?"

Eliot shrugged. "What choice do we have? If we refuse, Kerr's quite likely to kill us. If we agree, we simply grow richer, keep quiet, and see what happens."

Simon didn't like the ease with which Eliot proposed treason, but he had a good argument. Kerr could easily murder them all, yet he'd offered a deal.

Randolph's thought paralleled Simon's. "Why make this offer? Why not simply kill us?"

The answer came to Simon with a sudden certainty, and he spoke it aloud. "He wants us to advance his cause when we return to England."

Coulston was appalled. "What?"

"Kerr might be mad, but he is, as Eliot says, cunning. If we agree to wait here until he lays his proposal before his queen, we return to England his men, bound to him by the sops we've taken. In order to protect ourselves, we'd have to support his son's claim to the throne and press Elizabeth to accept the marriage peacefully. He's played this well."

"True." Randolph sounded defeated. "We stepped into his trap like rabbits into a snare."

"How did he know the details of our mission?" Coulston asked.

"He must have a confederate in England." Recalling Elizabeth's mention of spies, Simon didn't say that Kerr's helper might well have come with them, might even now be nearby.

Coulston drew breath to argue, but Randolph said, "I begin to wonder if this mad scheme might possibly succeed." He counted his points on his fingers. "Kerr has specific knowledge of affairs at the English court and the Scottish court as well. Judging from the meal he provided yesterday, he's no country bumpkin. And think how easily he tricked us into coming here."

"But the queen's lady!" Coulston exclaimed. "Was she fooled as well?"

"She was part of it." Simon recounted what he'd learned from Agnes that afternoon.

"All the more reason to do as Kerr asks,"

184

Eliot said when he finished. "Shall we admit to our queen we were tricked like children at a fair?"

"What should we tell her?"

Eliot bent and picked up a stone. "If we cooperate with Kerr, he will substantiate whatever story we tell to explain our delay."

Simon saw Eliot looking at him speculatively and knew he was being asked, in a subtle manner, if he would lie to Elizabeth in order to make them all look less foolish. Imagining her pale eyes fixed on him, he knew he could not.

Before he could answer, however, Randolph intervened. "We can discuss what we tell the queen once we are away from here. Kerr is the present danger." He glanced backward. "Is there someone of the household who might help us escape?"

"There's more than one who's unhappy," Simon answered, "but they are afraid of Kerr's wrath. We have nothing to offer that would counter it."

Coulston struggled to understand. "You say the son is a lackwit?"

"He seemed sane enough at dinner, though bored near the end," Eliot said.

"As were we all," Coulston said with a sniff.

"He was dosed, perhaps with poppy,"

185

Simon said. "Then whatever they gave him began to wear off, and he became agitated."

He told them how he'd spent the afternoon following Kenneth in his childish pursuits and the glimpse he'd had of the youth's tendency to become violent when crossed. "They have trouble controlling him. You note he did not appear at dinner, nor did 'Lady' Agnes."

"What do you think is wrong with him?" Coulston asked.

"Perhaps some fever in the brain stunted his mental growth. They probably calm his angry moods by giving him small doses of opium, but he'll need more and more of it over time. The effects on his health will someday be disastrous."

"And they want to marry this damaged offspring to their queen." Randolph glared at the tower as if he blamed it for their predicament.

Eliot seemed almost amused. "It would not be the first time a nation suffered a ruler with an addled mind, nor the first time an ambitious parent put a child on the throne to further his own interests. I'd guess Kerr intends to be the power behind the throne."

"Likely," Randolph agreed.

"Kenneth is handsome enough to turn any woman's head," Simon said. "If they can keep him from speaking overmuch, he might appear suitable."

"It's all clouds and smoke!" Coulston said, waving a hand dismissively.

Randolph took off his cap and rubbed his balding head. "I have often been at court. Clouds and smoke are quite acceptable as national policy."

Eliot raised his hands, palms out. "All that is nothing to us. The man's gold is good, even if his logic is not. If we delay our mission for a week, we continue as before, only richer. Let the others believe we await the queen's arrival. After some days, we'll announce to the others that her plans changed. We can then continue to Edinburgh."

"And when our host leaves for Holyrood two days hence? What do we tell our companions then?" Coulston scoffed.

"I never said we wouldn't earn the wealth Kerr offers," Eliot said with a grimace.

"I cannot agree to this." Randolph's tone was firm.

"If we do not," Eliot answered, "he will kill us, every one."

"There is another option," Randolph said. "We will leave by stealth tonight and journey on alone."

The idea filled Simon with dread, but he

saw no other way. Might Tavish or Nettie help?

"Speak to the others a few at a time," Randolph ordered. "Tell them to remain awake. We shall leave on my signal."

"They will pursue us," Eliot warned.

"We'll go at midnight, when it's full dark. That will give us until daylight, enough time to outrace them, I think."

Coulston frowned but nodded in agreement. Eliot spoke against it, attempting to argue Randolph's conscience into silence. When Simon agreed with the other two, he said grimly, "You've decided it, then." His tone implied whatever happened was on their heads, not his.

To Simon's disappointment, Nettie was not in sight when they returned to the hall. He'd had a faint hope he might enlist her aid, but it was probably best they trust no one outside their party. He caught a glimpse of her later as he laid out his cloak on the floor, but she was across the room and didn't look at him. They'd have to find their way alone, but Eliot, once he realized they were determined, had claimed he could lead them back to the seashore.

Randolph's signal came when sounds of snoring filled the hall and the fire had burned to embers. As if answering the call of nature, Matthew left the hall. A few minutes later Philip followed, then another man, and another, until they were all gathered by the window in the solar. Matthew eased it open noiselessly, and one by one, they dropped lightly to the ground.

But when they stole across the moonlit courtyard and approached the low wall that surrounded the place, a figure rose, taking a truculent pose. "Is this how th' English repay hospitality, then?" Dickie Muir said. Along the wall at least three dozen men stood up, weapons in hand. "We thought ye macht mak an improper decision," he said, his tone smug. "We'll extend our hospitality once more, but 'twill be a bit more confining this time."

Amid protests from Randolph and rough orders from their captors, they were forced back across the courtyard to the tower. "Climb," Muir ordered. "All the way to the top."

With spears at their backs, they had no choice. One after another they climbed the ladders to the top level, empty except for a foul-smelling bucket. When the last Englishman stepped onto the plank floor, Muir's head and shoulders appeared, a dark silhouette lit dimly by lanterns below. "Sleep well, masters," he jibed. "Our care is fer yer comfort, till the day ye die."

"Your master is mad, Muir," Randolph said coldly. "His scheme will fail, and you will suffer the wrath of both the Scottish queen and the English one."

"Mad he might be," Muir replied calmly, "but Geordie has a way o' getting what he wants. Fortune favors the brave, does it no'?" With that he disappeared, pulling the trapdoor closed behind him. They heard the sound of trapdoors on the other levels being closed and bolted as well. In a place designed so no one could get in, they were prisoners with no way to get out.

Henry convinced himself Calkin needed to know of Constable Fenman's suspicions, though he recognized in his heart that desire to speak to the guardsman again drove him. As he completed his tasks at home, he pondered how he might convince Calkin of Fenman's evil nature without sounding like a whiney child.

When he'd closed the shop for the day, he went to the inn, peering into the taproom. Calkin sat at a table with two local men, and when he looked up and saw Henry, his eyes flashed a warning. An almost imperceptible motion of his head indicated the back of the building. Henry got the idea, scanned the room as if looking for someone who wasn't there, and left.

He made his way to the rear, though a jumble of old furniture, food scraps, and chickens made the passage somewhat perilous. Calkin waited in the empty kitchen. Putting a finger to his lips, he took a candle from a shelf, lit it, and led the way up the back stairs to his room. "Your visit will have tongues wagging if they know of it, so speak softly."

Henry described his encounter with Fenman. "He doesn't believe you seek a cousin." Taking a breath, he added, "I don't believe you came to catch a cheating merchant, either."

Calkin grinned sheepishly. "It was the knife, wasn't it? I knew as soon as I said it."

"You were aware of the matter when you came."

"Aye. Simon told the queen, who sent me to do as he would if he were here."

"I want to help."

Calkin studied him in the candlelight. "I understand, lad, but there's naught you can do."

"I know who can be trusted." Thinking of Fenman he added, "And who cannot."

"Fair enough. If I need information, I'll find some reason to visit your shop." Calkin

191

leaned forward, resting his palms on his knees. "But hear this. I protect you — and Hannah and your sister." When Henry's eyes widened he said, "There! I see their safety concerns you, so think on it. If there's a murderer in Old Change, I don't want him harming any of you."

"He could as easily come after you."

The guardsman rubbed his hands together. "That will be his undoing or mine, but I am wholly prepared to wager on myself."

"Will you tell me what progress you've made thus far?"

Leaning until his back touched the wall, Calkin complied. "I looked first at the searcher who took your uncle's place, but he was unknown here until months after Clark was killed." He grimaced slightly. "That's not to say he's honest."

"Dodgson?" The man wasn't likeable, but Henry had never thought of him as criminal.

"He's willing to take a bribe. In fact, he encourages it." He told Henry what he'd seen in the grocer's shop.

"What made you suspect him?"

He shrugged. "There's gossip. And I've seen underhanded dealing around the palace, so I know the signs."

"Dodgson has never asked Simon for

money."

"Because Simon is an honest man and all know it. The searcher has neither a threat to hold over him nor a hope the guild would believe lies about him."

Henry sighed. "Why don't folk abide by the rules, so they aren't forced to pay bribes?"

Calkin smiled, and Henry realized the question was naïve. "There are many reasons men don't do as they should. Profit is certainly one. If Simon mixed a little sand into his physic it would go farther, and who's to say it would harm anyone?"

"That's why the guild has rules against it."

"Too many rules and too much power, according to some." Calkin shifted his legs to a more comfortable position.

"Will you arrest Dodgson, then?"

Calkin spread his hands. "Who will testify against him? Those who know his crimes are as guilty as he and would face the same punishment."

Recognizing the truth of that, Henry returned to his concern. "Who killed Will, then?"

Calkin replied with his own question. "Your uncle was an honest man?"

Henry shrugged. "Would Simon be his

friend otherwise, or Aunt Annie his wife?"

"You're right, though it would be easier to explain his death if he were dishonest." His hand went to his stomach and rubbed. "Your aunt can cook, I tell you!"

"Umm." Henry was tired of hearing about his aunt's skill in the kitchen, but the comment brought to mind her message. "I'm to tell you she'll make whatever dishes you'd like, if you let her know what they are."

"She will, eh?" Calkin thought for a moment. "Can she make fish with Galentyne sauce, d'you think? I had it once as a boy, and I've never forgotten it."

"It happens," Henry answered, "that I'm to take John fishing tomorrow. We shall catch a trout or two and see what she can do with them."

CHAPTER ELEVEN

By the time daylight sliced through the wall slits, Simon and his companions had explored the tower's highest room closely for a possible escape and found none. There was barely room for all of them to sit, but most slumped dejectedly against the wall. Randolph patiently answered and re-answered the questions of those who hadn't heard Kerr's proposal. Harold Empson, whose brother-in-law was on Elizabeth's Privy Council, found fault with Randolph's decision to steal away at night. "You should have proposed a second hunting trip," he said peevishly. "We could have ridden away into the forest and eluded them."

"And been chased down and murdered by bowmen who know the countryside well?" James Coulston shot back. "That plot would end with an arrow in your back!" He turned to Randolph. "Tell Kerr we'll do as he asks. We can always repudiate him later, when we are safe."

"It's unlikely he'll take anything we say now as truth," Randolph said darkly. "All he needs do is keep us locked up here until it's too late for us to press our suit."

"And then what?" Matthew asked. "Can he let us go, knowing we'll tell what he's done?"

"Kerr is convinced his plan cannot fail. He will not think we matter," Randolph answered. Simon wondered if he believed it or was merely soothing the younger man's fears.

"Where's Eliot?" Philip asked. There was a stunned silence as his absence registered.

"He was with us in the courtyard," Randolph said.

"Did they take him somewhere else, do you think?"

Having theorized an Englishman was helping Kerr, Simon guessed the truth. Eliot's smiles at Kerr's stories, his argument they should accept the bandit's offer, and Kerr's knowledge of their plan to escape. He met Randolph's gaze and saw the knowledge there as well.

Eliot had been working against them from the first. Recalling the rumor he'd killed a man, Simon reconsidered Munn's disappearance. He'd thought it odd the guide had left his bag behind. Had he truly run off, or was his body buried along the coast in a shallow, sandy grave?

Still looking at Simon, Randolph shook his head slightly. "Kerr might be questioning him in order to learn more about us," he said for the benefit of the others.

There was some discussion, but after a while they lapsed into silence, waiting listlessly for an unknown future to become the present. When the sky turned a pale blue, they heard sounds of activity below and stood, warily watching the trapdoor, which rose a foot, paused, and then opened all the way. Muir's head appeared and he said brusquely, "Who's the surgeon?"

All eyes turned to Simon, who stepped to the front. "I am."

"Come wi' me."

With a glance at the others, Simon moved to obey. As he descended the ladder, he caught a look from Randolph that seemed to suggest he do something to help them. *What would that be?* he wondered. *Am I expected to overcome a houseful of outlaws?*

When they reached the bottom of the last ladder, Simon told Muir, "Your master's plan cannot succeed. The queen will see what Kenneth is."

Muir chuckled. "Why should she? He has

writ her letters tha' reveal wide interests i' the world, a bit o' education, and a fine turn o' phrase." Raising a brow, he added, "They're nae bad, if I say so m'self." Leaving Simon to follow, he turned toward the house.

Kerr waited in the hall, feet resting on bricks wrapped in cloth. "Ye're the surgeon?"

"I am."

Assuming the outlaw wanted treatment for his poor circulation, Simon had already begun listing possibilities in his mind when Kerr said, "My son needs physic." He gestured at his daughter, who stood behind him. "This one is sometimes useful at keepin' him well, but she claims this illness is beyond her skills."

Agnes stared at him intently, nodding minimally, which Simon took to be a sign he was to agree. "I will do what I can." Sliding his pack from his back, he started out of the room.

As he passed, Kerr put a heavy hand on his arm. Simon felt the chill of the man's bloodless fingers through his clothing. "We leave for Holyrood tomorrow at daybreak. If Kenneth is nae well enough t' travel, I'll put ye in a wooden cage and hang it fro' the tower roof till I return. Ye'll probably nae live t' see me again, nor will 't be an easy death."

Gulping back his fear, Simon followed Agnes down the corridor, hoping the heir's illness was not beyond the power of an apothecary's skills.

The stench of vomit filled Kenneth's room. On the floor was a bucket that had caught most of the mess, but his clothing was stained and caked with it. He lay with eyes closed, obviously weak and exhausted, on a pallet of straw. He'd been covered with a woolen blanket, but he was so tall his feet stuck out the bottom. Simon bent to touch his forehead. He was not feverish. Pressing Kenneth's belly lightly, he got no response.

"He's fast asleep."

To his surprise, Agnes grinned. "He should be. I gave him monkshood t' make him puke, and now I've given him poppy juice, t' make him sleep the day away."

As Simon turned to her, he saw a red mark on her left cheek. "Who struck you, Agnes?"

"Who d'ye think?" She laid her hand on the mark as if to cool it. "I had t' say I couldna help Kenny, and it made Father verra angry."

"You made your brother sick on purpose, so your father would send for me?"

"He wouldna bring ye down for muther or one o' us girls. We can a' die for all he cares, but nae his precious son!" She sniffed angrily and tossed her head at the inert figure on the bed. "The next king o' Scotland!"

"What do you want of me?"

"If I help ye t' escape, will ye take me wi' ye?"

"Take you where?"

Agnes shrugged. "Anawhere but here!" She took a step toward him, her expression earnest. "When Mary came fro' France, Father took me t' court, hoping the queen would invite me int' her household. It was lovely there, wi' dresses like ye've nae seen." Her eyes hardened. "But ever' noble family in Scotland had the same idea. There were dozens o' girls seeking Mary's favor, and ever' laird o' Scotland stood aboot looking wise in hopes she might ask him t' advise her. Father was ignored, as was I." Her tone turned bleak, and she touched her shoulder as if remembering pain there. "He was verra angry, though I did the best I could!"

Simon imagined the rural, untaught girl competing with daughters raised in fine homes, girls who'd spent time in the courts of Europe. She was pretty enough, but could she dance, play an instrument, speak many languages, and comment on the latest styles? Not likely.

Agnes turned toward her brother, sprawled on the bed with his mouth open. "Father found one friend at court, an Englishman."

"Samuel Eliot."

She smiled grimly. "Tha' one. Though I failed t' impress the queen, Eliot took t' me. Soon he and Father were hatchin' a plan, an' I was sent t' help Muir bring ye t' Duns."

Eliot had again influenced them, Simon realized, accepting Muir and "Lady Agnes" at face value and promoting the trip to Duns.

"Father has convinced himself tha' the queen will fall in love wi' Kenny once she sees him." Agnes clenched her hands together, pacing the room. "Mother says he's mad, but she doesna dare oppose him. He's determined t' see it done."

Mad was the perfect word for it. Kerr was so hungry for power that his grasp of reality had become weak. The idea of setting his daughter in the queen's inner circle had been unlikely enough, but when it failed, he'd hatched an even more outrageous idea.

Was there any chance his plan could succeed? Simon doubted it but couldn't wholly discount it. What was called madness by some was renamed boldness once an enterprise was successful, and belief in a dream was often the impetus that made it into reality.

He looked at the supine form on the bed. "Your father wouldn't be pleased to learn this."

Agnes glanced at the doorway but set her jaw. "If I stay, he'll beat me when 't pleases him and one day give me t' Eliot as a prize." She took Simon's arm. "Here is what ye must do."

Simon listened as Agnes explained her plan. "Kenny will wake in a few hours, a bit weak but well enough. Tavish will take ye back t' the tower. On th' second level, ye must find a place t' hide. Tavish will bang about and make it seem he's taken ye t' the top, where yer friends are."

"They'll wonder when I don't return."

Agnes waved a hand angrily. "Who shall they tell tha' ye're missing? We will get away i' the morning, ye and me and Tavish. We'll send soldiers t' free them when we get t' Edinburgh."

"Your father might kill them before we can return."

"He intends ye'll die, but nae until he reaches the city, so he is wi' the queen herself when ye're slaughtered."

"Except for Eliot."

"Aye. He'll appear later wi' a tale of bandits and slaughter."

"And he the only survivor."

"Indeed."

His companions would probably decide he'd gone over to Kerr's side, but he could do nothing about that at the moment. "We must act quickly, then."

"In the morning, when Father has left for Edinburgh," Agnes instructed, "climb down through one o' the murder holes." Reaching into her sleeve, she brought out the end of a rope twined around her upper arm. As she uncoiled it, Simon wrapped it around his waist, pulling his tunic over it when he finished.

"Where the tower wall meets the house, there's a hiding place out o' sight o' the guards. I'll come for ye once I've given the men left behind a dose o' what I gave Kenny. Tavish will have horses ready on the far side o' the hill." She paused, glancing at his crippled arm. "We'll nae hae saddles. Can ye manage?"

Simon nodded grimly. He'd have to. "Will we go east, to the sea?"

She shook her head. "Father will go that way. Tavish knows of a trail t' Edinburgh tha' he says will get us there i' two days if we ride hard."

Picturing the servant's dour face, Simon asked, "Do you trust Tavish?"

Agnes smoothed her hair in an unconscious preening gesture. "He'll do anything for me, and I for him. When Muir finds us gone, he'll think we've run off together, but he won't guess we've taken one o' th' English prisoners wi' us."

A dangerous escape, a rugged trail, and a frantic chase for the capital. Was Agnes trying to trick him? Simon could see no reason for her to lie. Still, he was loath to leave his companions and follow the plan of a teenage girl angry at her father.

What choices are there? he asked himself. *I can trust Agnes or return to the tower.*

"I will do it."

She glanced at the stone walls of the room. "Then I'll soon be free o' this place."

"God willing, we'll both be."

Kerr was pacing the hall when Simon returned. "How does my son?"

Simon said what Agnes had told him to say: "It is but a stomach ailment, probably from the rich food yesterday. I have given him a sleeping potion, and he should wake well recovered."

The bandit's frown relaxed. "Good."

Simon made a last attempt at diplomacy.

"Your Worship, please speak with Master Randolph again. We did not completely understand your proposal —"

"Ye've had yer chance." Simon turned to see Eliot standing in the doorway of Kerr's office, arms folded across his chest.

"More opportunity than poor Munn did, I'll wager."

Eliot shrugged. "The world will not miss one such as Munn."

"Not the world, perhaps." Simon thought of the letter in the guide's belongings. "But someone will. Who will miss you, when your treason is discovered and you are put to death?"

"Enough!" Kerr interrupted. "Tavish, return him t' his proper place. We hae much t' do before morning, and I'll waste nae more time chattering wi' one who canna see a boon tha's dangled before his nose."

Tavish, stone-faced as ever, led Simon from the room. Following the man's rigid back, Simon wondered if he'd dare to defy his master's order when the moment came. With a blank expression, Tavish passed the men on guard, opened the first trapdoor, and gestured for Simon to ascend. When they reached the second level, he nodded at a stack of crates in a corner and continued upward, making a good deal of noise. Simon slid into hiding, watching as Tavish climbed the second ladder, opened the trapdoor, and repeated the process so it seemed to those below they'd both climbed all the way to the top. After a short time he backed down the ladder to the ground floor without so much as a glance at Simon, pausing only to close each trapdoor behind him. When the last bolt slid into place there was silence, and Simon was alone.

He tried to rest, but it was difficult to forget he might at any moment be discovered, that he must escape this tower without being detected, leave his companions behind, and travel across the bleak landscape with only a naïve girl and her morose lover for company. The night was long, and while his body was quiet, Simon's mind gave him no peace whatsoever.

After Henry Maldon went home to the apothecary shop, Calkin returned to the taproom interested in finding out more about the constable who was so interested in his presence. Though Henry hadn't said it, he sensed Fenman had long been a trial to the boy.

Calkin was a little disappointed to learn his performance hadn't been convincing.

He'd cultivated the idea he was in no hurry to locate his dissolute cousin. "My uncle has money," he'd said several times, "and he's paying. Denis can remain lost for another day or two." Men who spent their evenings in the alehouses, working men with no accounts to tally or preparations to make for the next day's business, were mostly simple types who didn't question a free drink. He should have guessed that Fenman, used to dealing with the seamier side of life, would become suspicious of a stranger who remained after it was clear he wasn't getting results.

The taproom was sparsely populated, with only a few of the most assiduous drinkers still there. Calkin listened quietly to their discussions of weather, the state of the roads, and the lack of understanding among wives, sisters, and daughters that a man needs to be left alone. He said little as he waited for an opening. When the conversation turned to the law and its faults, someone teased a man with whiskers almost up to his eyes about his most recent brush with the law, part of a long series of such events. Calkin saw his chance.

"Is your constable fit for his post? Some I've seen are painted figures, all color and no depth."

"Fenman is no painted devil." One fellow pointed at the whiskered man. "Ask Rob if he hasn't got a strong arm."

Rob snarled in response, but a discussion of the constable's effectiveness ensued. Most admitted Fenman earned his pay, and the complaints mentioned against him always began with wrongdoing on the part of the complainer, most often the whiskered Rob, and resentment at having been caught.

"Fenman thinks he's king," Rob said angrily. "Never pays for a meal or a bowl of ale."

The host turned from the spigot with a disapproving glower. "Why should he pay? Each time he enters this place, those that might have thought to rob me or cheat the serving wenches think better of it. I want him here, and I don't mind if he slakes his thirst on my ale."

"God's truth." A well-dressed customer stood off to one side, resting his foot against the hearthstone. "In the years since Fenman took the position, we've seen fewer beggars in Old Change, no vagrants, and no whores flaunting themselves on the street. He makes it known they're not welcome here, which keeps our families and shops safe."

"But he is a harsh man," Rob argued.

"Once I saw him hit a beggar with a club because he asked the baker for a slice of bread and could not show a coin to pay for it."

The host grunted disdainfully. "The law says them that won't work should be whipped, but the justices are often too weak to do it! If Fenman gives a beggar the beating the law demands, then he's more likely to take honest work and not go on with his wicked ways."

The merchant agreed with grim righteousness. "A harsh lesson to remind them of God's wrath to come, that's what sinners need."

CHAPTER TWELVE

As the black outside turned the tiniest bit
less black, Simon heard the sounds of Kerr's
party preparing to depart. Horses' hooves
sounded on the hard ground, calls of
farewell rang out, and cart wheels rumbled
at the front of the house. With deliberate
care, he eased from his hiding place and
put an eye to the arrow slit. He looked down
at the courtyard, his view somewhat
obscured by the roofed gateway. Men had
gathered there, some on foot and some on
horseback. A large cart packed with goods
was covered by a waxed blanket lashed
down on three corners with ropes, the
fourth left open for last-minute items. He
was surprised when Agnes hurried out, her
movements jerky in the torchlight, and
tossed a cloth bag onto the cart with a vigor
that revealed agitation. Simon's heart sank.
Agnes was going to Edinburgh with her
father.

Was he stuck in this place? No. He had the rope, and another hour of darkness. As soon as Kerr and his party left, he'd escape and go for help.

Agnes had not forgotten him. As she turned to go back inside, she glanced up to where he watched and gave him a small but encouraging nod. Disappearing from his range of vision for a few moments, she returned carrying a small earthen jug. With a jesting comment, she handed it to one of the men on guard duty, who took a drink and passed it on to his comrades. When they'd all had a share, Agnes glanced again at the window slit and shrugged, as if to say she'd done what she could. Then she climbed onto the cart, turning her back to the tower.

Kerr came out of the house with Kenneth beside him. Gesturing for his son to climb onto the cart beside his sister, Kerr mounted his horse, surveyed the assemblage critically, and urged his mount forward. As the party headed out, Agnes looked back once, and Simon thought he saw tears glistening on her cheeks. He guessed Kenneth's illness had made Kerr decide to take her along in case the boy needed care. Her plan had gone wrong.

As the creaks of the cart grew fainter,

Simon went into action. Agnes had done her part; now he had to do his. He'd spent much of the night figuring out which murder hole was least visible to the guards. Now he unlatched the half door that led onto the walkway, crawling out on hands and knees behind the parapet. Tying the rope Agnes had provided to a supporting beam, he let himself down through the hole. With only one arm that could support his weight, his descent was clumsy, and when he landed, his good hand throbbed from rope burns. But he'd done it.

Simon backed into the corner Agnes had described, unsure what to do next. Did Tavish know she was gone? Even if the young Scot was still willing to help, how would he find him?

The soft sound of branches brushed aside startled him, but a soft voice whispered, "It's Nettie. Come this way." Simon took a step toward her voice then paused. "Come!" She repeated, beckoning urgently. Lacking another option, he followed the girl along the stone wall.

As they passed the doorway, Simon saw one of the guards slumped against the wall, his face slack. He touched the man's neck and felt a pulse beating slowly but steadily beneath the skin. With an impatient gesture, she went on. Now they had to cross the courtyard, where shadows were beginning to lighten. Nettie seemed to know what to do, for she darted, waited, then darted again. The thought flitted through Simon's mind that she'd done this before.

Despite his dread, there was no shout from the tower, and no one stopped them at the wall. At the gate a second man lay full out on the rocky ground, head resting peacefully on his two hands. Nettie spared him hardly a glance, leading the way up a steep path that skirted the tower. Staying low, she ran from one dark place to another. Simon followed, trusting her experience.

Once they crested the hill, Nettie stood straight and slowed her pace somewhat. "Where are we going?" Simon asked in a low voice.

"Kerr keeps most o' th' stock in a byre dug into the hillside," she answered. "Tavish sees t' them. He's good wi' horses, better than any other."

"We thought Kerr had wealth hidden somewhere."

"There's a room in the house as well," Nettie said. "A false wall in his closet."

He recalled the wall that wobbled at a touch. No wonder the room had seemed small.

The far side of Duns hill sloped steeply for a way, then lowered gently and became densely wooded. When they reached the trees, Nettie turned from the path, walking confidently between the gray branches. She paused once to move aside what might have been a couple of broken branches, but she carefully put them back as they'd been after they passed. Nettie went on, her slight frame bending as she easily ducked under low-hanging branches. Stumbling along behind her, Simon was surprised when she stopped, apparently at a blank wall of rock. Looking closely, he saw there was an opening in the hill's face. It was difficult to see, since the entrance was hidden with woven branches. By himself, Simon would have walked right past it.

"Kerr keeps most of the livestock here," Nettie said. "Fat cows and fine horses, though of course they took the best mounts to Edinburgh."

"I saw how grand they looked," Simon said, "while his people suffer."

Nettie's chin rose a little. "We'd rather starve than be part o' his murdering an' thieving."

"But you're treated badly," Simon said. "I saw the bruises."

Nettie's fair hair shifted in the moonlight

as she tossed her head. "Dickie Muir thinks himself ma master. Still, he's a bit feared o' what we'll do if he goes too far."

"We?"

"Tavish and Agnes and me." He heard grim humor in her voice. "Agnes promised t' geld him if he troubles any woman o' the place wi' his so-called manhood." She lowered her voice. "If Tavish were nae so good wi' livestock, they'd have killed him lang ago."

Nettie whistled softly and Tavish appeared from the cave, leading three horses.

"He made her go t' Edinburgh with him," Nettie told him.

"No!" There was a wealth of emotion in the word. "What'll we do now?"

"This man can lead th' English warden here. He'll free th' others. Once the prisoners tell their tale, Kerr can nae longer hide his crimes."

"But Agnes —"

"They'll speak for her. She'll no' be punished when they tell tha' she tried t' help them."

Tavish looked to Simon. "We will," he promised, "if you help my friends escape."

Turning back to his sister, Tavish said, "Take Agnes's horse and come wi' us."

Nettie shook her head. "Those Kerr left

215

behind must think ever'thing is as it should be." She put a hand on her brother's chest, where it looked even smaller than usual. "I'll wake the ones asleep at their posts and shame them into keepin' quiet. I'll say ye've gone hunting."

"But what if Muir —"

She gave Tavish a push that didn't move him an inch. "I've handled him afore. If th' warden comes quick and quiet, he' tak th' place before they ken what's happening. Now go!"

He didn't like it, but Tavish slipped the rope bridle off one horse, turned it around, and sent it away with a smack on the rump. It trotted away, nickering softly, and answering sounds came from somewhere close. Simon had to admit Kerr's ingenuity. What could the wardens do if, when they chased the bandit home, they found no stolen goods at Duns Tower?

Tavish held the second horse steady for Simon, who made a clumsy attempt at mounting. Without a saddle, he ended up back on the ground. The horse shifted its feet nervously at his amateur attempt. To his embarrassment, Tavish simply picked him up and set him on the horse, more concerned with speed than Simon's dignity.

"Where are we going?" he asked, hoping

he'd be able to keep up with the Scotsman.

"South o'here's Beel," Tavish replied, pointing. "Th' English warden is there."

"We have no time to send for troops or cavil over jurisdiction."

"He can coome t' Duns on yer word, because Englishmen are held captive."

"I see. The Hot Trod."

"Aye."

Simon took up the reins, holding them and a clump of the horse's mane with his good hand. "Then let's go, as swiftly as we can."

Calkin approached Annie Clark's home at mid-day, when his shadow was small and dark on the dusty street. Noting an amateurish attempt to mend a broken window frame, he guessed Annie was too proud to ask her brothers for help with repairs. He vowed to fix the window before he left Old Change. It wouldn't take long, and it was the least he could do for her.

Knocking at the door, he called, "Goodwife Clark?" He sniffed deeply as a delicious aroma reached his nostrils. Could it be?

Annie appeared, wiping her hands on her apron. "Come in! The fish is almost ready."

"I regretted my mention of the dish," he

told her. "I feared it would trouble you."

"No trouble!" she said. "Henry and John caught six fine trout this morning, and the sauce is a-boil." She turned to the fire. "The boys are in the back. You might call them, if you will."

"I'll be glad to." Calkin had been pleased to find Annie's children neither too shy nor too bold. They spoke when it was warranted but didn't interrupt, as some children did. The boys came in at his call and soon they sat at the table, enjoying the best fish he'd had in his life.

When the meal was finished, the children went off, and Calkin sat watching Annie clear away the remains. "You've had no luck finding your cousin?" she asked.

"None, but I am willing to be patient."

"Yes," she said. "Patience gets a person through when naught else can."

"Hannah told me you're twice widowed," he said. "I was sorry to hear it."

"Thank you." Annie stopped with a bowl in each hand, gazing into the past. "I was lucky to find two good men, and it was hard to lose them."

"Your last husband was a searcher?"

"Yes." She wiped a bowl with a cloth as she explained. "As a boy, Will was apprenticed to a tanner, but his heart wasn't in it. Instead, he taught himself to read and write and went to work as a clerk for the guilds. When next they needed a searcher, his experience and his reputation as an honest man led them to hire him."

Calkin wanted to ask more, but he reminded himself Annie didn't know he might have been murdered. Instead he said, "The death of those we love reminds us life on earth is fleeting."

"True." Annie continued clearing the table. "Our plans mean nothing to God." Turning to stack some bowls on a shelf, she added, "My Will intended to go on a trip the next day. He'd packed some things in a bag in case he had to spend a night somewhere." She looked at the floor, adding, "I've kept it as he left it."

"Such things are a comfort," Calkin said, sorry for her pain. "Where did he intend to go?"

"To an almshouse some distance from here. He'd received a letter from the man in charge of it, saying they needed him to come there when he could."

"And he intended to go the next day?"

"Yes." Looking up at the ceiling, she conjured the memory. "A man had been brought to this place. He was unable to speak, and they could not identify him. He

219

had in his clothing a bit of paper with Will's signature and the wax seal he used for official documents."

"He had no idea who the man was?"

"None. Will showed the letter to the constable, who thought it was some scheme to get him away from home and rob him. He'd almost decided not to go, but he changed his mind."

"Why?"

"He said if he could help some poor soul he should do it, and he thought the constable over-cautious. 'Why should someone write to a man such as me to lure me away?' he said." Annie pressed her lips together. "I confess I didn't pay much attention. Arthur was just a few weeks old, and my mind was on managing without him."

"Might I see the letter?"

Annie's eyes met his for a moment, and he saw her assessment of him shift slightly. He might have known Simon Maldon's sister wouldn't be easily misled. After a long look at him, however, she went to a chest and took out a small cloth bag. Returning, she handed Calkin the letter and then went back to wrapping the leftover food.

November Ten, 1588

To the honorable William Clark, greetings and wishes for every good fortune from Daniel Etheridge at Hope House, Servant of man by God's Most Holy Sufferance.
Good Master William Clark, Greetings.

Through the grace of God and in His service, I provide a place for men to begin life anew when they have fallen into paths of wickedness. It is called Hope House, and here I have developed my small skill in healing both the mind and the body. Knowing this, some neighbors brought a man to me a fortnight ago. They had pulled him from the Caine River, and he was almost dead. I feared for many days that God would not spare him, but the pitiful creature has, by God's mercy, recovered somewhat in recent days.

I have no way of knowing what kind of life the fellow has led, but he is very fearful and exhibits the most abject terror when I inquire about his past. He either cannot or will not say who he is or where he comes from, but he had in his possession a document. Though the water had blurred much of it, your searcher's

221

seal and signature were visible. It is my firm hope that you can tell me who this man is or at the least provide some clue that will help to establish his identity. It pains me to think that somewhere a family grieves for him, so I beg you most humbly to contact me at your earliest convenience.

God's servant and yours,
Daniel Etheridge

"What do you think?"

Calkin realized he'd been staring at the letter for some time. "It is intriguing."

"The writer drew a map on the back."

Turning the paper over, Calkin dutifully examined the map, though he didn't need to. He'd heard of Hope House, and he'd seen Daniel Etheridge many times, at Elizabeth's court.

Tomorrow he would visit the place. At best, he would learn something about Will Clark. At worst, he and his horse would get a bit of exercise.

As dusk and fatigue blurred the colors and outlines of their vision, Simon and Tavish came into Beel, more a fortified garrison than a town. At its center was a tower every bit as grim as Duns, surrounded by an assortment of spare structures that served the needs of the hardy residents. As they passed through a barbican gate into a large courtyard where dully clad people moved about, guards eyed them suspiciously. Simon warned Tavish to let him do the talking.

They presented themselves at the warden's home, where they learned he was at his dinner. After showing the letter Elizabeth had provided, they were led to a small, square room where a man and woman sat, sharing a tray of meat and cheese. The woman retreated with discreet grace to another room, and they were left with the warden, William Heaton.

From his appearance, the warden of Beel might have been either Scot or Englishman. Heaton had pale hair, an equally pale complexion, and a large mustache that hid his mouth unless he was speaking, when his bottom teeth flashed in a slightly jutting jaw. Simon explained the situation and answered Heaton's questions, gratified when the warden took his story seriously.

"Kerr has plagued us for some time," he said. "Even with the Hot Trod, we have not caught him at his crimes."

"What exactly does this law allow?" Simon asked.

Heaton shoved the bench where his wife had been sitting out with a foot, indicating that his guests should sit. Once they had done so, he pushed the tray of food toward them. Simon took a chunk of cheese gratefully, having had nothing to eat but some dry bread Nettie had given them before they rode away. Tavish merely stared at the warden as if willing him to speak.

"Border Law gives us six days to cross into Scotland and capture criminals with their plunder. Kerr and his men strike quickly and retreat to Duns Tower, where they hide what they've stolen before we arrive." He tossed a scrap of meat to a hound that appeared to be sleeping nearby. The dog opened its eyes, caught the tidbit with no wasted movement, swallowed it whole, and closed its eyes again.

"When we ride over that cursed hill, Kerr seems always to be at leisure, and he greets me like an old friend. The place appears poor, the wife and daughters dressed no better than servants." He pointed a gnarled finger at Simon. "You no doubt saw that he and his fighting men show no sign of hunger or want."

"Tavish can show you where to find stolen animals, and there is a secret room in the house where he keeps the goods."

Heaton leaned across the table, fixing his eyes on Tavish. "You have seen these things?"

Tavish's answer was typically brief. "Aye."

Leaning back, Heaton nodded to himself. "Then mayhap we can end his evil." His eyes rested on some faraway spot. "I could tell you tales of the horrors Kerr and his reivers leave behind, but there'll be time for such things when he is dead."

"You won't find him at Duns," Simon said. "He's gone to Edinburgh." Briefly he told Heaton the plan Kerr had for his son.

The warden chewed on his moustache for a moment. "That will make the taking easier, I trow, but I wouldn't have minded dropping a noose around Kerr's neck m'self." He turned to practicalities. "How many are left to guard Duns?"

"Half the usual, I'd say. Kerr took two dozen men with him."

"There's an advantage for us, then." Heaton chewed again on his mustache — or his lip; it was hard to tell which — then rapped sharply on the table. A man appeared in the doorway, and he ordered, "Find Eric." The man went off without a word, and Heaton turned back to his guests.

"The law requires we proceed with hue and cry, a great racket that lets folk know

225

we come under Border Law. Since the lives of Englishmen are at stake, we'll dispense with that in this instance." He turned to Simon. "Did Kerr's conniving steward go or stay?"

Simon turned to Tavish for the answer. He was silent for a moment, his brow deeply furrowed. He must feel like a turncoat, Simon thought, helping the English attack his people.

Tavish's answer surprised Simon, both in its length and the emotion it revealed. "Muir is there, and if I macht, your honor, I'd be pleased t' spill his guts m'self, when we coome."

Heaton examined Tavish as if taking his measure, but a stocky young man appeared in the doorway. The warden turned to give him a summary of the situation. "We will leave early in the morning and take Duns tomorrow night. Muir must not have time to kill the captives."

The warden and Eric, his second-in-command, argued briefly about bringing along the "slew dogges," hounds trained to follow a trail. "The dogs' baying would give us away," Heaton said. With a wave in Tavish's direction he added, "Nor do we need them. We have a guide." Eric nodded, but Simon sensed his disappointment. It was

226

his job to handle the valuable hounds, and he was obviously proud of them. His glances at Tavish revealed mistrust of the Scot's honesty. Tavish finally turned his eyes to meet Eric's, and the Englishman looked down at his hands.

Rapping the table again, Heaton barked orders, and men hurried to obey. "Rest," he ordered. "Tomorrow will be a long day. Eric, find room for them in the barracks."

Eric led the way to two unoccupied pallets and told them where they might find breakfast in the morning. Without meeting the eyes of anyone in the room, Tavish rolled his tattered plaid around himself and turned his face to the wall.

Covering himself with his doctor's cloak, Simon struggled to find a comfortable position on the hard wooden bed. He couldn't help but think about the coming fight. Though he'd been forced to defend himself a few times in the past, he'd never ridden into battle. Would he panic when the fighting started and freeze, or worse, run? He frequently practiced with his throwing knife, but once he'd thrown it, what more could he do to help the warden subdue the reivers?

The barracks felt alien, with unfamiliar noises and constant movement that kept him awake and on edge. Simon thought longingly of the softness a wife — his wife — added to their home: curtains at the windows, cozy quilts, and her own warm flesh next to his. How did men live like this, all hard surfaces, rough blankets, and no reassuring female presence in the night?

In the end he drifted into slumber, telling himself if God willed it, he'd soon be home again. Each day must take care of itself. Heaven already knew what would happen, and Simon would learn what kind of soldier he was when it was his time to know.

A motley party of rescuers assembled the next morning, and Simon guessed from their eager chatter that the Hot Trod was a welcome diversion. They were mostly volunteers who gathered before the warden's house, local men led by a half-dozen professional soldiers. Most had bows slung over their backs. Some had swords, spears, or wicked-looking knives, and one carried a musket as proudly and lovingly as if it were his first-born son.

Just before they left, one of the men fastened a clump of peat to the head of his spear and set it afire. "A sign we're on Hot Trod," Heaton told Simon. "Our six days begin now." Simon bit his lip, knowing they had at best two or three days. Kerr would arrive in Edinburgh tomorrow or the day after. Once he was in the presence of the Queen of Scots and could not be blamed for their deaths, his prisoners were doomed.

CHAPTER THIRTEEN

As Calkin rode away from Old Change, the huddled community with narrow streets and busy to-and-fro gave way to open country. The air was scented with a variety of flowers and, less welcome but necessary, the dung that farmers spread on their crops.

He passed Hampstead Castle, the rundown, neglected estate where he'd first met Simon Maldon and Elizabeth, then a forgotten princess. It was odd, Calkin thought, that one never knew on first meeting who'd be a passing acquaintance and who'd become part of his life. He might have worked for the royal family his entire career and never spoken directly to Elizabeth, and Simon might have lived out his years without ever catching her notice. Yet the three of them were connected. He and Simon had become friends, and though the queen could not be friends with the likes of them, she valued their abilities. She trusted them, too, which was satisfying. Many folk were valuable to Her Majesty, but how many did she truly trust?

After a half mile, he might have forgotten that London was so close. The land rolled gently, clothed in the striking green of early summer. Sheep dotted the hillsides and grazed the roadway, a few of them cantankerous obstacles that lay close to the path and refused to move so the horse had to step around them. As he crested a small hill, Calkin saw the almshouse below, a prettier picture than he'd expected. According to what he'd heard, Hope House had once been a monastery. Now, instead of busy monks working to sustain themselves, men in rough tunics performed many of the same tasks.

As Calkin rode up to the largest building, a man put down the rake he was repairing and stood to greet him. "Welcome, friend."

"I thank you. Is your —" He stopped, unsure what Hope House's founder called himself. "Is Daniel Etheridge here?"

The man pointed to a group at work in the vegetable garden. "He's there. Shall I take your horse to the water trough? The day has become warm, and he looks thirsty."

Calkin hesitated. This place was full of criminals. Was the man a prigger who'd steal the horse? Chiding himself for such thoughts, he said, "I thank you," and handed over the reins.

He approached the garden plot, where the men had stopped work to examine him. Some were shifty eyed and surly-looking. Others seemed distant, as if they didn't fully comprehend what went on around them. A few were watchful but earnest, as if they'd learned to hope for the best in this place. The youngest, a smooth-faced man with merry eyes, tilted his head to regard Calkin. "I know you, I think."

"I've seen you at court many times, Your Worship."

Etheridge's smile dimmed momentarily. "I am called Daniel here."

Calkin bowed slightly. "Very well. I am Sergeant Calkin, of the queen's guard." When some in the group shifted nervously he added quickly, "I mean your people no trouble."

"Then we will help if we can." Turning to the others, Etheridge said, "Masters, go on with our work and I will rejoin you soon."

As the young man led the way to a shaded area, Calkin took stock of this most unusual nobleman. The son of a duke, Daniel had often come to court in his youth. When he stopped attending his father, rumors sped through the palace that were soon confirmed. The duke's youngest son had announced he wanted nothing to do with affairs of state; in fact, he wanted to be a priest. This his father did not allow, but the boy refused to wear fine clothes, would not consider a brilliant marriage, and claimed he meant to serve God rather than the queen.

In the end, he'd disappeared from London. Gossips said he'd gone to live among the wrecks of society at an old monastery he'd renamed Hope House.

As they walked, Daniel pointed out areas of interest, first the long brick building where Calkin had stopped. "That's the barracks, where the men sleep. Over there is the hall, where we take our meals and where the men learn simple trades: pot-mending, rope-making, and the like."

"So they do not have to steal to live?"

Daniel smiled placidly. "Exactly so. I try to change the lives of men who lose their way."

"And they are criminals?"

"Some," he admitted. "Others have fallen into drink or other sinful ways. This is a stopping place where they may turn their hearts to God and begin anew."

"Who pays for it?"

"I do." Daniel smiled shyly. "In fact, my father does, with a certain understanding."

Seeing his guest's confusion, Etheridge explained. "The duke has plenty of land and other sons to serve his ambitions. I begged this small estate for my own, and he agreed on the condition that I remove myself from his presence forever." His tone was mild, but Calkin sensed the hurt that had come with the promise.

Looking down at his dirt-spattered clothing, Daniel went on, "I believe it is more important to please my Heavenly Father than the earthly one. Serving these men, working alongside them and seeing them find new hope, is far better than dancing attendance on an earthly king or queen."

Though he knew no insult was meant, Etheridge's statement dismissed Calkin's entire career as well as the duke's. "You have a fine site," he said.

"When Henry seized the Church's properties, my grandfather bought this land from the crown. He had no use for the buildings, but God's hand was in it, for now I have the means to do the work He put me on earth to do."

"Commendable."

Etheridge's smile was patient, and Calkin realized he was used to being doubted.

"These men want to work, Sergeant, but employment has long been difficult to find. Our present queen seems to be leading us back to prosperity, but until there is work for all, I must do what I can."

Calkin turned to the question he'd come to ask. "I recently met a woman whose husband received an odd letter from you some years ago." He told Etheridge about Will Clark's death.

"He was killed? I thought my words had failed to touch his heart. Praise God, and may his soul rest in peace!" Bowing, he mouthed a prayer while Calkin stood uncomfortably by.

"Do you know what happened to the man you wrote of?" he asked when it was finished.

"Carl? Why he's here still. I could not turn him out, for he never fully recovered."

Calkin couldn't believe his luck. "Might I see him?"

"Of course." Etheridge led him inside, where three men sat making belts. Two were passable craftsmen, but Calkin was surprised at the quality of the third one's work. Though he kept his face lowered, he was clearly disfigured. His left cheekbone was sunken, the eye missing.

One of the other men looked at Calkin

suspiciously. "Who is that?"

"One who wants to see what good work you do," Etheridge said.

"He'll set the guilds on us!"

"He was not sent by the guild, James." Turning to Calkin, Etheridge explained, "The goods we make cannot be sold in London, where the guilds hold sway. We take them into the countryside, to local fairs." He added in a low tone, "It helps them when they earn their keep, and some of the better craftsmen are offered employment at some castle or country estate."

It wasn't a bad idea to show a beggar or petty thief how to make himself into an honest workman, Calkin supposed, though he wondered how many successes Etheridge had. Did these men return to their old ways when he was no longer nearby to encourage them?

The suspicious James was still glaring at him, so Calkin told him, "I am not from the girdlers' guild or any other. I'm only an old soldier, come looking for a friend." That seemed to pacify the man, and he went back to pushing his awl through the thick leather.

The one-eyed man paid no attention to the conversation as he worked at edging the belt he was making with smooth, even stitches.

Etheridge touched his arm to get his attention. "A fine effort, Carl."

"Thank you." He glanced up briefly before returning to work, and Calkin saw the full extent of his injury. It was hideous and pitiful at once, and he looked away.

"Carl is our miracle," Etheridge said, patting the man's shoulder. "God took pity on him, and now see what he can do."

"Most wondrous," Calkin said dutifully. "What happened to him?"

Etheridge led him a short distance away, though Carl appeared uninterested in anything but the leather in his hands. "Someone beat him mercilessly and threw him in the river to die. By God's grace, he crawled to shore, where he was found and brought to me."

"Might I ask him about it?"

Etheridge considered. "It upsets him, but I will ask. He knows I will not hurt him."

Moving back to the table, he said, "Carl, do you remember when you were hurt?"

Fear lit the man's eyes, and he dropped the leatherwork, raising his arms over his head as if to fend off blows. "I will not come back! I will not, on my word!"

Etheridge touched his arm, speaking softly. "You are safe, Carl. This man only wants to know if you remember what happened."

"I meant no harm, master!" He began sobbing. "I won't come back! I won't! I swear it!"

Though it took some time, Daniel managed to calm the man's fears, reminding him again and again that he was safe. When his cries stopped, he picked up the leather, located his needle, and went back to work. In a short time, though tears remained on his face, Carl's expression revealed only concentration on completing his task.

"Most of the time, he's as you see him now," Etheridge said. "It's only when he remembers what happened he shows emotion, and it's always terror."

"And he had a piece of paper in his clothing with Will Clark's signature?"

"Yes. It was a letter on some minor matter of business. The signature gave us someone to contact, but I don't know why Carl had it in his possession or why he was attacked."

"Do you have the letter?"

Etheridge shrugged. "I doubt it. We use and reuse paper, teaching the men to sign their names." He smiled like a proud father. "Some even learn their letters."

"In the years since, you've discovered no

more about Carl and what happened to him?"

"It is my belief he fell afoul of ruffians near the riverbank." He shook his head. "Carl was a poor man, judging from his clothing, so he'd have had little money. It was cruel sport, I suppose, for men with no conscience to empty his pockets and toss him in the river."

"Cruel indeed." Daniel was partly correct, but Calkin had deeper suspicions. Someone found sport, not in stealing a man's earthly goods, but in taking a more precious gift — life itself.

CHAPTER FOURTEEN

Once again Simon rode unwillingly over rough country and through isolated but thickly wooded tracts. At least someone had lent him a saddle this time. He and Tavish traveled in the middle of the group, whether to protect them or to guard against possible treachery, he didn't know.

When the sun finally came up, the day turned bright, and he saw the best of a Scottish summer, with blue skies and temperatures that warmed but did not grow hot. Flowers he hadn't noticed before caught his eye, tiny white specks and tall, bright purple blooms that dotted the way as if created for their pleasure. It was hard to keep in mind that they rode toward danger with the glory of the land spread before them.

They pushed onward as fast as possible, leaving behind those whose horses were more suited to plows than distance. Heaton seemed to share Simon's fear that the prisoners would be killed before they could reach them, though he never said it aloud. From time to time he dropped back to consult Tavish, who gave terse but helpful replies. The day waxed and waned with only brief stops. Conversation was minimal as the men prepared their minds for the coming fight.

When the sun had almost sunk behind the hills, Tavish spurred his horse to the front and spoke to Heaton. Raising his hand, the warden signaled a stop. As the men dismounted, a boy of perhaps twelve came through, gathering reins and leading the horses away into the trees.

"We'll wait here for deep night and continue on foot," Heaton ordered. The men sought out comfortable spots and sat, most leaning against trees and closing their eyes. A few stared into space or at their hands. Pausing as he passed, Heaton advised, "Rest if you can."

Obediently Simon sat, leaning against a small hillock. Tavish crouched nearby, looking not in the least relaxed. His hands formed fists, as they had the first time Simon saw him. "You hate Geordie Kerr," Simon said in a low voice.

Tavish didn't speak for some moments,

but finally he acknowledged, "I do." Simon thought that was all he would say on the subject, but he added, "He murdered a man who was like a father to me and Nettie, and he killed our muther as well."

"The old lord of Duns Tower." It was a guess, but Tavish nodded.

"Ma muther kept his house. When his wife died, she became his leman and later his wife. We hardly remember our father, but Malcolm Kerr treated Nettie an' me as if we were his ain."

A laird who took a servant to his bed wasn't uncommon, especially in rural areas where there were few women of the correct social class. The name he'd mentioned registered. "Kerr! Malcolm was —"

"Kerr's own uncle."

"Tavish, tell me everything so the pieces come together in my head."

At first haltingly but with growing confidence, Tavish told the story. Geordie Kerr's father had been, as Kerr admitted, profligate and irresponsible, the opposite of his brother Malcolm, who'd been granted the small holding at Duns for service to James IV. Geordie took after his father, despite Malcolm's attempts to help him. He'd arranged a marriage for Geordie that should have established him at court, but for years he'd chosen the carefree life of a soldier of fortune, coming home only long enough to get his wife with child before leaving again on some adventure. By the time Agnes was twelve, Geordie's name was so black he was in danger of hanging. Malcolm and his old friend Menteith had convinced him to bring his family to Duns, where they hoped he would settle down and stay out of trouble.

"Malcolm promised Geordie the holding would be his in time," Tavish said, "but he didna want t' wait for it. One day when the two o' them were oot hunting, Malcolm fell from his horse. He was dead when Geordie found him — at least, tha's what he said." Tavish shook his head as if Simon intended to argue the point. "He was a fine rider. He wouldna fall, nor would his ain horse throw him. Tis an insult t' them both t' say so!"

From what he knew of Kerr, Simon didn't doubt Tavish's word. "And your mother?"

Tavish pressed his lips together as if to steel himself before speaking. "When Geordie came home wi' Malcolm draped over his saddle, head dented like soft fruit, Muther went wild, screaming he was a murderer." His gaze swept the ground. "Geordie ordered Muir t' take her away — t' calm her, he said." His face went still.

"How she raged as he carried her fro' the hall!"

There was nothing Simon could say, so he merely waited for the rest of the story.

"I tried t' stop them. That's how I came by this." Tavish touched the scar on his forehead. "When I came t' myself, Muther was dead. Geordie said she took her own life i' grief for Malcolm, and nae dared say else. When I called him murderer and swore I'd kill him, he put me i' the tower wi' nae food or water. It was a week, maybe more. If it hadna rained, I wuld hae died." He said it calmly, but Simon felt a chill go down his back.

Tavish rubbed his face with one hand. "Finally, Kerr sent Nettie t' tell me he would treat the people o' Duns fairly if I accepted him as laird. He knew they'd do as I did, y'see. If I didna agree, he'd leave me t' starve." His eyes met Simon's. "Tha' was nae stop t'me, but I could see fro' ma sister's manner tha' t'was nae only me he threatened. When I made her tell me a', Nettie admitted Geordie told her to say he'd give her t' Muir if I didna agree." Tavish ran a hand through his shock of pale hair. "I see th' way Muir looks at her, and I see th' sma' things Nettie abides fro' him, caresses she cringes at an' blows when it pleases him t' hurt her. She willna admit it, but I ken. I ken."

With sudden impatience, Tavish rose to his feet. "We must haste. When I dinna return, she'll suffer for 't!"

"Heaton seems to know his business, while you and I do not," Simon said reasonably.

They lapsed into silence, Tavish brooding, Simon wondering how men like Kerr and Muir got away with their crimes. Could the people of Duns Tower have done something about their lord's murder? Probably not. They were part of the land, in effect owned by the laird. With Malcolm dead, Geordie had the right of blood, and once the housekeeper was silenced, the others would have feared a similar fate.

As if he could no longer keep the words inside, Tavish said, "Muir beat her unconscious and hanged her from a stable crossbeam." He touched the knife at his belt. "Tonight I give peace t' ma muther's soul. Malcolm's justice will coome later, but I'll see tha', too."

Leaving Tavish to his dark thoughts, Simon sought out Heaton. "We might find the people of Duns are not so loyal to their laird as they might be." He explained Tavish's contention that Geordie had murdered the rightful owner.

There was some mustache chewing, barely visible in the growing gloom. "Some will remain loyal to the laird, though, when Englishmen arrive at their door."

Simon nodded. "Muir, for one. But Tavish will know who can be trusted."

The warden's grunt indicated little trust for any Scot. "We'll be ready, whatever comes."

A man approached, and Heaton asked, "Have you got it?"

"I have." He handed over a sack that made Simon's nose wrinkle.

"What is it?"

"Meat for the dogs. To keep them occupied until we are in place."

Simon realized that this was how he might be of real help. "I will take it to them. They know my scent already, which might keep them from barking."

"Oh, they'll bark," Heaton said, "for they are hounds. Still, you know the place." Simon guessed two things weighed on the warden's decision, Simon's inability as a fighter, and the fact that if he were caught, it wouldn't give away the presence of the rest of them.

Minutes later, Simon hurried from shadow to shadow, a sack of half-rotted venison slung over his shoulder. A dog began to bark, and another joined in and then another, but he kept going. A voice called, "Quiet, you hounds!" but the dogs kept up their racket. Reaching the pen, he tossed the meat over the fence, aiming for different sections. All the dogs but one stopped barking and went for the food. He managed to hit the remaining animal directly with a piece of meat, and she went quiet. In the relative quiet he could hear the clacking of jaws and the low growls of warning as one canine came too close to another's meal. He threw the last bit into the pen and wiped his hand on the grass.

Keeping to the darkest areas, he made his way back to the wall. Heaton and his men were there, crouched on the outer side. Twenty feet away, a man stood guard, his posture indicating boredom and fatigue. Heaton touched the arm of one of his men, but Tavish put his own hand over Heaton's. After a brief hesitation, the warden sat back, giving tacit permission for Tavish to handle the situation.

Tavish moved closer, whistling softly. "It's me, Jack."

The guard tensed, peering into the darkness. "Tavish? Muir looked for ye ever'where."

"I've brought help tha'll turn Kerr and his hounds out o' Duns for aye."

There was a pause. "Ye mean to tak the holding, Tavish?"

He stood, letting himself be seen. "I do."

A longer pause followed before Jack spoke. "Muir is in the hall wi' them he calls friends. As usual, when Kerr is gone, we're made t' do a' the work."

"All the better for us, laddie," Tavish said. "All the better for us." To Heaton he said, "Muir has done as I hoped, putting our lads on duty while he and his friends drink Kerr's ale. I'll wager ye'll face few enemies outside the hall."

"Good." Tavish and Jack moved off along the wall, and Heaton and his men entered the courtyard. Simon watched as the warden signaled and men left the group at intervals. By the time they reached the house, what had once been twenty men was down to seven. They seemed to read each other's minds, and Simon merely followed, as quietly as possible.

The wait made him clench his teeth with apprehension, but finally Jack and Tavish rejoined them. "All the men on guard know Geordie Kerr's time at Duns Tower is at an end." Tavish rubbed his knuckles. "One wouldna listen, but he'll be nae stop t' us now."

Heaton's men now ringed the tower and the house. Heaton turned to Simon. "You must climb up and free your friends while we see to the men inside."

Simon nodded, realizing he was again being put to best use. The English prisoners would recognize him and obey his commands.

Luck did not favor them completely. The two guards inside the doorway were Kerr's men, and one managed a shout before the warden's man put him down. "Hurry!" Heaton ordered, and Simon started up the ladder, trying not to think about the chaos that erupted below.

In response to the shout, voices rose, first in question but soon in calls to action. As he opened the first trapdoor, Simon heard running steps. He pushed himself upward, imagining the battle that would soon ensue below.

Before the second trapdoor, he paused. If there were guards in the tower, they were likely to be on the next level, the highest except for the one where the prisoners were confined. They'd hear the commotion below, which made it clear something was wrong. Standing directly under the trapdoor

249

Simon shouted in his best Scottish burr, "Muir needs help! We're under attack!" Quickly he scurried to a corner and covered himself with a blanket.

In only seconds, lamplight showed in the room. Through the fabric Simon saw the light begin to descend. Next he heard muttering voices, two men who argued briefly about what they should do. In the end they decided to proceed by stealth. Setting the light down on the floor, they descended the ladder to the next level.

As soon as they were gone, Simon closed the trapdoor, leaving them nowhere to go but down to where Heaton's men would deal with them. It was good of them, he thought, to have left a lamp with which he could light his way.

Climbing to the top, Simon slid the bolt and opened the last trapdoor. When he raised the light to let his friends see him, there were gasps of surprise. "Maldon!" someone said, "We thought they'd killed you!"

Philip asked in a smug tone, "Did I say he would not leave us penned like cattle?"

"Hurry!" Simon said. "There's an English warden below who'll take the place if he can."

By the time they reached the ground level,

the battle was over. Heaton's men were rounding up those who'd opposed them, roping them together with hands tied in front. One body lay slack on the floor, a pool of blood spreading from it, but other than that Simon saw only minor wounds: a broken arm, bulges on foreheads, and cuts, most on the surprised defenders.

Simon introduced Heaton to Randolph, who expressed his thanks for the rescue. Members of the household who'd fled when the battle began came to peep cautiously into the hall. One, bolder than the rest, asked what had happened.

"This holding is forfeit," Heaton told them. "Geordie Kerr has attacked and imprisoned a solemn delegation sent by the queen of England. These men will face many charges, and your queen will decide what will become of them."

"But wha' shall we do?" an older woman asked.

Heaton considered. "For the nonce, do as you've always done. Keep the holding ready for the new owner your queen will name."

In the torchlight Simon saw confusion on their faces. "Tavish will tell you what to do," he assured them, and relief replaced confusion. They were used to taking orders, and Tavish was someone they trusted.

A woman asked, "Kerr will not return?"

The warden gave a huff of disdain. "Not when these men reveal what he did."

"Will the queen punish us?" The youngest of Kerr's daughters stood uncertainly at the edge of the crowd. Simon wondered if her mother had sent her, hoping the warden would be merciful to a child. Nettie, who stood nearby, placed a protective arm around the girl's shoulders.

Randolph raised his voice so all could hear, even those still cowering inside. "We will tell your queen the servants and women of Duns Tower did no harm to us. I know not what she will decide, but I will speak for you."

They didn't cheer — they were Scots, after all — but a few nodded in appreciation. Catching Simon's eye, Nettie almost smiled, but her expression changed. "Where's ma brother?"

"And Muir?" Heaton asked, looking around. "I saw him when we entered the hall."

There was a hurried search of the courtyard, but Tavish wasn't there. The warden's men turned the bound captives to the torch light to better see their faces. Muir was not among them.

"Tavish!" Nettie said in a voice filled with

dread. "He's gone after him."

"How would he escape?" Heaton asked. "The horses are guarded."

"There's a boat on the shore." As soon as she said it, Nettie was running, bursting out the doors as she called her brother's name. Taking a torch from a bracket at the entryway, Heaton followed, the small crowd trailing him as they murmured questions. When they'd skirted the solid bulk of the house, sounds of a struggle echoed across the waters of the tarn and back at them. Simon hurried forward to catch up with Heaton in order to see what his torch revealed. His foot kicked something, and he paused. A knife lay on the ground, Tavish's knife. Stooping, he picked it up and hurried forward.

At the edge of the lake, Tavish and Dickie Muir were locked in a deadly contest. A rowboat bobbed along the shore nearby, loose from its moorings. Tavish had apparently reached Muir before he could get the boat away. Now they faced each other, bodies tense and faces grim.

Muir brandished a sword at Tavish, who defended himself with one of the boat's oars. Though long enough to hold off the sword thrusts, it wasn't made to hold up against the heavy blade of a Scottish sword.

As they approached, Simon heard a crack. Ahead of him, Nettie cried out in anguish as the oar broke in half. The paddle end flew toward them, and Heaton ducked with a cry of surprise as it landed at Simon's feet.

Without turning, Tavish called over his shoulder, "Hold! This fight is mine!"

Muir gave a guttural laugh. "Aye, let me spear this poor fish afore ye come for me." He lunged at Tavish, who scrambled out of the way. The piece of wood he had left wasn't long enough to fend off a sword, but he used it to deflect the blow, twisting out of the way.

"Give him a sword!" one of the Englishmen shouted, but Tavish cried, "Nae!" He'd probably never used a sword before, much less faced an opponent skilled in its use.

He did, however, know what to do with a knife. "Tavish!" Simon called.

Tavish turned slightly, watching Muir but aware of Simon's movements. Simon tossed the knife, and he caught it by the haft. To Muir, he said softly, "Now I'll finish ye!"

It was horrible to watch, yet no one turned away. Tavish spent most of his energy avoiding the sword. With the fragment of oar in one hand, he managed to block the overhand blows. When Muir tried an upward thrust, he twisted away, avoiding the blade by mere inches. Twice he tried to strike a blow of his own as he danced by, but Muir was as quick as he. On Tavish's second attempt, Muir knew what to expect and turned the sword to deliver a backhand blow that caught Tavish just under his ribs. He grunted in pain but turned quickly, raising the dagger to keep Muir from stepping in to finish him.

"Stay!" he warned as one of the warden's men stepped forward. With a ragged breath, he again twisted aside as Muir jabbed at the place where he'd been a moment before.

The struggle seemed to go on for hours, and Simon's fears for Tavish grew. He was obviously in pain and defending himself against a sword with only a knife and a bit of wood. "Help him!" he urged the bystanders, but Tavish gasped, "Stay back!"

Muir's grin showed white in the torchlight. "Aye. Stay back while I finish this." Stepping forward, he lunged at Tavish, who barely avoided the blade, wobbling out of the way as if unable to remain upright. Emboldened, Muir followed his own thrust, making a second attempt at the backhand blow that had succeeded earlier. This time, however, Tavish twisted in a circle so he faced Muir head on as he stepped forward. With a swift movement Tavish stabbed his opponent in the heart, exhaling with effort at the same moment Muir released his final breath.

For some moments there was no sound at all except Tavish's ragged breathing. Then everyone, English and Scot alike, began to cheer.

CHAPTER FIFTEEN

He might have known it, Calkin thought as he led his horse into the stable at the inn in Old Change. Henry Maldon waited in a corner, curiosity leaking out his eyes though his face held its usual closed expression. He greeted the boy cordially, realizing he might be of help.

He told Henry about Carl, hoping he might remember him. Not surprised when he didn't, Calkin said, "Probably a vagrant. He'd have been missed, else." Rubbing his neck, he asked, "Might your uncle have hired this Carl to carry a letter for him?"

"Yes," Henry replied. "Will said a few errands might put a man onto the right pathway."

"So Carl was probably on his way to deliver the letter Etheridge found on him. That is lucky, for it tells us he was attacked near Old Change."

"By the same person who killed Uncle Will?"

"The killer thought Carl was dead until your uncle showed him the letter from Etheridge. He had to stop Clark from going to Hope House. Desperation made him kill Will in broad daylight." He glanced toward the river. "I'll wager his earlier crimes were secret."

"Earlier crimes?"

"A man such as this loves to kill," Calkin said. "If I'm right, he's been doing it for years, telling himself he is acting in the name of the law."

The boy's eyes grew big. "Fenman?"

Calkin nodded. "He knew about the letter. He tried to talk your uncle out of going. Clark must have told him that day at the procession he'd decided to look into the matter."

It took Henry a few seconds to process the information. "Will you arrest him, then?"

"What would the good folk of Old Change say if I told them their constable is a cold-blooded killer? They sing his praises because he keeps the streets safe and empty of vermin."

"Then what will you do?"

"Deal with him," Calkin said. "He thinks

he's too clever to be caught, but we will see."

When Constable Fenman went into the pie shop the next night for supper, Calkin followed him, taking a seat where he faced him directly. All day long he'd shown up wherever Fenman happened to be. In the morning he'd stood watching as Fenman left his lodgings. Several times he'd leaned against a post as Fenman passed on the street. And if the constable entered a shop, Calkin followed, standing at the back and watching.

At first Fenman had ignored him. At the third instance, he made eye contact, his expression curious. Calkin merely looked at him. The next time the constable tried smiling. Calkin didn't smile back. When his smile turned to a glare, Calkin stared back, his expression blank. Fenman began pretending he didn't notice, but his manner was false, his laughter forced.

Every few minutes, Fenman's glance found Calkin. Each time his brow knit briefly, and he ran a hand around his collar. *He won't let things go on much longer,* Calkin thought.

Finally Fenman rose from his bench, taking a deep breath and letting it out before starting toward Calkin. Though he would betray nothing in public, it was clear he needed to know what had changed in the last twenty-four hours. When he reached the table, Fenman's features were set in a pleasant expression. "Good evening, Goodman."

Calkin merely looked at him expectantly.

"I have begun to wonder what your business is in Old Change." Fenman smoothed the front of his tunic, glancing around the room as if aware of curious eyes. "I'm the constable, you see. It's my job to assure that strangers are no threat to folk."

After letting a long silence develop, Calkin said softly, "I think you are the threat here."

It took Fenman a moment to decide how to respond to that. In the end he chose insulted innocence. "I am no threat to those I am sworn to protect. Only criminals should fear me."

"Good to know," Calkin said, "for I intend to expose a criminal. A murderer."

"You have no jurisdiction here," Fenman said, keeping his voice low. "If you have suspicions, you should report them to me."

"Oh, I have suspicions."

"Then present some document to prove you are an agent of . . . the crown." It was a good guess, and Calkin's respect for the man's intelligence rose a little.

"I have no documents." It was a lie, but he needed Fenman to believe he was on his own.

The constable's shoulders relaxed, and his voice rose. "Then I advise you to leave Old Change, for I dislike your idle presence. If I find you here tomorrow, things will go hard for you." With that Fenman walked out just as a girl came with the bowl he'd ordered in her hand.

"I'll take the ale," Calkin told the girl, "and bring me a bowl of soup as well." He smiled to himself, satisfied he'd goaded his opponent into action. When Calkin appeared on the streets of Old Change tomorrow, Fenman would begin plotting how to get rid of him.

The two days that followed the taking of Duns Tower were an extension of Simon's nightmare. The trail to Edinburgh was long unused, and before they started, Tavish confessed it had been years since anyone actually traveled it. They had to depend on instinct, for at times it appeared there was no trail at all.

Warden Heaton rode with them, leaving his men to guard the prisoners until the crown decided what would be done with them. Randolph was determined to complete their mission, and they were all anxious to reveal to the Queen of Scots the perfidy of her subject, Geordie Kerr.

All but one, of course. Eliot was missing, and Nettie reported he'd left with Kerr. "He was dressed as a groom," she said, curling her lip in disgust. "But I knew 'twas him."

Randolph's disgust equaled Nettie's. "The queen will deal with him."

Exhausted, Simon let his horse have its head. He soon ended up in the rear, often batted by branches those ahead released as they passed. He was becoming a better rider, however. Tavish taught him some tricks, so he no longer needed a stump to stand on in order to mount. He'd also become practiced at sliding lightly to the ground when they stopped to rest.

Tavish, though wounded and battered, insisted on leading them to the capital. "Ye'd be lost in two hours' time, else." It was true he had a sense for finding the way, but Simon thought he knew another reason the lad was determined to go.

If he'd had his way, Tavish would have traveled day and night, but Randolph insisted, "We shall do ourselves no service if we arrive so fatigued we cannot frame an intelligent sentence." Though he accepted that announcement without argument, the stops were not particularly restful with Tavish pacing and biting his lip to keep from urging them onward.

They reached Edinburgh just after noon on the third day, having become lost only once and then briefly. However, Tavish's keen sense of direction in the woods deserted him when they entered the city. His eyes widened at the sight of so many buildings, and he seemed to shrink from the warrior who'd killed Dickie Muir to the awed peasant he actually was. "I dinna think t'waud be sae grand," he said wonderingly.

Randolph took over, eyes narrowing as he got his bearings. "Holyrood Palace is near Edinburgh Castle." He pointed at the huge stone structure that dominated the city, looming over it like a watchful parent.

Keeping the castle before them, they easily found Holyrood, situated west of the abbey for which it was named. "It's a quadrangle," Randolph said for the benefit of those who were new to the city, "built by James IV, the queen's grandfather, to celebrate his marriage to Margaret Tudor, sister to our own Henry Eight."

Warden Heaton took his leave at the palace gate. "I'll deliver my report of events at Duns Tower and let the Scottish authorities decide what should be done." Apparently forgetting that he stood on the streets of the nation's largest city he added, "I must return to England with all possible speed, for God knows what mischief the Scots will make in my absence!"

Randolph made a pretty speech of thanks, and they all wished Heaton god-speed on his journey home. Embarrassed by their gratitude, he waved it away. "I pray Queen Mary deals harshly with them who imprisoned you, for it will serve as a lesson to the rest of them."

When he was gone, Randolph turned to Matthew. "Find a place we can stop for several nights," he ordered. "James and I will arrange an audience with Her Majesty."

Once they'd found an inn, Philip returned to the palace to guide Randolph to it. A few hours later, the three men rejoined them. "The queen will see us day after tomorrow," Randolph reported. "She regrets it cannot be sooner, but there are pressing matters she must deal with."

"Did you tell them what Kerr did to us?" Empton asked in a tone that managed to hint Randolph might have forgotten.

The look he got told Simon that even an ambassador could be irritated by a long ordeal and a lack of tact. "I told MacIver we'd been delayed by a misguided Scot who intends for his son to marry the queen."

"And what did he say to that?"

Randolph's brow furrowed. "He laughed."

"He laughed?" Philip asked in wonder.

"As if I'd made the most amusing jest. He said we shall hear more of Geordie Kerr."

"God's elbows!" Empton exclaimed. "Their queen invites a murdering outlaw to court, a man who kidnaps an entire delegation."

"Do they not understand?" Matthew asked.

"Twill serve her right if she marries that beef-wit!" Empton stormed. "The boy's addled!"

"We wouldn't know that if Simon had not spent time with him," Randolph reminded him.

They fell silent, fearing their mission had failed before it began. "What shall we do?" someone asked.

"What we can," Randolph replied. "When we see the queen, I'll outline the wrongs done to us and ask for redress."

Empton huffed sarcastically. "If the Scots have decided to support Kerr's son as their candidate for Mary's hand, they'll invent some excuse to explain what's happened."

Matthew nodded agreement. "Since our

purpose is to suggest an English bridegroom, he'll claim we mean to discredit him."

Simon had a hopeful thought. "Agnes is here. She knows what Kerr did."

"Will she speak against her own father?" Randolph asked.

"I don't know," Simon replied. "If she knew Tavish is here, it might make a difference."

"We'll see what happens when we meet with the queen," Randolph decided. "If we need the girl's support, we will locate her and request her help."

On the morning of their audience, each man pulled together what finery he had for the visit to court. Randolph checked his papers at least four times to be sure he had any document that might be requested of him. Philip examined his reflection in the polished brass mirror several times. For his part, Simon brushed his mud-spattered clothes and cleaned his teeth with a twig, chewing some spearmint leaves to sweeten his breath and possibly settle his nervous stomach as well.

As they entered the palace, they saw that Kerr had been truthful about one thing: the queen was preparing to go on a progress.

Flurries of activity abounded, with carts drawn up at several gates, the longest outside the queen's apartments in the south range. Servants carried out an amazing assortment of goods: trunks, sacks, jars, and even a bird in an elaborate cage.

"When does the queen leave?" Randolph asked the boy sent to guide them.

"Tomorrow, by her plan, though it's hard to say." The child's comment echoed one he'd not doubt heard from his elders. "There's yet much to be done."

The boy guided them into an audience hall filled with people. Simon hadn't thought much about how the queen would receive them, but he'd had a vague idea it would be fairly private. Surely marriage plans should be discreet, at least until details of Elizabeth's offer were presented. Would Randolph be forced to list Robert Dudley's qualities as a prospective husband in front of a hundred Scotsmen? It would make the task much more difficult, and Simon was glad he was simply an observer in the background.

After they'd waited half an hour or so, trumpets sounded and double doors at the front of the room opened. First, two boys in livery came through and set their backs against the doors to hold them open. Next came four uniformed soldiers, two of whom took a stand beside the front doors while the other two marched to the doors at the back and took up posts there. They were followed by several dour-looking men dressed in unrelieved black. The queen herself entered, followed by more solemn men and two ladies who kept their eyes modestly downcast. The newcomers arranged themselves across the front of the room with practiced grace. One man offered a hand as Mary stepped onto a raised platform where an elaborate chair waited.

The Queen of Scots was a lovely woman, though Simon thought she lacked Elizabeth's regal presence. Mary was graceful and elegant, but her gaze was soft, almost shy, and she often tilted her head to the side in a deferential manner Elizabeth would never have affected. Her gown was black and gold, a departure from the mourning white she'd worn for so long after the death of her husband, the king of France. Now that "The White Queen" had set her mind on remarrying, white was no longer appropriate. Her hair was almost completely covered, but he thought it was reddish, a reminder of her Tudor blood. What struck him most was her height, for she towered over most in the room. Bidding the assembled crowd good morning, she sat, signaling the day's business would begin.

There were some tedious matters to be dealt with, as was always the case. Simon stopped listening as clerks read reports on the queen's intentions for travel, recent decisions regarding trade and shipping, and a decree concerning the city's curfew. He studied the people around him, the noble and powerful of Scotland, comparing them to what he knew of English nobility.

They were less showy, and he guessed it was due to the influence of John Calvin and the recent exhortations of John Knox, who'd been so bold as to scold the queen for her elaborate dress, her Catholic ways, and her love of dancing. Simon guessed it was a trial to a woman raised in the brilliant court of France to be now subjected to the disapproval of her own subjects.

Simon's woolgathering came to an abrupt end when a name penetrated his consciousness. "Laird Geordie Kerr!" a page announced.

There was a shuffling of feet in the crowd, and people turned to look. Simon couldn't see the rear doors from where he stood, but he heard Coulston mutter, "Scoundrel!"

He was pressed almost against the wall as Kerr's party entered and those already in the room were forced back. In the lead were two men he'd seen at Kerr's banquet, now dressed in black caps with long feathers pointing backward, white capes trimmed with blue, green doublets cinched with wide leather belts, snow-white hose, and black boots trimmed with rosettes.

The two men parted at the front of the room, taking opposite directions. Two more dressed exactly the same marched forward, then two more, and two more. Soon the front of the room was lined with Kerr's henchmen, all smartly dressed and standing at attention. Last came Kerr himself, flanked by his son. Their colors were similar to those the retainers wore, but the outfits were more elaborate, with chains of gold and fur-trimmed cloaks despite the month and the temperature.

Kerr bowed low, and after a moment Kenneth did the same. "Yer Majesty," Kerr said loudly. "It is an honor t' be called into yer presence."

"Scoundrel!" Coulston said a little louder, and Randolph gave him a glance of warning. Always cautious, he waited to see which way the wind blew before choosing a course.

What happened next surprised them all. Through both sets of doors, armed soldiers entered, pushing spectators aside. A gray-haired man stepped from his place beside the throne and said in a firm voice, "Geordie Kerr, ye're a disgrace t' yer nation, an outlaw and a murderer. Ye and yer men are under arrest, and two days hence, ye shall hang on the gallows, every one!"

Resistance was brief. Kerr's men had surrendered their weapons, as all did when entering the queen's presence. One had secreted a knife in his boot, but he'd barely pulled it free when a trooper laid him out with a heavy blow from his sword hilt. The rest froze, uncertain what to do. Kerr himself stood open-mouthed as his men were herded together and escorted away.

"Yer Majesty! What treachery is this?" he finally managed.

The queen remained silent, and the man who'd made the charges spoke again. "Ye'll be an example to the marches, Kerr. We'll have nae reivers preying on our English brothers."

Randolph shifted his feet, and Simon, too, began to understand. Kerr's very public arrest and condemnation had been arranged to show the English two things: the Scots were in control of their own people, and they valued peace with England. It was royal theater at its finest.

Kerr turned to the queen with a dramatic

sweep of his hand. "But I hae yer letter sayin' ye'd hear ma suit!"

Mary remained silent, lowering her eyes, and the minister answered for her. "Criminals dinna press suit wi' a sovereign. Yer fate is decided and wilna be changed."

Kerr opened his mouth, but nothing came out. Putting a hand on his father's arm, Kenneth said, "Shall we gae home now, father? I dinna like this place, and I miss ma hounds."

The man in charge spoke to the waiting guardsmen. "Take them away."

When Kerr and the rest had been pushed from the room, still protesting, the gray-haired man turned to Randolph. "Are yer complaints answered, master?"

"Most completely, Your Worship," Randolph said with a low bow.

"Then we shall retire to a private place, where ye may present yer greetings t' the queen."

There was some discussion of numbers, and Randolph accepted the suggestion that only he and one other attend the queen and her council. Simon was relieved when he chose Coulston. They waited with the others in an anteroom, hardly knowing how to react in the presence of Scots who might privately applaud Kerr's actions against

Englishmen.

As his initial shock faded, Simon's thoughts turned to Agnes. What would happen to her now? She'd saved him and the others from certain death. He could not let her be taken unaware and punished for her father's crimes. Telling his friends he would rejoin them at the inn, he went looking for someone to ask how he might find her.

After glares and blank looks from several people he approached in the palace hallways, Simon found someone willing to answer his questions. The man was seated behind a small table in one of the corridors, apparently taking the names of people going in and out. He was a talker, a veritable chatterbox, and he was thrilled to meet an eyewitness to the arrests. "We heard rumors something bold was afoot," he said, leaning over his table eagerly. "Were ye no' impressed by the cleverness o' it?"

"It was indeed clever," Simon admitted. "They suspected nothing."

The clerk chuckled at the trick. " 'Twas nicely done, d' ye agree? Nicely done."

"It must have been some time in the planning."

The man put a finger over his lips. "I am not privy t' their secrets, o' course, but His Lordship has said for months something must be done about the border reivers if we are to keep peace with England. This Kerr, it is said, does not care if a place is English or Scots. He became bolder and bolder as time passed."

"They knew of his raiding?"

"They had no proof, do ye see?" His eyes narrowed. "Nae witnesses left alive, they say."

"So your queen called him here to account for his deeds?"

The man smirked. "The queen is often unaware what must be done t' rule a nation." He sounded like a child repeating what he'd heard from his betters. "She was raised to be a consort, not a monarch, ye see."

"I see."

The clerk blinked as if realizing he'd overstepped his place. "She is our queen, o' course, but a woman, too. Our councilmen do their best t' relieve her o' the strain o' leadership."

"So the council called Kerr to Edinburgh."

The other man folded his hands primly. "He might have kept his life, since he's married to an earl's daughter. But a warden from the marches appears with a tale of kidnapping and murder, and your party of Englishmen comes on his heels with the

same complaint." He shrugged meaning-
fully.

"They decided to make an example of
him."

"And well they might," the fellow said,
raising a finger indignantly. "Bandits scour-
ing the countryside, frighting landowners
and travelers? It's uncivilized." He ended
the conversation where it had begun. "It
was nicely done, was it not? Verra nicely
done."

Simon almost felt sorry for Kerr, despite
his crimes. He'd marched into the queen's
presence proudly, anxious to begin the brilliant life he'd imagined. Now he would
hang.

That reminded him of Agnes. "Will they
kill them all, even those not in court today?"

The man frowned. "By day's end they'll
find the rest. No doubt they'll hang them,
too."

CHAPTER SIXTEEN

Calkin knew something was wrong when he left his inn to find Henry hurrying toward him, looking as close to panicked as he'd seen the boy look. "What's wrong?"

"There's a woman at the shop." The boy's mouth didn't seem to want to work. "Hannah bowed when she saw her and sent me to find you." He gulped. "I think it's the queen."

"By the sweet blue eyes of Christ!" Calkin swore. "How did she manage this?"

Henry merely shrugged. Calkin strode off at a pace that was half-hurry, half-irritation.

They came to the shop together, where a sedan chair sat outside with four sturdy men standing idly beside it. Calkin went on, but Henry seemed reluctant. "She won't bite, lad."

"No," he replied, but his tone revealed uncertainty. "I'm afraid I'll do something wrong."

Calkin paused. "It's hard if you haven't been around them all your life." He put a hand on Henry's shoulder. "Stand behind me. Bow when I bow, and if I back up, get out of the way."

They went inside. On a stool in the center of Simon's workshop sat Elizabeth, the plain black dress she wore insufficient to disguise her royal manner and Tudor bearing. Behind her were two women and two men, each dressed plainly. The men were guards Calkin recognized, and he thought with some relief that at least she'd chosen a pair who knew enough to keep what they saw to themselves.

Some distance back from the queen Hannah stood, her face pleasant but her spine tense. She held a tray of tarts, and the queen munched on one while one of the ladies nibbled at another. In a corner Susan sat on the floor, her eyes wide with wonder.

"Ah, Calkin!" Elizabeth said. "I've come for a report on your progress."

He glanced around, and the queen took the hint. "You may all retire . . ." She looked around the small room. "Somewhere."

"Will you come into my home?" Hannah said, and the queen's ladies obediently followed her to the doorway. Hannah looked to Henry and touched Susan's arm as she passed. The girl rose and went with the others. The guardsmen took up positions at the doorways, setting their faces in neutral expressions.

"Your Majesty," Calkin said when they were alone, "is there something wrong?"

"Of course not," she answered. "I want to help, and you have sent no word, so I came."

He bit his lip to keep irritation from pouring out. "It has been my practice these last days to establish myself as a man of no import. How will the local folk react after this?"

Elizabeth huffed in disgust. "They know nothing. I came veiled."

"With attendants and guards."

"Who might be any woman's protection on the streets of the city."

"You are . . . noticeable, Your Majesty."

She shrugged. "One hopes so. A monarch must look regal, or people lose faith in her."

He sighed. How could he explain to her the stir such a visit would cause in Old Change? There was no help for it now, he told himself. Best get the visit over, so the gossip could circulate and die away. He told her what he knew and what he'd guessed about the constable and his activities. "Folk around here admire him, because he keeps the peace. They don't know how far he goes to do so, and some, I think, don't care."

"The wicked must be punished," the queen said primly, "but it must be done by the law, or we'll have no need for government." Wiping her lips with a bit of cloth Hannah had provided, she asked, "How will you deal with him?"

"I don't know. I have no proof he's killed anyone, certainly not Simon's brother-in-law."

"If you have need, I'll send more men."

"I thank you, Your Majesty," Calkin said with a grim smile. "But the fellow will run at the first sign he's found out. I prefer to track him down myself."

Her lips twitched slightly. "You're an independent sort, Guardsman Calkin."

"My mother reminds me of it often, Your Majesty. I do not like to trouble others with matters I can see to myself."

Elizabeth licked her lips. "You must be certain you can see to it alone, else you might put yourself in danger."

"Better me than those I care about, madam."

Elizabeth's gaze lit on Henry, who had remained when the others left, whether on purpose or because his limbs wouldn't obey him, Calkin didn't know. "And who is this?"

The boy obviously could not answer, and Calkin said, "This is Henry, Simon's son."

279

She spoke kindly. "Henry, of course. Your father speaks well of you, and I trust his judgment above that of most men."

Henry's face turned bright red, and he opened his mouth, but nothing came out. "He's a good lad, Your Majesty," Calkin said. "If I have need of help, I will send him to Whitehall to let you know."

She seemed satisfied with that, and Calkin told himself he'd neatly solved two problems. Both the queen and the boy thought he would consider asking for their assistance, and while he had no such intention, it would keep them out of his way until he'd obtained proof of Fenman's guilt and brought him to justice.

It took Simon the rest of the morning to set his plan in motion. First he located Tavish, who'd retreated to the stable where they kept their horses. Cowed by the city and the crowds of people, he found comfort with the animals and declared he would not budge until it was time to return home. Simon found him sitting on a block of wood, exchanging views with an old groom. He was so focused Simon had to pull at his sleeve to get his attention.

Rising, Tavish said to the man, "I thank ye for the advice, and I'll remember ever' scrap o' it when I coome back home."

Simon related what had occurred, watching as confusion, surprise, and disbelief crossed Tavish's face. "But the queen promised to hear his proposal."

"That was before they kidnapped a delegation from England," Simon reminded him. "It is good news for you, for your stepfather will be avenged."

"Aye." He didn't sound convinced, but Simon thought it was best Agnes's love for Tavish would never be tested by the knowledge he'd killed her father.

Reminded of his purpose, Simon said, "I hope to give Agnes the chance to return safely to Duns, if you are willing to help."

Tavish grasped Simon's arms, his grip painful. "She is in danger?"

"Since she's here with her father, she'll be considered part of his schemes."

"I must find her!" Tavish touched the knife at his belt. "I will fight them all!"

Simon didn't try to explain how many that would be. "We need no fighting." When Tavish appeared ready to argue, he said, "It's best if I bring her here to you."

"I see." It was clear he didn't see, but to his credit, Tavish was willing to try.

"The council doesn't know Agnes is here. If she disappears, she might escape her father's punishment, though the estate will be confiscated by the crown." He put a hand on Tavish's arm. "Someone must take her home, where she can say she was unaware of Kerr's crimes."

To Simon's great relief, Tavish saw the logic of that. "I will do it."

"Good man. When I bring her here, be ready to leave as soon as possible."

After making Tavish promise to wait in the hayloft and not even peep out the window, Simon began searching the streets of Edinburgh for the makings of a disguise. Using a little of Elizabeth's gold, he bought a woolen cap that came so far down on his forehead he had to squint to see. From a cart he purchased a plaid in brown and black. With the merchant's help, he wrapped himself so his withered arm, his neck, and most of his chin were covered. As an added distraction, he made himself an eye-patch with a leather thong and a bit of cloth. When he finished, he thought even Hannah might not recognize him if they passed on the street.

The first part of his plan was easy: returning to the palace, he asked a guard at the gate where the prisoners had been taken.

"The Tolbooth," he replied. "The council has ordered a new prison built, but I say, let 'em make do with the auld place. Them as don't like it shuld keep t' the law!"

He gave Simon directions, adding with a smirk, "You macht reconsider your visit. After a night in the Tolbooth, a man is grateful for death!"

It was indeed an awful place. Simon had seen prisons before, but this one was almost beyond description. He smelled it long before he reached the entry, and it was all he could do to make himself go inside. Peering in, it seemed he was looking through the gates of hell.

Steeling his resolve, he asked the guard at the entry if he might see the men due to be hanged the next day. He was, he said, a writer of news sheets anxious to get the story of the outlaw Geordie Kerr from the man's own lips.

The guard hesitated, making humming noises that indicated neither yes nor no. Taking the hint, Simon handed over a coin he thought would suffice, but the man merely sucked at a tooth and stared at the sky. Another coin brought a change of expression but no agreement. When Simon put a third and a fourth coin down, a hand swept them away so quickly he almost missed it.

"Carry this," he said, holding out a stick with figures carved on it. "The others'll know ye have leave t' visit. Through the main room and climb the stairs t' th' east wing. Ye'll find them there, dead men all." He laughed at his joke as Simon took the stick and entered the least welcoming place he'd ever been.

Dread deepening with every step, he followed the directions, passing through an open area where perhaps thirty prisoners sat, most in poses of dejection. They were not confined, and a few worked at arranging and cleaning the space allotted to them. Farther on were individual rooms where he assumed wealthy prisoners lived in some privacy. One even had a bed and a fire with something cooking over it.

Beyond the open room, more prisoners were confined in horrible cells, whether due to their crimes or to lack of funds to buy a little freedom, Simon didn't know. They were empty of furniture and smelled even worse, if that was possible, than the area he'd just left. At the end of the corridor he found a set of stairs so filthy he had to pull the plaid over his mouth in order to continue. At the top of the first flight was a locked apartment, but upon peering in, he saw it was empty. Continuing up a second stairway, he found a guard at an oaken door. After showing the wooden token he'd been given and passing over more coins, he was let into what the guard called the iron room, reserved for those under sentence of death.

The room was bare, and a pile of straw in one corner that might have been intended as bedding was so old and dirty it was more like compost. When Simon entered, all but one set of eyes turned to him. Kerr stood alone in a corner; his men stood in groups of two or three, though one sat dejectedly alone, his back against the stone wall. The one who did not turn to look at him was Kenneth, who stood with his forehead pressed against a stout wooden door on the far side of the room, peering through the crack at a sliver of daylight.

"Who are you?" Kerr came forward, his tone truculent. There was a fear beneath the anger. Simon pulled the patch off and unwrapped the plaid so they could see his face.

"It's the surgeon!" one man said.

"Have ye come to mock us, Englishman, now we're fallen?" Kerr asked.

The man who'd been struck by the guards in the audience room sat with his back to the wall, and two of his companions crouched beside him. His head was bloody, his gaze unfocused. Simon went to him, bent down, and looked into one eye then the other. "He's badly hurt."

Kerr said grimly, "What difference if he kens when they put the rope around his neck?"

Simon retreated, leaving the dazed man to his friends. "You have it right, I suppose."

"Why have ye come, surgeon?" Kerr asked again. He tried for a casual tone, but his voice was thin. "Have you brought physic that will save us?"

"I cannot save you," Simon said honestly, "but I would save your daughter if I can."

"Agnes!" Understanding dawned in his eyes. "She helped you escape." Simon didn't deny it, and Kerr said in a rush of anger, "Why should I save th' ungrateful bitch? Let her hang wi' the rest o' us!" He pointed to where Kenneth stood. "There's a platform beyond yon door. At daybreak we'll be taken oot there so the whole city may watch us die."

Simon resisted the pity that rose in his heart. "How many have you killed, Kerr? I cannot change your fate, but I can save your daughter if you tell me where she is." When Kerr hesitated, Simon added, "Agnes does not deserve to die!"

Kerr pointed at his son. "And Kenny? He will hang with me, when he has done nothing!"

Some of his father's emotion apparently reached Kenneth, for he turned. "Shall we go home now, Father? I dinna like this place. It smells."

It tore at Simon's heart to see how little Kenneth understood of what had happened and what would happen. He knew, however, that saving him was not within his power. Only Agnes.

"Your son is in prison, locked and guarded. Your daughter is, if it please God, still free. Tell me where she is, that I might save her life."

Kerr's jaw worked as he stared at the son he couldn't save and considered the daughter he didn't care to. Simon waited. The outlaw had to know in his heart that Agnes was the best part of him. Could he admit it?

In the end, Kerr heaved a great sigh. "Ma feet have plagued worse than usual the past few days, like two lumps of cold meat. Agnes planned t' go out t' buy cowslip and other herbs for physic." He smiled grimly. "There'll be no healing the ailment I face tomorrow, but it might be ye can find her before the queen's men do."

"Where?"

"At our inn, the Thistle and Corby."

Simon put a hand on Kerr's shoulder.

287

"You have done right by her."

Kerr's attempt at a brave smile was only half successful. "Mayhap she'll say a prayer for us on the morrow."

Grateful to leave the stink of Tolbooth Prison behind, Simon retraced his steps on the theory that Kerr's inn was close to the palace. It had started to rain, adding to the chill he felt after leaving the doomed outlaws. The cobblestones turned dark and slippery, and he walked as most did, with hands out to break a possible fall. Near the abbey, a woman selling strawberries gave him directions to the Thistle and Corby Inn. As he'd guessed, it was only a short distance away, on the other side of Holyrood.

When he reached the inn, Simon was dismayed to find two soldiers at the corner of the building, apparently idle. He stopped abruptly, guessing they waited for others of Kerr's party in order to arrest them. Did they know, he wondered, that there was a woman in the group? Even if they did, Simon had an advantage over the soldiers, knowing Agnes on sight. Taking up a post some distance away, he waited. If he was lucky, the girl's return path would come past him, and he could stop her before she reached the inn. If not, he'd have to improvise.

Luck wasn't on his side. When he spied Agnes coming along the muddy street, the inn and the waiting soldiers were between them. His only piece of luck was that she'd covered herself with her plaid to keep the rain off, hiding the black hair and pretty face the soldiers would have been told to watch for.

Taking off at a run, Simon brushed past the soldiers and stopped the surprised Agnes some distance from them. "Brenda!" he cried joyfully. "Darling, I have returned!"

"What?" Agnes's cloth bag fell off her shoulder, and she clutched at it to keep it from falling onto the ground. There was no recognition in her eyes, only suspicion.

"It's me," he whispered, keeping himself between her and the soldiers. "Simon!"

"Who? Simon —"

He covered her confused utterances by clasping her to his chest. "They've arrested your father, and those two are waiting to arrest you." He tilted her slightly so she could catch sight of the soldiers, who watched with amused interest.

Agnes's struggles ceased. Putting her arms around his neck, she said fondly, "My own!"

Putting his arm around her as a lover might, Simon led Agnes away, forcing himself to walk slowly and appear relaxed.

Once they were out of sight, he stopped in an alleyway and told her the whole story.

When he finished, the girl's face was white. "Father!" she said. "What can I do?"

"I promised him I'd help you return to Duns," he told her. "Randolph will explain to the queen that you and your mother had no part in the crimes."

She began to cry. "I thought I hated him, bu' I nae wanted him dead!"

"Of course you didn't." Hoping some twisting of the truth would help, he added, "He says he is content if you are safe."

"Then he does care for me, a little." Her eyes went wide. "But will they kill Kenny as well? Ye've seen him, Simon. He's like a child."

"I know." Once again he felt the wrong of it. "There is naught either of us can do for him. I can only see that you get home." He didn't mention the probability Duns wouldn't be her home much longer. She'd have to face that when the time came.

Looking up from her tears, she asked, "How would I get there?"

That he had an answer for, and he smiled a little. "Someone waits to take you, and I know he'll do his best to see you safe."

CHAPTER SEVENTEEN

All day as he made his deliveries, Henry watched for Calkin. There was no sign of him, and he returned home late in the day, disappointed. He'd hoped to learn if the guardsman was making headway in the investigation, and, if he was honest with himself, hoped Calkin might have questions he could answer about the people and places of Old Change.

In the shop he made quick work of closing, shuttering the window and making sure the place was secure and tidy. When he went through the curtained doorway into their living quarters, Hannah was letting out the hem of Susan's skirts.

"She grows taller every day," she said, but her tone was fond rather than complaining.

Henry looked around for his sister, and Hannah went on, "She's out with the pigeons, collecting eggs for tomorrow." Unlike most commoners, apothecaries were al-

291

lowed to keep pigeons because their eggs were essential in many medicines.

As Henry went to the larder to get himself some bread and cheese, Hannah asked, "Have you been dogging Calkin's steps again?"

"I haven't seen him. Did he stop here today?"

"No." One brow rose. "Susan says he spends a fair amount of time at Annie's."

"That's where I saw him last." Henry scowled in the direction of his aunt's house.

Hannah broke off a thread and examined her work, pressing the fabric flat with her fingers. "Perhaps he has questions concerning his investigation." The twinkle in her eyes belied her words. Reading his face, she added gently, "Henry, Calkin knows what he's about."

Though he knew it was childish, Henry wished Calkin depended on him for information rather than his aunt. Changing the subject, he asked, "Were you busy in the shop this afternoon?"

She ticked off the items on her fingers. "I sold some juniper for a cough, some coriander for Goodwife Taylor's daughter, who has worms, a little lady's mantle for the woodcarver's gashed thumb, and . . . the constable wanted some belladonna."

"Fenman?"

"Yes. I suppose he's giving us his custom in order to impress Annie." She gave another smile that made Henry frown. "With a stranger in the area, Annie's admirers will try a little harder, I think. He bought one of Annie's cakes, as well."

Henry frowned. "Fenman bought a cake and some belladonna?"

"Yes." Hannah raised a hand, anticipating his comment. "I warned him about the dangers. Apparently his father had pain in his back and legs and now he has it, too, poor man."

With a sense of foreboding, Henry went to the shop and took a book from a drawer in the worktable. Though almost certain he knew the properties of the herb, he wanted to be sure. William Turner's *New Herbal* was an invaluable aid, listing all the "simples" available to apothecaries along with their effects. He didn't find belladonna in the "b" listing, but under the more common name, "deadly nightshade." He read the passage, saying the last few words aloud. "One dose causes hallucinations, two brings insanity, and three is certain death."

Closing the book, he returned to Hannah. "I must go out again."

"Henry, Calkin said —" Her voice

betrayed mild annoyance.

He cut through her objections. "Calkin thinks Fenman murdered Uncle Will."

After a moment, Hannah understood. "The queen's business is Simon's business."

"I suppose he told her about it and —"

"Does Fenman know he is suspected?"

"A visit from him seems to indicate he might be."

Hannah rose, her hands clasped before her. "Calkin must be warned."

Without replying, Henry turned to go, taking up his cap as he passed. When he opened the door, Hannah's voice stopped him. "Henry."

"Yes?"

"I'm going with you."

"There's no need —"

She put up a hand to stop his argument. "If Fenman is a killer, it's best the three of us face him together."

They started at the inn, where Henry tiptoed up the back stairs and rapped gently at Calkin's door. No answer. Returning to Hannah, he suggested they split up to check the alehouses and pie shops. He was in none of them. When they met again, Hannah said, "He might be at Annie's house."

Henry nodded. "I should have thought of that."

"I'll go and see. You wait at the inn, for he's bound to return there."

If he can, Henry thought, but he didn't say it aloud.

When Hannah was gone, he waited for a time in front of Calkin's lodgings. A sense of urgency made it impossible for him to keep still, and he walked up and down in front of the place until he realized he was probably attracting attention as he paced like a gander missing his flock. When there was no one nearby, he faded into the narrow alley, telling himself Calkin might have come back and gone up the back stairs.

Slipping past the open windows of the taproom, where people sat drinking, talking, and playing dice, Henry stepped carefully around the cast-off items piled at the side and back of the building. The day was dying, and the back garden was hidden in shadows cast by the surrounding buildings. Opening the door a slit, he peered in and looked into the kitchen. A woman worked at a table, her back to him as she sliced sausages into small bits and threw them into a pot beside her. As Henry tried to decide if he could get past without her seeing him, she picked up the pot, grunting with the effort, and left the room. As soon as she was gone, he hurried up the narrow staircase to

Calkin's room.

The top of the stairs was dark, with only a dim light behind him and a slightly brighter one from the front staircase. He rapped lightly on the plank door. As before there was no answer, but this time he laid his ear against the wood. Inside, someone made low sounds. Rapping again, Henry waited a few moments. The sounds continued, and he became alarmed. Either the occupant was having a nightmare, or he was in pain. He opened the door enough to peer in.

Calkin lay on the bed, eyes glazed and pupils dilated. Mumbling incoherently, he didn't seem to recognize Henry when he bent over him.

"Calkin!" No response. "Sergeant Calkin!"

Belladonna. Delusions, insanity, then death. How much of the poison had he taken? The room was dark, and Henry fumbled for the candle and tinderbox beside the bed. With shaking hands, he achieved a light and used the candle to search the room. On a stool beside the door was half a small cake, the tiny oak leaf in one corner attesting to its maker. Calkin groaned, and Henry went to the bed, putting a hand on his forehead and checking his eyes. There was no sign the guardsman knew where he was or who was with him.

Henry spoke Calkin's name again, but he only rolled his head and moaned. What should he do? Go back to the shop for an emetic? Call for help? He rejected both those ideas. A call for help was likely to bring Fenman, and that was no help at all. And who knew how much time he had? Calkin might die in the next few minutes.

Hannah! She was probably waiting for him. She would know what to do.

He hurried downstairs, pausing only to see that the kitchen was still empty. He hurried to the front of the inn, where he found Hannah peering in, looking for him. When he told her what he'd found, she ordered, "Let me see him. Quickly!" He led the way to the back door.

The kitchen was still empty, and he guessed serving of the evening meal was well under way. They made their way upstairs, where Calkin lay much as he'd been when Henry found him.

Hannah made a quick assessment, looking at his eyes and smelling his breath. "We have to get as much of the poison out of him as we can and hope he hasn't absorbed too much."

He should have thought of that himself, Henry chided silently. He'd panicked at the sight of Calkin lying there helpless, but Hannah, used to medical emergencies, remained calm.

Rolling Calkin onto his stomach, they pulled him sideways until his head hung over the side of the bed. Hannah pulled the chamber pot out from under it and positioned it below him, which Henry thought irrelevantly was something only a woman would think of. While he held Calkin's head up by firmly gripping his hair, Hannah stuck her fingers down the guardsman's throat, pulling them back quickly as his gag reflex went into action. When Calkin was done retching the first time, she did it again and again, until nothing more came up.

Lifting Calkin's head, Henry looked at his eyes. The pupils almost obscured the blue, but he thought the man seemed a little more aware. Hannah used the blanket to wipe his face and chin, and he mumbled, "Thirsty."

Henry picked up the pitcher of water on the table and held it as he drank deeply. Once he'd finished, Calkin looked up at them. "What?" he asked, his lips barely forming the word.

"Fenman poisoned you," Henry told him, speaking distinctly.

Calkin's brow furrowed, but he gave a tiny

nod, leaning back and closing his eyes. "Thought he'd meet me man to man. Stupid."

Henry glanced at Hannah, who shrugged. "We've done the most important part, getting rid of the poison. It's up to Calkin's body to restore itself now." She touched her forehead as if trying to recall. "Do you think fennel boiled in wine would help?"

Again Henry chided himself. He was the apothecary's assistant. He should have thought of it, might even have brought some along if his thoughts had been less scattered. Hannah's mind was working, even though he'd seen in her face that she, too, feared for Calkin's life.

"Will you go, or shall I?"

"I will." She looked at Calkin. "He'll sleep for a while."

Once Hannah was gone, Henry sat quietly, watching Calkin breathe, but the rush of energy brought on by fear made him restless. Picking up the chamber pot, he dumped the remainder of the cake on top, added a little water, and went to the window. As he was about to empty the pot, he noticed movement below. It wasn't unheard of for a person to be doused with filth when pots were emptied without care, so Henry waited to allow the person to pass.

The figure that traced the inn wall was familiar. Drawing back from the window and looking aslant, Henry watched, able to see but not be seen. It was Fenman, no doubt coming to make sure his plan had worked.

Poison was a tricky business, with the possibility of the victim taking too little, none at all, or getting help when he began to feel ill. Henry guessed if Fenman found Calkin still breathing, he'd take advantage of his helpless state to finish him.

Again he had to decide what to do without Hannah to advise him. If he called for help, would those in the taproom believe him or side with the constable? Fenman was an officer of the law. Henry was the orphan Simon Maldon had taken into his home. He imagined that Fenman would say what he'd always said: Henry was born to be a liar or worse.

He couldn't take the chance, at least not until Hannah returned. Quickly Henry returned to Calkin, shaking him. "We must go." He pinched the candle wick to extinguish the flame.

"What?" Calkin's eyes focused on him. "Henry?"

"We must go!" Urgently, he tugged on Calkin's feet, setting them on the floor and

300

pulling him to a sitting position. "He's coming to kill you, and you're too weak to defend yourself." Could he delay Fenman long enough for Calkin to get away, or would the constable swat him aside like a fly and finish them both?

"Help me stand." Calkin stumbled to his feet, listing dangerously toward the window.

"Lean on me," Henry ordered, catching his arm. Together they staggered to the door. In the narrow landing outside the room, Henry stopped, unsure where to go. Fear shot through him when the scrape of the door against the stone floor sounded. Then a woman's voice called out in a cross tone, "I said I'd get it. Be patient!" The door closed again, and Henry imagined Fenman hovering outside, waiting for the serving wench to get whatever she'd come to the kitchen for. He had only moments to get his father's friend to safety.

"Up." Calkin's voice was all breath and no voice. "Up." He nodded at a rough staircase that led to the top story, and Henry saw immediately what he meant. They could hide there until Fenman left.

"A moment." Leaving Calkin leaning against the doorway, Henry quickly re-entered the bedroom, emptied the chamber pot onto the ground below, set it under the bed, and returned. It was best if the constable couldn't tell if his plan had succeeded or not.

Moving quickly, Henry helped Calkin up the steps to the cramped space under the roof. It was quite dark, but he saw the shapes of four pallets and a table with a wash basin. The inn's serving wenches would sleep here once their workday was done. Leading Calkin to one of the pallets, Henry eased him onto it. His breathing was slightly slower than normal but not labored. It seemed they'd gotten the poison out of his system, though his body needed time to recover.

Hardly daring to breathe, Henry followed Fenman's movements by sound. He came up the stairs, his steps almost silent, listened at the door of the room they'd just left, and cautiously opened it. Henry thought he went inside, but he didn't remain there long. He paused almost directly below them, apparently thinking through the change of plan Calkin's absence necessitated. Finally, light steps whispered down the back stairs.

Seeing that Calkin was asleep, Henry slipped down the stairs to assure Fenman was gone. There was no one in the corridor or on the landing below. He crept down, one step at a time, and looked out the back door. The constable was nowhere in sight, which was a relief. He'd feared Hannah might meet him as she returned with the medicine, and he had no illusions about what Fenman would do to anyone who knew or even suspected his crimes.

He went around to the front of the inn, peering cautiously into the street in time to catch a glimpse of Fenman as he disappeared inside. At the nearest open window, Henry watched as the constable's gaze searched the room, no doubt looking for a sick and dying man. He didn't find Calkin, but his gaze lit on the searcher, Dodgson, who sat alone, sipping at a bowl of ale. Approaching, Fenman said something that made Dodgson frown in confusion. Fenman jerked his head toward the door, indicating they should go outside. Dodgson obeyed, his expression revealing uncertainty and a hint of fear as well. A few patrons turned to watch them go, but they soon returned to their ale and conversation.

Fenman pulled the searcher away from the doorway, which brought them close to where Henry crouched at the side of the building. Dodgson, whose face showed clearly in the light of a torch outside the inn, looked like a man who wished he were somewhere else.

Fenman got right to the point. "The stranger in town, Calkin. I want you to find him."

"He has a room upstairs, someone said."

"He's not there. I believe he wanders the area, sick and confused in his mind."

"Why would he — ?" Dodgson stopped, probably afraid of the answer. "What have I to do with him?"

"Calkin is the queen's man, here to uncover crime. Are you willing to face charges for taking bribes and allowing businessmen to cheat honest folk?"

Dodgson tried for outrage. "Who says such things of me? I am —"

Fenman looked at him with contempt. "I know exactly what you are, and if you don't do as I say tonight, everyone else will know it as well."

Abandoning outrage, Dodgson wrung his hands. "I never hurt anyone! If I've been too lenient with the guildsmen, I'll remedy my practices immediately."

Fenman huffed disdainfully. "I care not for your schemes, if you do as I tell you tonight."

Dodgson looked up at the stars as if for guidance and help. "I'm no criminal."

"You love fine clothes and finer wines. I

know it all." Fenman gave his shoulder a shake. "Now, listen. Calkin is dead or close to it. He cannot harm us if we make sure he's finished."

Dodgson rubbed his nose with a knuckle. "I could not kill a man."

The pause that followed was so long it made Henry twitch. He was unable to see what Fenman was doing, and all sorts of fears raced through his mind. Fenman had seen his shadow. He'd heard Henry breathing. He'd sensed someone was listening.

Apparently it was none of those things, for Dodgson finally said, "What must I do?"

"Bring the man to me. Afterward you can return home and forget tonight's business. Will that help you swallow your conscience?"

The searcher was caught between fear of discovery and reluctance. "I suppose so."

"Well, then. Find Calkin. Convince him to come with you to the old bridge."

Dodgson shuddered. "How am I to do that?"

"Tell him I'll be there at midnight," Fenman said smoothly. "Convince him you'll help to arrest me. If the dose I gave him is working, his mind will be weak, and he won't question you."

Fenman had to repeat his instructions and

his threats, but finally they parted, Dodgson heading away from Henry. Fenman stayed a few moments, apparently watching his new partner go. A sigh told Henry he'd made a decision, and he went away with the air of a man who had things to do.

Henry went back inside to where Calkin slept soundly in the attic room. He crouched beside the bed, watching the guardsman's chest rise and fall. His breathing was regular, and his rest seemed unbroken by the delirium they'd seen earlier. Hearing soft steps below, Henry went to the stairs and beckoned. Hannah had returned with a stoppered phial, and waking Calkin, she made him drink the fennel and wine mixture. When he revived somewhat, they led him down the stairs to his own room.

Not yet in control of his limbs, Calkin leaned on his rescuers heavily. As they passed the stairway to the taproom, they were illuminated in the light from below. Calkin's face was gray and his jaw set as he forced his suffering body to function. Entering the dark room, they set him on the bed. Slumped and weak, he put one hand on his stomach and the other at his throat. On top of almost being poisoned, Henry guessed his gullet was raw from retching. Hannah offered another drink of the wine, which he swallowed gratefully before turning to Henry. "Tell me what you know of tonight's business, all of it."

Henry recounted everything he knew. Calkin listened carefully, leaning forward to catch every word. When Henry finished, Hannah's nervous shifting signaled worry. "We should leave here," she urged.

"Yes," Henry agreed. "One of them is likely to come back."

"We can take him to our house," Hannah said. "He'll be safe there."

Calkin put up a hand. "Now that Fenman knows we're on to him, no place is safe. When they don't find me in the shops, they'll come to your house or to Annie's."

"I can't believe he's a killer," Hannah murmured. "A hard man, people say, but still —"

"He's probably been murdering helpless folk for years, beating them to death and letting the river take their bodies."

"The poor men must have washed ashore somewhere." Hannah shivered. "Wouldn't someone investigate?"

"The corpse of a ragged beggar doesn't stir much outrage." Calkin's tongue obeyed him only minimally, and he had to concentrate to get the words out. "How should folk learn where a homeless, feckless man entered the river, and who's to say he didn't end his own useless life? Fenman gets away with it often enough to slake his need to kill."

"We'll go to the justices in the morning," Hannah said. "They'll arrest him."

"It must be tonight," Calkin answered. "Once he knows I'm alive, he'll be gone. He must have heard by now about your mysterious visitor."

Calkin was right. Having any man suspect him was bad enough, but Fenman had guessed Calkin was the queen's man. He had to either kill him or disappear. "What can we do?" Hannah asked.

"Fenman must believe his plan is succeeding," Calkin said after a moment's thought. "Tell Dodgson where he can find me."

"You can't fight them!" Hannah protested. "You can hardly sit upright."

"Time will take care of my weakness," he told her calmly, "and Dodgson is no adversary." Putting hands on his knees he rose, not gracefully but with success. "Hannah, return home, get your daughter, go to Annie's house, and lock yourselves inside. Once Henry's done as I ask, he'll join you. Let no one in but him. Who knows what hold Fenman has on others."

"Shouldn't we raise the alarm?" Hannah asked.

"And warn our murderer?" Calkin shook his head. "At this moment he believes he can still prevail, which is as it should be."

"Then I will come with you," Henry said. "I can be a witness —"

"As can I —" Hannah added.

Calkin gestured them to silence. "Simon Maldon is one of my oldest friends. When he returns from Scotland, shall I tell him I let his wife, his son, his sister, or all of them be harmed?" He looked from Hannah to Henry. "Capturing this killer is my task, given to me by the queen herself. I charge you in her name to obey my orders. Do you understand?"

Henry tried again. "Fenman is a killer!"

"Of helpless men," Calkin said grimly. "I am a soldier, and I will be ready."

Seeing the determination in the guardsman's eyes, Henry gave up. "What should I say?"

Laughter and a snatch of song reached their ears a short time later as Hannah and Henry slipped quietly out the back door. Henry found it hard to believe normal life went on for others: a song, a jest, a taste of ale. They had no idea a killer walked among them, hiding his evil deeds behind the mask of authority. If they told them, who among the inn's patrons would believe them?

When they reached the street, Hannah asked, "Will you do as Calkin said?"

Henry paused, unsure if he should tell the truth or not, but Hannah didn't wait for his answer. "Once I lied to the queen." She looked down at her hands. "She was not queen then, only a princess. But I was her servant, an orphan taken from an alms-house."

Hannah was an orphan? Did she know, then, the doubt that came with being no one's child, the feeling one was never as good as those with parents, grandparents, and more?

"Why did you lie to her?"

"To keep her from going out to meet a killer. I locked her in a storeroom, and when she asked me later how it happened, I said the door must have closed accidentally."

"You lied to keep her safe."

"Yes." Her voice grew more confident. "Is a lie that keeps someone from harm a sin?"

"I think not."

"Even if that person holds rank or privilege of birth?"

A smile formed on Henry's lips. "Even then."

"Calkin told us to go to Annie's. I don't remember him saying we had to stay there."

"That's true."

"And even the queen could not object if a woman and her son feel the need to take a walk on a warm summer evening."

Henry felt a smile bloom as they parted. For the first time ever, it seemed they truly understood each other and were in complete agreement. Calkin would not face Fenman alone.

It took Henry a while to locate Dodgson. When he spotted him coming out of an alley, his expression serious, Henry ran at him, bumping against him as if panicked.

"Pardon me, Master Dodgson," he said, speaking hurriedly. "I seek the constable."

"Is something wrong, boy?" Dodgson peered at him in the darkness, and Henry lowered his face, hoping the searcher wouldn't recognize him.

"There's a man down there who is either mad or sick," Henry said, pointing back the way he'd come. "I don't know what to do for him."

"Is it the stranger who came a seven-night ago?"

"The very one. He's raving, and he can't walk very well."

Dodgson patted his shoulder. "You are a

good boy. Now go home, for I will see to him."

"Are you certain? He seems very sick."

The man's beakish nose lifted. "If he is, he needs a man's help, not a boy's. Go home."

Henry went on, slumping his shoulders as if disappointed to miss the excitement. As soon as he was out of Dodgson's sight, he stopped. Now he had to find Fenman.

He was headed toward Annie's house, and Henry again put on an anxious manner. "Constable, you must come. My friend Calkin has lost his senses. He's like a wild beast."

Fenman tried to hide his pleasure, but Henry saw his lips twitch. "Where is he?"

"I don't know. I met the searcher, Master Dodgson, and he went to find him." He made his voice hopeful. "Likely he will take him to a physician."

Henry could almost feel Fenman's satisfaction. "I'll find them and help if I can."

"I can come with you," Henry suggested.

"What good will you be?" Fenman said with a disgusted grimace. "Begone, orphan."

Assuming a glum expression, Henry went on. As soon as Fenman was gone, however, he turned back, went to Annie's door, and knocked lightly. "Hannah," he said, "it's time."

CHAPTER EIGHTEEN

Henry and Hannah made their way to the bridge, Henry leading the way along the familiar path. It was an almost moonless night, but the skies were clear, and they had little difficulty.

"What did you tell Aunt Annie?" Henry asked, keeping his voice low.

"Everything," Hannah answered. "She cannot be left out of it now, since Fenman might come looking for Calkin."

"Does she understand the danger?"

"She does. She'll stop the door with furniture, and she took up a fire iron and carries it with her." Hannah made a sound that might have been a chuckle. "At first she was a little angry that we'd kept secrets, but I think she would forgive Calkin anything. She said 'Richard' had to do what he thought best. I had to think to recall that 'Richard' is Calkin."

As they neared the bridge they slowed,

stepping carefully to make no noise. A good distance back from the bank, Henry turned into the trees and continued toward the river until there was no more cover. Peering through the branches of some half-grown alders, Henry saw a black ribbon of movement that shone as an occasional ripple reflected the available light. The river. As his eyes adjusted, he was able to discern the bridge's nearer end, where Fenman waited, much as he'd waited for Henry a few days earlier.

"He's there," he whispered to Hannah.

"Waiting to kill Calkin," she said. "We should have brought help."

She was correct. "You must go and find someone. They'll believe you."

"Henry —" Hannah apparently thought better of arguing, but it was too late. Someone was coming down the path, brushing aside branches that had overgrown it. Turning, Henry saw a light that wavered as the holder wove back and forth, pausing every few steps. Soon John Dodgson came into view, holding a burning rush in one hand and supporting Calkin, who seemed unable to keep his feet under him, with the other.

Henry fought the urge to leave his hiding place and go immediately to Calkin's aid.

What if his friend had misjudged his condition? What if they hadn't gotten enough of the poison out? Calkin seemed so weak, so confused.

Beside him, Hannah seemed ready to step out from the protection of the trees. Henry put a hand on her arm, at the same moment she touched his shoulder. Each had reminded himself that Calkin wanted Fenman to think his plan was working.

"Where — where are we?" Calkin mumbled, his words amplified by the water.

"At the river, friend," Dodgson replied. "You were ill, and I thought a walk would help."

"Yes," Calkin mumbled. "There are horses. Can you hear them?"

Calkin teetered to a stop, using the smaller man's shoulder to hold himself upright. Dodgson leaned forward, speaking to Fenman. "I've done as you asked. You said bring him —"

"Help me get him onto the bridge."

Dodgson hesitated, knowing there was evil afoot. In the end, however, he stuck the torch into the soft soil of the riverbank. Fenman inserted himself under Calkin's other arm, and the three sidled onto the bridge's narrow deck. Dodgson grasped the rail with his free hand as they went, letting go for the briefest possible period before grabbing it again farther along. He muttered something, but Henry picked up only the tone of complaint, not the words.

With the torch left behind on the bank, Henry couldn't see much. The men on the bridge were not even shadows against the black water, only voices. Calkin muttered incoherently for a while before he said clearly, "I hear them! I hear the horses."

"Is he armed?" Fenman asked.

"He was," Dodgson replied. "I took the knife from his belt and threw it into an alley."

"Good man."

Calkin appeared not to hear them. "Someone must help the horses, or they will drown."

"No horses, friend," Fenman said.

"I hear them!" Calkin insisted. "They are there, in the water!"

"And you are here, where you and Master Dodgson must fight to the death."

"What do you mean?" Dodgson's tone was sharp, but the answer was a grunt, followed by a short cry and the crash of something — or someone — falling onto the bridge.

Fearing Calkin was dead or hurt, Henry left the trees, crawling toward the water on

317

hands and knees. He heard Hannah gasp as he left her, but he hissed, "Stay there!" and she obeyed.

The men on the bridge were focused on each other. Closing to within a few feet, he was able to distinguish their dim figures. Dodgson lay unmoving on the bridge deck. Fenman leaned over Calkin, who slumped against the rail. He swayed perilously, but Fenman caught his arm, leading him toward the center of the bridge.

"Birds," Calkin muttered. "Keep them away from me!"

As he got closer, Henry saw there was something in Fenman's hand. "Folk need to understand their place in this world," he said to Calkin. "When they don't, I help 'em."

Henry saw him silhouetted against the night sky as his arm rose. The weapon was a straightstick, a truncheon used by law officers to subdue and control criminals. He brought it down at Calkin's head, but the guardsman turned at the last moment, taking the blow on his shoulder. It was undoubtedly painful, but not disabling. Calkin fell, curling his body defensively.

"You hit me!" he cried, pain evident in his voice. "I've done nothing to you."

"They all say that, every one of them!"

Fenman ran a loving hand over the club. "But the 'nothing' they do? There's the rub! What good is a man who lives by begging, who lets the poor tax support him so honest folk must pay his way?"

Henry eyed the distance between himself and Fenman. Why didn't Calkin fight back?

Fenman aimed a vicious kick at Calkin, who covered his head with his hands. "When someone won't earn his way, I perform a service in addition to that which the law asks of me." He leaned over the recumbent Calkin. "I remove men from the world who are no use to it."

Another blow of the truncheon brought a howl of pain from Calkin. "Mostly I see to those who are no use to the world," Fenman said. "You're not like them, but the river will take you, as it took them." He looked up, and the faint glow of torchlight from the bank caught the eagerness on his face. "A rope, a rock, and a corpse, and the world is less one troublemaker."

Fenman raised his arm to strike a third blow, but this time was different. With a lightning-quick movement, Calkin caught his wrist, twisting the hand that held the club until it dropped into the water with a hollow plop. Grunting from pain and surprise, Fenman twisted free of the

319

recumbent Calkin and scrambled for solid ground. His escape was thwarted when Henry stuck out a foot, sending him sprawling onto the bank. Calkin was on him in a flash, and the two men faced each other grimly.

"You killed Annie Clark's husband."

Fenman chuckled humorlessly. "He's why you're here? The fool deserved what he got."

"And Carl?"

"I don't know how the wretch saved himself, but I couldn't let Clark speak to him."

Calkin said clearly, "Peter Fenman, in the name of the crown I charge you, submit to arrest."

"And hang like a pear on the gallows tree?" Fenman leaned to the side, grasped the torch Dodgson had implanted in the mud, and lunged at Calkin. Dropping back, Calkin managed to avoid the flame, but Fenman swung his improvised weapon in varying half-circles, making it hard to predict where the fire would be. From time to time he jabbed it at Calkin, who seldom deigned to move his feet but simply swayed back or to the side far enough to evade Fenman's reach. Calkin had no weapon but seemed unperturbed by the inequality.

Realizing he couldn't intimidate his opponent, Fenman backed away from the river. Henry guessed he would toss the torch away and take his chances in the dark woods.

Calkin saw it, too. "You won't get far." He crouched like a cat, ready to spring the moment his opponent let down his guard.

Fenman shrugged. "I know the land; you don't. I have desperation on my side; you have only duty. It's worth the gamble, I trow."

Movement surprised Henry, and it was a few seconds before he realized what had happened. Calkin's crouch had been more than simple readiness. He'd been reaching for something neither Henry nor Fenman guessed he possessed.

Henry saw Calkin's arm move, and Fenman dropped the torch to the ground. It lay on the ground, still burning, and he saw the constable's face contort with pain. It took him a bit longer to understand the reason: a small knife protruding from his shoulder.

Fenman tried to run despite the injury. Calkin was ready for that, however, following the path of his knife and catching the man before he could take a step. With a grunt of pain, the constable fell to the ground. Calkin planted one foot on his chest, removed the knife from Fenman's shoulder, and slipped it back into his boot. Looking up at Henry he commented, "A fellow learns to carry a spare."

Henry untied the rope belt he wore and held it out. "Here."

Turning Fenman over, Calkin pulled his hands behind his back and began tying them together. Still breathing heavily, he managed a smile. "I hope you can keep your arse covered until you get back home, lad."

Hannah appeared at Henry's side. "He can borrow my girdle if he needs it."

Calkin paused, his foot still on Fenman's back. "Both of you?"

"We —"

A cry interrupted Henry's weak attempt at excusing their presence. "Help!"

The shout came from the bridge, and the voice was Dodgson's. "See to him," Calkin ordered. Henry took up the torch and stepped cautiously onto the bridge. He heard Dodgson's gasping breath but couldn't see him until he reached the middle. There the torchlight revealed a white hand grasping one of the rail supports. Dodgson's body lay atop the fast-moving stream like a floating leaf as the current pulled at him. "Help me!" he begged. "I can't hold on!"

Needing both hands, Henry laid the torch

aside. Squatting, he wrapped one arm around the upright and took Dodgson's forearm with the other hand, repositioning until he felt he had the strongest grip possible. "Bring your other hand up and grasp my arm," he told the struggling searcher. With some difficulty, Dodgson obeyed, and Henry pulled him toward the bridge. "Move your hand farther up my arm."

"I can't!"

"You must." With a strangled sob, Dodgson obeyed, moving his hand up Henry's sleeve. Henry then moved his own hand, pulling Dodgson closer as the water fought to pull him away. After several such maneuvers, he was close enough to reach the man's collar. Taking a firm grip and hoping the searcher's taste for fine clothing meant it was strong stuff, he shouted over the current, "I will stand, pulling you up as far as I can. You must roll yourself onto the bridge."

Dodgson's breathing was labored, and his grip on Henry's arm seemed to be weakening. Could Henry pull the man's dead weight from the fast-flowing water? If the rotten wood of the rail broke or Henry lost his balance, they might both end up in the black, dark river.

Feeling Dodgson's strength waning,

Henry cried, "One, two, three!" On "three" he set his feet beneath his body and gave a mighty pull. Dodgson came out of the water, his chest bumping the bridge deck with a sodden thud. His flailing free arm found Henry's tunic, and he managed to throw his weight forward, getting all but one leg out of the water. Once he was more on the bridge than off it, Henry let go of the collar and grabbed his belt, pulling him sideways until he rested wholly on the bridge, gasping and dripping.

"Henry?" Calkin's voice came out of the darkness.

"I have him," Henry replied, picking up the torch. Pulling the coughing, retching man to his feet, Henry again took hold of his collar, pushing Dodgson ahead of him toward the shore.

Calkin stood over the prone Fenman, whose hands were now tied behind him. Hannah stepped to Henry and hugged him, relief evident. "I was so afraid," she said into his hair. "You were very brave. I am always proud of you, but never more than tonight." Her motherly instincts took over and she added, "Still, you should have waited for help. You might have drowned!"

Seeing Fenman stretched out on the ground, Dodgson began babbling in an attempt to establish his innocence. "Good-man," he said to Calkin, "I never wished you any harm. This man forced me to lie." He stabbed a finger at Fenman. "If I'd known he intended to harm you, I'd never have agreed. And see what he did to me! I might have drowned —" Anger got the better of him, and he kicked at Fenman, hitting him a glancing blow on his back. Fenman grunted a curse.

"Enough!" Calkin growled, but Dodgson, terrified by his brush with death, lost control.

"He'd have — killed me — blamed — crimes — on me!" Each phrase came with a kick.

Pressing one arm against the hysterical man's chest, Calkin pushed Dodgson away from Fenman. "He will face justice," he told him sternly. "As will you."

"I never killed anyone!" Dodgson shouted, his voice rising. "He tried to murder me!" He pointed dramatically, and Henry automatically followed the gesture with his eye.

"Calkin!" he called, but it was too late. Taking advantage of Dodgson's outburst, Fenman had risen to his feet and run onto the bridge. He ran awkwardly due to his bound hands, but his aim was clear. He rushed forward, crashing into the half-rotted rail. They heard a crack, followed by a splash. Then there was no sound but the river, continuing on its way.

CHAPTER NINETEEN

Agnes refused to leave Edinburgh until the executions were over. "He deserves t' die if the law says so," she insisted. "But he is ma father, and I'll stay wi' him till it's done."

Geordie Kerr, his son, and two dozen of his men were hanged at mid-day. Rumors circulated that some of his party were still at large, but the soldiers sent to the Thistle and Corby had found no one. Word had apparently reached Kerr's servants early enough to allow them to disappear into the city or, more likely, the countryside.

Simon, Agnes, and Tavish watched the hangings from a large window in the hayloft. Though removed from the grim scene, their height gave them a clear view of the scaffold over the heads of the crowd. Simon didn't see it as an advantage, being unsure how he felt about public punishment, but it gave Agnes some comfort while protecting her from discovery.

Finding courage for the last act of his life, Kerr walked boldly and silently to the scaffold. Following his example, his men did the same. Only Kenneth spoke. Simon couldn't hear his words, but the youth's manner revealed he had no idea what was about to happen. As an official read out the charges and warned those assembled below that this was what those who broke the queen's law deserved, Kenneth fidgeted, apparently trying to get the noose to lie in a more comfortable position on his neck.

Agnes turned away at the last. Tavish put his arms around her as she cried into his shoulder. Simon, too, turned away, but Tavish watched until the end, his expression unreadable. Simon guessed he'd found the small sense of peace that comes when balance is restored.

The Queen of Scots consented to a second meeting with the delegation from England before leaving on her progress. Simon guessed the details of Elizabeth's offer had been minutely examined in the past twenty-four hours, but when they were ushered into her presence, Mary revealed neither pleasure nor disappointment with the proposal.

They met in the same room as before,

though this time there were few in attendance outside Randolph's party and a dozen or so of the queen's men. At first, members of the council asked questions, some seeming interested in Elizabeth's suggestion, some affronted. There was great concern about exactly how the English would acknowledge the Queen of Scots as heir to their throne. There were also questions about the lands and titles Robert Dudley would receive to elevate him to acceptable rank for a queen's consort. Randolph replied patiently, using courtly language that never failed to irritate Simon. Why didn't they simply say what they meant to say?

When the old gray men ran out of questions, Mary, who had waited patiently throughout, spoke in a soft voice. "Who among you knows Robert Dudley well?"

Randolph began a carefully considered response. "His Lordship is a great man, Your Majesty, well versed in the ways of governance —"

Mary's gesture was minimal, but Randolph got the idea. He looked around the group, apparently considering which of them might provide the kind of information the queen obviously wanted. Simon was surprised when Randolph said, "My surgeon, Simon Maldon, has met His Lord-

329

ship on several informal occasions."

Simon's first instinct was to argue. While what Randolph said was true, he could hardly claim he knew the man. Their meetings had been focused on helping Elizabeth, not becoming acquainted. All he could attest to was that Dudley had been loyal to Elizabeth long before she became queen. That wasn't likely to be what this queen wanted to hear.

Mary's lovely eyes rested on him. "I would speak to Master Maldon alone."

Neither side liked it. Mary's council undoubtedly wanted no secrets kept from them, and Randolph probably had not imagined she would question Simon privately. Still, Mary was queen. They left the room, each group by its own set of doors.

Simon had no idea what he should do. Was he expected to approach now that he and the queen were alone? It would be ridiculous to shout across the room, and she probably didn't want the two men still on guard to overhear, but he dared not move without permission.

"You may approach." Her voice was soft and carefully modulated, and he imagined the training she'd had as a girl, designed to make her appealing, attractive, and amiable.

Perhaps Elizabeth was lucky her father had so often ignored her. Instead of striving to be the jewel of some man's court, she'd developed her mind and become a jewel in her own right.

Simon moved forward, but the next question was how close. Should he stop at the usual distance for conversation, or farther back, since their stations in life were so different? He chose the latter but wondered if he was expected to bow once he'd done it. Deciding it couldn't hurt, he bowed low, putting one foot behind the other as he'd seen Randolph do.

"Rise, and come closer."

Keeping his head lowered, Simon peeped at the queen from under his lashes. Her hand fluttered to her chin, and she licked her lips. Her Majesty the Queen was nervous!

Simon's distance vision had faded somewhat over time, and his view of Mary thus far had been blurry. Closer, he saw she was indeed lovely, with perfect skin and even features. Today her hair was pulled back from her face and fastened with a jeweled band. Her gown, deep green silk with huge skirts, was studded with gems at the bodice, the collar rising to her ears. Her pink cheeks and constantly moving hands reminded him, however, that beneath all the finery was a young woman who'd been offered a bridegroom. Mary wanted to know about the man she might marry.

She didn't start with a direct question, however. "Where you are living?"

It was a throwaway, a question that gave her time to assess him as he answered. The phrasing was odd, and Simon said, "If you prefer, Your Majesty, we might speak in French."

Looking relieved, she asked in her customary language. *"Où habitez-vous?*

"London, Your Majesty," Simon answered, "with my wife, son, and daughter."

"You have a wife."

"Hannah, Your Majesty. She was for a time your cousin's maid."

"Ah. So you know the queen well?"

He'd expected that question. "These days only as a subject knows his monarch, but when we were young, she and I spent some time together in study."

Her head tilted with interest. "What sort of study?"

"Her Majesty of England was anxious to perfect her knowledge of languages." He shrugged. "My father had encouraged me to read and study, and when he learned of her desire to practice foreign speech, he offered me as a . . . companion." It wasn't the right word for what he and Elizabeth had been to each other, but he had no better word for it. They'd at times behaved like friends. They were certainly more than acquaintances. How many acquaintances put their lives in jeopardy to save each other?

"What did you gain from this?" the queen asked.

The question jarred Simon back to the present, irritating him as well. Members of the nobility seemed to expect that no person did anything for another without some sort of payment. He chose an answer she would understand. "She let me borrow her books, Your Majesty."

"I see." He guessed she didn't, but she asked, "Through my cousin you met Dudley?"

"Yes, Your Majesty."

Mary tilted her head again, calling on the charm that made men leave her presence singing praises. "What do you think of him?" At Simon's horrified look, her eyes turned pleading. "I won't repeat what you say, but must know the man who would be my husband."

Simon swallowed. Elizabeth had not meant for him to be her agent in this matter, and he didn't know what she wanted

333

the result to be. Did she mean to give up her long-time friend and possible lover for political reasons, or had she woven some tangled plot to fool the Queen of Scots, to punish Dudley, or both?

All he could do was tell the truth. Elizabeth surely knew that while Simon could play a role convincingly, he had no talent for outright falsehood. She wouldn't expect him to lie to a queen. He hoped.

Beginning with a brief physical description, he told her about Dudley: his love of horses, his impressive bearing, his clever mind, and his willingness to listen to the views of others.

"Lord Robert has been, as long as I have known him, constant in his concern for England and its monarch." He didn't know if that was a recommendation or a condemnation, but it was the truth as he knew it.

After Mary thought for a while about what he'd said, she asked the question Simon had dreaded. "Did he cause his wife to be murdered, do you think?"

"Your Majesty, no man can see into another's heart. Should you ask, however, if the Robert Dudley I have seen is the kind of man who would kill a woman, especially a woman he loved, I would say no."

Mary nodded slightly. "I thank you for your honesty." Tapping her knuckles on the arm of her chair, the queen let the guards know the interview was concluded.

The council and the delegation were invited back into the room, and Mary addressed them, turning again to English. "Goodmen, I thank you for your pains in presenting my cousin's proposal, and I add to the council's apologies my sincere regret that you suffered abuse from one of Scotland's more" — she paused over an unfamiliar word — "barbarous citizens."

"We are content that the matter is concluded, Your Majesty," Randolph assured her.

"As to my cousin's proposal, I must think on it. It is my hope to meet with Elizabeth within the year, when I may give her my answer in person." She watched Randolph's face, perhaps trying to gauge if such a meeting would ever occur. When he didn't react, she went on. "But that is a matter for another day."

There was more flowery language on both sides, but eventually the queen rose. Everyone bowed as she exited the room, leaving behind the minister who'd done most of the talking. "Master Randolph," he said, "I would have some conference with you and your surgeon."

The rest of the party was ushered out, and Simon watched them go enviously. Would they try to pry out of him what Mary and he had discussed?

"I wish to know more about the matter at Duns Tower," the man began. Apparently there would be no fine words and hidden messages here, for the man's iron-gray eyes focused on Simon directly and he folded his age-spotted hands under his chin in a listening pose.

After a nod of affirmation from Randolph, Simon told the story as he knew it, taking care to highlight Agnes's innocence, the physical abuse she'd endured from her father, and the help she'd supplied. The man listened without comment until he'd finished.

"And where is Agnes now?"

Now he couldn't tell the whole truth, and he stammered a little over the words. "I cannot say, Your Worship." Strictly speaking that was true, though he knew she was somewhere between Edinburg and Duns, following Tavish.

"And this Tavish who led you here, he is not one of Kerr's men?"

"No, Your Worship. He was used as a servant, but the old laird married his mother late in life and considered Tavish and his sister stepchildren." He thought of mentioning Geordie Kerr had killed his own uncle, but that was unproven, and Kerr had already paid all for his crimes.

The man looked at Simon sharply. "You say Malcolm married the lad's mother?"

"You knew him?" He shouldn't have been surprised. They would have been of an age, and Scotland was a relatively small country.

"Aye. He was a decent man, but I fear he greatly misjudged his nephew's character." He looked at the wall behind their heads. "We've both suffered for our blindness."

Simon saw a way to perhaps aid those who'd helped him. "Tavish is a fine man, Your Worship, and he and Agnes are fond of each other. Is it possible he might marry her and manage the estate? He's very good with horses and could provide stock for the queen's needs. And he's an honest young man. Together he and Agnes could help to stabilize the marches."

The man didn't speak for some time, and Simon felt a blush creep up his neck. Who was he to give advice on governing to a councilman of a foreign nation?

To his surprise, the response, though delayed, was positive. "Agnes wed to Malcolm's stepson, eh? It might serve, surgeon. The idea might well serve."

Emboldened by success, Simon drew Munn's tattered letter from his doublet. "A man hired to guide us here disappeared early in the voyage. We thought he'd deserted us, but it's almost certain he was murdered so Kerr could turn our path toward Duns Tower." He didn't add that one of their own party, George Eliot, was the likely instrument of Munn's murder.

The man shook his head in disgust. "Another sin on Kerr's head."

"I ask that Munn's mother, who sent this letter, be told what happened to her son. While it will distress her to learn of his death, I believe it's kinder than leaving her to wonder why he doesn't return." Nodding gravely, the man took the letter from Simon and promised to see to it.

As they left the audience room, Simon noticed that the usually serious Randolph was trying to suppress a smile. "Have I offended someone?" he asked.

Randolph chuckled. "Not at all! In fact, you're a marvel, telling an earl how Scots' matters should proceed and getting him to see it's in his interest."

Simon wasn't sure where the humor came from. "Tavish and Agnes will treat the people of Duns fairly. The raids will stop.

And Agnes might even come to court from time to time, which will please her. What's wrong with that?"

"Nothing, nothing at all." Randolph chuckled again. "Do you recall Kerr's banquet, when we were informed that Anne Kerr is the daughter of a duke?"

"Yes, of course."

Randolph's eyes twinkled. "You've just met that duke, Menteith. Agnes is his granddaughter."

Simon had to laugh along with Randolph. His innocent suggestion fit precisely into the old duke's desires, providing for his daughter and granddaughters, bringing peace to a section of the marches, and providing a source for reliable horses, which he would no doubt profit from in some way. It worked out nicely for everyone, and the duke was almost certain to see it was done.

CHAPTER TWENTY

The Queen of England was in council, but when Calkin asked if he might see her, he was told to wait. Escorted to her closet, a small personal room, he waited, looking out the window at the city below. When the door opened and he heard her skirts brush the floor, Calkin turned and bowed. "Your Majesty."

"Sergeant." She gestured her attendants away. "It is good to see you."

"I trust your evening was pleasant?"

"Well enough, though it was a tedious affair. Have you come to report on your errand?"

"I have." He gave a brief account of his adventures, ending with a mild huff of disbelief. "Simon Maldon is a peaceable man, but murder seems to seek him out."

"He will be pleased to know we have settled the matter for him, I think."

Calkin hid his amusement at her use of

the word *we*. "No doubt, Your Majesty."

She looked at him speculatively. "Will you be glad to return to the guardhouse, Calkin?"

He found himself answering honestly, though she'd probably asked out of politeness rather than curiosity. "I have been thinking, madam, that I should like to retire."

That surprised her. "Retire?"

He hadn't really thought the matter through, but as he spoke, Calkin realized he meant every word of it. "I returned from Old Change to find that my mother has died."

"I am sorry to hear it." Elizabeth's voice had an odd tone, and Calkin wondered if she knew about his wretched family. He couldn't imagine she would take interest in such things as her guards' private lives, but then, she was Elizabeth, a singular person if ever he'd met one. He didn't elaborate on his mother's death, the sudden stoppage of her heart. He kept to himself the relief he felt, and the grim judgment he'd given his sister and sister-in-law. They could have everything in the house, but he was done with them. He felt some guilt and a modicum of pity, but most of all, he felt free. For the first time in his life, his family was not a weight around his neck, and he could think about what he *wanted* to do, not what he felt he *had* to.

"Things I've never done seem to beckon these days. I'd like to catch a fish, and perhaps learn to carve clever things from wood. I'd like to decide when I wake up in the morning what I want to do. I might even like to grow things in the earth, for I believe it's a miracle how one plants some tiny thing and it becomes a bush or a stalk or even a tree."

She smiled, and he saw in it the princess he'd first known. "Calkin, you're positively poetical!" He felt his face grow warm, but she said, "It is a good life you have in mind."

The moment had become personal, and he forgot his sovereign stood before him. "Do you ever wish for such things? A simple life, lived only as you will and not for others?"

Her eyes went soft. "Sometimes, yes." A moment later, she was queen again. "But what would I say to my father and his father if I neglected my duty to England?"

"Of course. The nation needs you."

"You have served well, Calkin, your nation and your sovereign. If you decide to leave us, I will remember you as a good soldier and a trusted one."

"Thank you." He turned to go, but her voice stopped him at the door.

"Is there perhaps a woman who's set your mind on this new course?"

Calkin shook his head. "Your father used to say you were too clever, Highness. Her name, should you care to know it, is Annie Maldon."

The English party returned to their inn to prepare for departure, which meant Simon had to climb to the barn loft. He'd lent Agnes his cloak to add a little comfort to her stable bed, and she'd promised to leave it there for him.

The place was silent except for the soft huffs of horses breathing, and Simon saw no sign of the boy who cared for the place. He was sorry, for he'd meant to give him a coin for his silence at Tavish's and later Agnes's presence.

Simon found the cloak, neatly folded, near the window. As he slung it over his shoulder and turned to go, a hand stopped him. "Maldon."

Turning, he met the eyes of George Eliot, who'd apparently been hiding in the dark corner of the loft. "Your Scottish scoundrels are dead, and you have no friends here."

Eliot tightened his grip on Simon's arm.

"Where is the daughter?"

Surprise made him slow to comprehend the question. "Who?"

"The girl, Agnes! Where is she?"

"Gone."

Eliot grabbed Simon's shirt, pulling him forward. "Where has she gone, cripple?"

Simon tried to twist away, but Eliot struck a blow to the spot where his neck joined his shoulder, causing his knees to buckle. "Tell me!"

Simon knelt on the wooden floor, trying to decide what to do. He was probably no match for Eliot in a fight, but he was determined not to tell. "Have you not hurt her enough?"

Eliot apparently reconsidered his approach. Letting go of Simon's clothing, he stepped back. "Listen, Maldon. We spoke once of reward, and you seemed a reasonable sort then. My position is perilous since Kerr's plan went awry. I never imagined they would —" He stopped, unwilling to say aloud what had happened to Kerr.

Simon glanced around, his mind working feverishly. The stable was empty. His friends were inside, gathering their belongings. Eliot had a knife at his belt he hadn't bothered to draw. He could easily kill Simon with his bare hands and walk calmly away afterward.

"Kerr had a great deal of wealth," Eliot said, his voice turning from threatening to coaxing. "It is hidden in his house, and a man with courage might yet make a profit on this enterprise." He added with a grim smile, "Or two men."

Simon forced himself to appear interested. "How?"

"You take me to the girl. We use her to get Kerr's wife to give up the goods in the secret room. The woman is no cleverer than my right shoe, but she does love her children. If we threaten Agnes, she'll do anything to get her back."

Simon didn't think it wise to agree too easily. "And then where would we go, with the Scots and the English on our trail?"

Eliot laughed. "You're the linguist! With your French we might start in Calais, but men with money are welcome everywhere." He shifted his feet impatiently. "Now where is she?"

Simon had no illusion Eliot intended to take him on as a partner. "If I tell, you'll kill me as you killed Munn, to get him out of your way."

Eliot's eyes hardened. "And if you don't, I'll kill you now. You will live exactly as long as you serve my purpose."

Simon had been readying himself. Still

kneeling, he raised one knee as if to get his balance. Eliot stood between him and the open window, about ten feet back from the opening. Setting his hands on his knee, he steadied himself, knowing he had one chance to defeat Eliot. It had to be a surprise, and it had to be over quickly, or the larger man's strength would win out.

With a sudden move Simon rose onto one foot, keeping his head low. Pushing off with the other foot, he butted Eliot's stomach with his head, centering his assault for maximum force. Pumping his legs and taking small but continuous steps, he forced the larger man backward, toward the window behind him and the ground below.

Sensing Simon's intent, Eliot tried to stop his backward motion. The loft was mostly empty, and there was nothing to grasp. His own unbalanced weight coupled with Simon's pushing carried him toward the gaping opening behind him. He had time for a curse before his foot found air instead of floor beneath it. His hands flailed for a hold on the window frame, but Simon gave one last push before reaching out his good hand to stop his own forward progress. Eliot teetered on the edge for what seemed a long time. Then he was gone.

Panting from exertion, Simon recovered

enough to look below, uncertain whether he'd see a broken corpse or Eliot's retreating back. The man lay writhing on the ground, trying to regain his breath, while Thomas Randolph stood over him, one foot on his neck. "Master Eliot," he said calmly. "You almost missed the boat back to England, which would no doubt have distressed the queen no end."

When they reached the docks of London, Simon said his goodbyes to the delegation. Randolph and Coulston would make their official report to the queen. His summons would come later. Randolph shook Simon's hand in his usual, dignified manner. James Coulston thanked him for the tenth time for his part in their rescue. Philip Coulston clasped him in an enthusiastic hug and promised to visit soon, which, though unlikely, Simon took as a measure of the young man's regard. The rest shook hands and offered their thanks. Even Empton bowed stiffly and allowed they were beholden to Master Maldon for their lives.

Old Change looked exactly the same, which seemed impossible to Simon. It felt as if years had passed, as if the buildings should be crumbling with age, the people wizened and ancient. But it was he who'd entered a different world, not they. Things here had no doubt gone on as they always had.

Not unexpectedly, it was Susan who saw him first. Simon saw a flash of movement through the imperfect glass of the shop's front window, an abundance of blond hair that disappeared briefly only to reappear in the doorway. "Father!"

In a trice she was in his arms, hugging and talking at once. There was something about gladness followed quickly by words he could make no sense of. Someone was caught then he was dead, his body washed up downstream and brought to Old Change for identification. Her last words surprised him. "Calkin says it was best, for he was an evil man."

"Calkin?" he repeated.

"Simon!" He looked up to see Hannah coming out the door at a run. Close behind her were his son and his sister. Behind them, a man stepped shyly into the street, his freckled face showing both joy and hesitation at Simon's return. Calkin, sergeant of Elizabeth Tudor's guard.

The call came the next morning, and Simon was ready. He followed the same man who'd come for him the first time, carefully side-stepping puddles left by the previous night's rain. One could never tell what was in them, and it wouldn't do to enter the queen's presence smelling of filth.

He didn't wait long in the anteroom this time. Several foreign-looking men exited, their expressions dour, before he was called into Elizabeth's presence. With her were Cecil, Dudley, and two other councilmen he didn't know by name. The queen dismissed them and the two guardsmen at the door as well. Dudley cast a wishful look backward as he left, and Simon guessed he might soon be called to another private meeting. No doubt Dudley had questions about the Queen of Scots he couldn't very well ask Her Majesty.

When they were gone, a young man in livery brought in a tray and set it on a small table near the window. He'd obviously been told what was wanted, for he set two chairs and backed out of the room, closing the door behind him.

"Try the cakes," Elizabeth urged. "They're quite good."

It was an understatement, at least as far as Simon was concerned. He'd never tasted anything like what Elizabeth informed him were called jumballs, small cakes with lemon and almonds. They were so sweet he could hardly believe it.

"Sugar," Elizabeth informed him. "Much better for folk than honey." He made an effort to stop at one for politeness's sake, but she ordered, "Try the pink ones. They're my favorites."

Then the questions began. Simon had to stop eating in order to answer without puffing crumbs on the queen's table. She asked his impressions of Queen Mary, and Simon answered honestly. He and Randolph had discussed the private audience and agreed the truth was best. Elizabeth listened closely as he reported the questions Mary had asked about Robert Dudley. He couldn't read her response, but when he finished, she asked, "Does she seem to you the sort to lay schemes and plot rebellion?"

He found himself using words similar to those he'd used with the Queen of Scots. "No one can say what lies in another's heart, Highness, but she did not seem calculating. I got the impression —" He stopped, unsure whether he should state what was only a feeling.

Elizabeth spoke sharply. "Simon, I sent you to use your powers of observation and sense of people. You must say what you think."

He sighed. "I have no basis for it, but I

think your cousin is perhaps ruled by emotion. She is a woman first and a queen after, while —" He stopped, horrified by what he'd almost said.

"While I am a queen first and a woman second." Elizabeth chuckled. "I am not offended, Simon. Your words might be considered a compliment."

He bowed. "They were intended as one, Highness."

She brushed crumbs from her hands. "Now to the matter of the Scottish bandit. Tell me."

He told the story of their capture and escape, emphasizing where he could that Randolph and the others had acted in good faith on information they believed to be true. The queen asked questions to clarify several points, shaking her head at Eliot's betrayal. "We knew he was a violent man, but we thought to balance Randolph's gentleness with a bit of practicality."

"You could not have known, Highness. And he will surely pay for his crimes."

"This very morning, I think," she said casually.

Though Eliot deserved his fate, the thought of him going to his death while Simon ate sweets with the queen was disconcerting. To change the subject, he said, "I think you have a story for me, now, Highness."

Pleasure showed in her eyes. "Were you surprised, Simon?"

Shocked was more like it, but he'd calmed himself with the knowledge everyone had come through alive — at least, everyone but Fenman. "I was indeed surprised, Highness, but I have not yet heard your part in it. Perhaps you have time to tell it to me?"

"I have made time," she said, unable to hide the eagerness in her voice. "After you left, I began thinking about Blackie and his strange confession. It seemed there was something to investigate in Old Change, and I decided to set Calkin on it, knowing him for one who likes a puzzle almost as much as you do." She stopped. "Has he asked your sister to marry him?"

It had been another shock, but Simon was reconciled. "He has."

"Then I have settled several murders and made a match as well," Elizabeth said with satisfaction. "It is more than I accomplish most days in this place."

"You're a marvel, Highness," Simon said. "I always knew it; now England knows, too."

"But they cannot know that I dabble in solving murders."

"Nor would they believe it, I think."

"It's enough that you and I know," she said. "Now take the rest of these cakes for Hannah and your children." She rose with a comical moue. "I must convince the ambassador of Sweden once again that his hopes for my marriage to his prince are not quite dead." Putting a hand on his shoulder, she said, "I am glad you returned safely, Simon."

He bowed. "Thank you, Highness. I hope you meet your cousin someday, and the two of you do well together."

Elizabeth smiled. "That is my hope as well, for we are cousins in blood and sisters in function. Still, if one is given her greatest hope, she must not ask for more. I have become England, and I will do what must be done to protect it."

Did that mean she'd give up Robert Dudley? As he walked home, Simon thought again how glad he was to not be in Elizabeth's place. Each decision she made affected so many, and she dared not let herself be swayed by love or hate, blood or affection. As he turned a corner and saw his comfortable little home ahead, he thanked God he'd been born a common man.

AUTHOR'S NOTE

A work of fiction is simply that, but I try in the Simon and Elizabeth mysteries to remain true to the spirit of the times and to Elizabeth Tudor's character. In 1563 she did propose her favorite, Robert Dudley, as husband to Mary, Queen of Scots, sending Thomas Randolph to Scotland with the proposal. We will never know for certain what her reasons were, since Elizabeth learned at a very young age to keep her thoughts to herself.

The match never occurred, nor did she ever meet the cousin she eventually sentenced to the executioner's ax. It was a wrenching decision for her, and she longed to know what sort of person Mary really was. I found it intriguing to imagine that Elizabeth sent her old friend Simon to get a look at the Scottish queen and give her a report unbiased by political, religious, or personal concerns. Once Simon was a member of the party, all sorts of imaginary events came to mind. The story took on a life of its own, as they tend to do.

If the idea of an outlaw being arrested when he comes to court with all his men in all their best clothing seems odd, read the poem "Johnnie Armstrong" and learn of a case in the 1500s where that very thing happened.

ABOUT THE AUTHOR

Peg Herring writes the award-winning Dead Detective Mysteries, the critically acclaimed Simon and Elizabeth Mysteries, and the intriguing Loser Mysteries. Peg lives in northern Lower Michigan with her husband of many decades. They love to travel and garden, pastimes that are not particularly compatible.

The employees of Thorndike Press hope you have enjoyed this Large Print book. All our Thorndike, Wheeler, and Kennebec Large Print titles are designed for easy reading, and all our books are made to last. Other Thorndike Press Large Print books are available at your library, through selected bookstores, or directly from us.

For information about titles, please call:
  (800) 223-1244

or visit our Web site at:
  http://gale.cengage.com/thorndike

To share your comments, please write:
  Publisher
  Thorndike Press
  10 Water St., Suite 310
  Waterville, ME 04901